THE
ADVENT OF
ELIZABETH

In memory of
my own "Elizabeth"

ACKNOWLEDGMENTS

Thanks to Carol Squicci, *mi enamorada,* my first reader, and my graphic designer, who creates all but the words and even then, will suggest a few. Her support goes far beyond her designs, and without it, *The Advent of Elizabeth* would not exist.

My deepest appreciation to Gary Miller, my editor, whose attention to character, story, and narrative technique made this a better story and a truer work.

It was my pleasure again to work with Anne Fox whose insistence on correctness and a sense of place put me to the test.

Thank you to my fellow writers, Davyd Morris, Bruce Coyle, Kitty Fassett, and Bill Weinreb, who gave me unparalleled insight to how one views a tale and a life. And more thanks to my early readers, again, Davyd, Bruce, and Kitty, as well as Marylene Cloitre, James Richter, Mary Walfoort, and Jennifer Dwight for their careful reading, discussion, and critique of *Advent.* My appreciation to Ted Allen, my colleague in teaching and my musicologist for this novel.

My gratitude extends beyond this particular work to the thousands of readers who, by reading and loving my previous novels, have given me reason to continue to explore fiction. These are for whom I write.

They would not know my work, though, without the hundreds of independent booksellers and librarians, my book-people, who recommend, circulate, and also enjoy my work.

I acknowledge the support and assistance of many friends and writers: members of my critique circle, the writers of the California Writers Club, the Berkeley Branch in particular, the friends and writers of the Bay Area Independent Publishers Association, and the always supportive David Beard, associate professor, University of Minnesota, Duluth.

JUNE, 2016

Pronunciation Note

The Finnish surname Pyykönen is nearly unpronounceable, at least correctly, by native speakers of American English, so much so that some Finnish Americans of that name have adopted an English pronounciation: (Pie-ko-nen).

The Finnish word Tytär (Too-ta) should be translated "daughter" where it appears here.

Author's Note

The treatment of the clergy and educators in this novel may be a concern to some. The characterization is not typical of either calling, nor should it be taken as an indictment of these professions.

Since the setting of this novel, 1967, several changes have improved prospects for protection of students, children, and innocents. That noted, none can say change has yet gone far enough.

Like all that happens in daily life, these incidents become the concern of fiction.

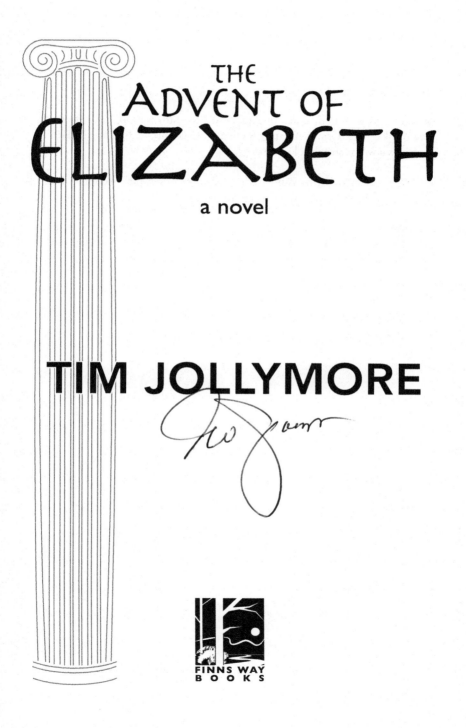

THE
ADVENT OF
ELIZABETH

a novel

TIM JOLLYMORE

FINNS WAY
BOOKS

Printed in the United States of America. For information, address Finns Way Books™, 360 Grand Avenue, Suite 204, Oakland, California, 94610; or contact www.finnswaybooks.com

For information on Finns Way Reading Group Guides, please contact Finns Way Books™ by electronic mail at readinggroupguides@finnswaybooks.com

ISBN 978-0-9914763-5-0 print
ISBN 978-0-9914763-6-7 electronic version (Dec. 8, 2016)

THE ADVENT OF ELIZABETH

1

Reunions

Bobbie had left my toast on the table, a little dry but suitable for dunking, and the coffee pot held a couple cups yet. She was off somewhere, shopping I supposed.

Between dunks and chews I'd been thinking about reunions, seeing as how the paper was full of articles about the one coming up in Santa Reina which is one of those small towns where any gathering of four or more is newsworthy. The fact was that some of my Frisco friends, south of town about fifty miles, raised eyebrows and snickers when I mentioned our centennial celebration. Seems none of them had attended their big-school fetes over the years and wouldn't, they maintained, even if it were the hundredth anniversary of their school's birth.

Now that's the difference between a town and the city: small town people, even if they've moved on and live outstate or outside of their state, settle their hearts, if not their persons, in the nest of their hometown, and the high school is the center of that life for them in a way unparalleled in a big-city school. So every class here has a great turn out for reunions. For this particular one, there isn't a room unrented for twenty-five miles in any direction. It's that big. I made my reservation early even though I live right here in Santa Reina. I'm hoping to use that room, too. Being an honored guest has its privileges.

You don't see my name in the paper, but I am referred to on page three of the *Santa Reina Republic* in the following article by Finn Pyykönen, one of our finest, athlete-turned-journalist, having interviewed Elizabeth Moore, PhD, another of our finest academic products, and a fine physical specimen, too.

My name is not mentioned in the article, of course, because the whole thing is a great big secret.

DIGNITARY TO HONOR LONG-TIME TEACHER

By Finn Pyykönen

Santa Reina– Elizabeth Moore, PhD, will present the keynote address at the Santa Reina High School Centennial, Saturday evening, 7:00 p.m. at the school gymnasium in culmination of a three-day celebration of the school's history.

Dr. Moore, now the Superintendent of Schools in San Francisco, a Santa Reina High graduate (1961) and former teacher (1965-67), has served as superintendent in Fresno and Sacramento. During her address, Dr. Moore will announce State Board of Education choice for California Teacher-Emeritus Award.

The honor, infrequently bestowed (last in 1985), goes to a long-career teacher who has continued through retirement to support public education, his/her students and school in meritorious ways.

"The award," Dr. Moore said, "is supported by nominations of former students, members of the community, and state board members. Recipients' names," she told the Chronicle "remain well-guarded secrets, unknown prior to announcement day."

Dr. Moore earned her bachelor's degree from the University of California, Berkeley, her master of education and doctorate at Pennsylvania State University. She served on the California State Board of Education, 1986-1989.

The Santa Reina Republic
JUNE 12, 1991

One thing that I should make clear since we are on the topic of reunions is that despite the fine attendance at these shindigs not everyone comes to Santa Reina happy, and most certainly all do not leave content. That may be especially true this time for those connected with what we call "the event" which was a murder perpetrated on the music room stage in 1967. Even though it was a horrid event, too lurid to say much about, you should know what happened as it affects nearly all the people you are about to meet. Except me, I suppose, and while I'm at it, I'll apologize for the lack of introduction. I'll do that later. I'm making an attempt here to be objective.

Here is what is known about that morning twenty-four years ago when Denise Hagerty, a student at Santa Reina High School in the spring of her freshman year, was stabbed to death:

She came early to practice. Denise was working on Mozart's *Divertimento in D*. She'd done that most of the spring semester. Some of the women in the teachers lounge, after the event, of course, were gassing about why she came early, and from what I gathered Denise was escaping a dicey homelife with daddy. Actually though, Denise was quite a dedicated clarinetist, first chair at Santa Reina, and played often over at The Sacred Heart, the church and parochial school. She came early to Santa Reina High regularly, before any one else, and I bet she wished she hadn't.

Someone was waiting for her. He stabbed her repeatedly, nineteen times the papers reported, with a knife that was never found, and got clean away even though he was interrupted in his labor by the music teacher, Elizabeth Moore, yes, the same Dr. Moore mentioned in the article here though she was Miss Moore back in '67.

Well, Elizabeth went down almost immediately in a dead faint, toppling into the pool of Denise's blood.

3

The murderer fled but left behind a weird calling card: one of the baseball team's catcher masks. That led police almost immediately to question the Wildcats backstop, Douglas Brandling. Miss Moore identified him, and he confessed during the first hour of questioning.

"The event" was tough on everyone. The families, who lived on the same street a block apart, suffered most. Denise's twin brother was sent away, and the family followed not too long afterward. As you might guess, reunions aren't their thing. The Brandlings were well-to-do but had little to do with Doug's confession and all, outside of the brother's presence at the sentencing. The brother, Warren, graduated that year, about two weeks after the murder.

It also went poorly for my colleague, Elizabeth. I call her Biz. Not only did she lose a great musician and ruin a suit of perfectly good clothes, but her identification of the catcher precipitated the break-off of her engagement to Wildcats baseball coach, Finn Pyykönen, yes the soon-to-be journalist. Biz stayed another year. He left town even before the Hagertys or Brandlings and within six months was married to a Pasadena girl.

Win some lose some, Biz.

Clearly, I'm tired of being objective, so let's move on while I tell you a little about myself.

2

Snub Speaks

I'm not going to tell you your business, but listen, I've been teaching English almost fifty years, and not telling people their business is anathema to me. That means foreign, alien, out of my bailiwick. So bear with me. If I grate on your nerves from time to time, don't stop reading. Otherwise, you could miss some very interesting detail, and I don't mean about me, exactly.

I am telling the god-awful truth, mainly because at this point I have nothing to lose. "How about reputation?" you say, but if I cared about reputation, I would have quashed all the rumors about me circulating at Santa Reina High. My girls would never tattle on me, so getting caught in the act was the only thing I feared. Hence, while in the darkroom, I kept the door locked, not always for photographic reasons. Public exposure I could've lived with—surprising how one gets used to almost anything, except abstinence—now, though, none of it matters.

I'm dying, you see. Prostate cancer. No. I'm not going to let them hack up my sexual mechanism and drop it into a surgical pan. No impotence for me, thanks. Furthermore, incontinence is for the less fortunate or for those who opt for a few more miserable years in diapers. Pampers are not my style. No thanks. No thank you, ma'am. Not for me, Snub Randall, and that's for sure.

Pushing seventy-six, I still have a formidable desire and the ability to follow its course, mostly. I'm what a student long ago, inaccurately trying to explain what Chaucer meant in describing his scholar as "a lusty bachelor," blurted out: "He's a sexpot." That is me, though I have the impression that this term is applied more to the feminine person, one of which you will meet in this story. Whatever you call me, I will cop only to being bountifully sexed up and sexy as well. Leave the "pot" for her, my Biz.

My follow-through has not been as easy as in my younger days. I have accepted medical assistance, pills and such from time to time, if you need to know, but I would rather die than give up sex—two-way, two-person, reciprocal sex. I guess that's what I'm going to do at the end, though: give up the ghost. So they say. I suspect that if there is intercourse in the "afterlife," having had my eternal share already, I am not going to be allowed no matter which place I'm sent to.

My part in this story will be what they call posthumous, meaning, I am compelled to tell you, that if you are reading this, I am dead. It all comes out after I'm gone, or as soon as. And maybe you wonder, so I'll tell you. I'm not trying to protect anyone, me included, but I'll hold it back from my townsfolk until I'm gone, just because I don't want to trifle with the inevitable questions that people will have: "How many were there? Why? Didn't you think it wrong?" All that crap would be too inconvenient and bothersome. After a man has died, though, all that "stuff," the muck he stomped around in while living, seems less important. Who really gives a damn anyway? Some pretend to, but really? If they'd cared so much, why didn't they stand up to speak when I was alive?

In any case, that big secret will be out. No, not that I, an award-winning teacher, seldom read my students' papers. That's been true enough and rumored enough, and there's no secret there. That I have lusted after my students has really never been unknown either. I liked the girls, and I didn't hold back. I flirted with them in a serious, manly, and lascivious way, appealing to newly realized sexuality, inborn curiosity, and, to be completely honest, especially as the years passed, their sympathy. No, everyone knew that.

Now only at the end, though, I'll admit this: when I could seduce one of my teenage admirers, I did. Oh, don't be shocked. The count for teacher-on-student seduction, adding in, perhaps, the fairly frequent student-on-teacher debauchment, is hardly greater—if it were known and not tacitly tolerated—than priest-on-altar boy (there seems to be little altar-boy-on-priest action, the boys having their eyes raised toward heaven for the most part). I maintain that the former are far less damaging in the long run. After all, a teacher represents himself, not a deity.

Besides that, in my practice sex was never forced. My God, that would have been rape, wouldn't it? I am not a rapist. By the same token, as you'll see, I am not relying on consent as an excuse. They were always—I'm not really that sure, so let's say mostly—seventeen or older, but not out of high school. After all, if they had been out of school, they would have been beyond my influence, and that was paltry enough, though I may claim otherwise at times.

These girls, no matter what anyone says, wanted sex. Maybe they didn't really want sex with me, but sex was something they wanted. Despite other girls' or their boyfriends' (more on one of these later) scruples, and beside concerns of the parents or the mumblers at the rumor mill, the so-called authorities (though I am more an authority on the subject than any notepad-carrying official you could name) all seemed to turn a blind eye to teenage sex. Like I say, they wanted it.

Let me restate that. It was an experience they wanted.

Their boyfriends were just too gawky, too scared, too loose-mouthed, too inexperienced, or too jack-rabbit-fast to help them out. So I made myself available, handy, helpful (especially in preserving my partners' reputations), and, above all, kind. I could not be accused of being unkind. In fact, even as one by one each of my girls graduated from high school and moved out of town, I went out of my way to help and encourage, to keep in touch, to inquire how college was going, to ask what they were studying, and all. I never, knowingly or intentionally, courted any but the college-bound (they left immediately after high school, which, as I moved on to the next school year, made life less complicated for me, I would say). Even though they were safely away having adventures of their own, I made a point to remember birthdays and important holidays. A couple times a year, I sent packages of candy bars, fancy crackers and cheese, munchies like wholesome chips and nuts. It was a transition for each of us, so I usually established a two-year limit.

Usually. The notable exception was Biz, now Elizabeth Moore, PhD. Our initial fling started her junior year, 1959. After her stories about home life, I had a talk with her father. I told him over Biz's objections to keep his hands off her fanny and stop hanging around at pajama-time. He was the adult for God's sake and her father, to boot. And he did back off. Then I took Biz for myself.

She broke it off eighteen months later, when she took up Pyykönen the summer after their graduation. Theirs didn't last through college, and Biz later came back to me, with some prompting, for my help navigating the shark-infested teaching-credentialing waters of 1965. We then had two lovely years after she joined the teaching staff at Santa Reina; her thanks seemed boundless. But in the middle of her third year, up shows Pyykönen again, to fill in as baseball coach.

The Advent of Elizabeth

That was the most difficult year, 1967, my toughest.

Oh, that year, I suppose, was harder for Denise Hagerty, who as you know, got herself murdered on the music room stage spring semester. And a stressful one for Biz, discovering the body and all.

Nineteen sixty-seven was challenging for Finn Pyykönen, too, who lost Biz again and, by choice, his hometown and job all at once. It was a harsh time for the family of confessed murderer, Doug Brandling who'd been a junior that year. For me, though, the year of that event was a beginning and an end.

After that I swore off helping out the girls, though when Biz left town a year later, my pledge wasn't all that successful.

I might break in from time to time to have my say about other characters besides the alluring though more-than-somewhat-loose Elizabeth Moore, who some now call Doctor PhD. She's my favorite. But another is that cream puff, Farley Pike. Between you and me, old FP earned his name from the face powder he wore during his initial interview at the school covering god only knows what. I might not say too much about my Father confessor and drinking buddy, Berach Phelan, since he's fallen on hard times in the last few years. Hardening, maybe pickling, of the gray matter. On the darker side, of course, are the Brandling brothers, one an MD, the other doing time for murder one. And there is Finn.

One more thing about 1967, and please don't think it is pay-back for my suffering. With this centennial coming this weekend, actually a three-day affair, I've been dipping my oar in the waters and my pen in the ink in more than a lusty way. My swan song wouldn't be satisfying were I not to stir a bit of mischief for some of what we call "the class of '67," those at the school the day of Denise Hagerty's murder. I am pinning a deserving few to the wall with that pen, using the U. S. Postal Service and staying anonymous, of course. Otherwise, "the event," (Miss Hagerty's stabbing, you know) might go completely unremarked during the all-school backslapping. That would be unseemly. So I hope some objective truth comes out.

That, you'll have to take for what it's worth.

3

Elizabeth

Elizabeth Moore woke annoyed. Snub was snoring—open-mouthed, rumbling drones—and he'd flopped his arm over her chest, now breathing right into her face.

Two hours earlier, her eyes had sprung wide open. I'm dying. Palpitations shoved her heart insistently against her ribs, pulsed up her throat, pounded in her head.

Once again, the dream had seized her:

On the music room stage, the goggle-eyed girl writhed and coughed blood. The boy ran. She knew that boy behind the mask, and she saw herself, as she had actually done, go down. She saw herself crumple to the wooden floor, wetting her clothes in the flow of the girl's blood and of her own urine. As if it were happening again, Elizabeth saw her own head hit with a horrible thud. I'm dying!

It had been the note that brought on the dream.

> Clear your sight!
> Who's Mr. Right?

That cryptic message had been mailed in a red envelope to The Stanford Hotel, the place in downtown Santa Reina, where she was staying for the centennial. Packaged with it was a *Republic* clipping of Finn's '67 baseball team.

Earlier this night, after the dream, she'd lain wide-eyed, piercing the dark room air, lying motionless in bed. Had she been wrong about who killed Denise Hagerty? After twenty-four years, she was suddenly unsure. Four o'clock. The dead of night, she thought. She breathed herself to calm. Guilt pushed sleep away. She tried to drain the horrid dream of its power, but "He wasn't the one" beat in her mind like a judge pounding a gavel. That she had slept again surprised her, but she had and soundly at last. Snub hadn't been sawing wood yet.

When   Elizabeth woke annoyed, Snub snorted and snored. My God, she thought, his breath stinks. I hadn't noticed that earlier. A rotted tooth, she decided. Elizabeth turned her head and shifted away from Snub, pushing his veiny arm off her. He grumbled but did not wake.

His presence, though it held her mindless of the bloody dream, grated her pride. Why did I let this happen? Again. Heavens, Biz, she chortled, can't you just say no? Had those been Sarah Petroski's words? Her therapist—her sex therapist, Elizabeth called her—preferred "no" to the regret and resentment Elizabeth seemed to instinctively choose. She sniffed the acid musk clinging to the pillow. Christ, Biz, the man is seventy-three. He's an old man. Surely you have it in you to say no. Her own compulsion held her vexed.

Of course, Snub was different. He had been her first, taught her everything she knew about it all. He'd also blocked her knowing the beauty in sex and love. Pride rebelled. No, I didn't go down willingly. Well, I did want it, yes, but not from someone twice my age, not really.

Yes, he was older, at that time, forty to her seventeen. Forty! Ha. That, too, could have been a lie, but age seemed unimportant at the time. Here you are yourself now forty-nine. Not young. Not so old either. She couldn't, though, imagine what it would be like to be as old as Snub. When she was retired, would she be chasing then? Not likely. Men were different. They suffered less.

The Advent of Elizabeth

When she was just a girl, Snub Randall had been mature and handsome, had that racy reputation, and all the senior girls drooled over him. The boys, well, they were just boys. Now those boys were men, mannish and comely. And Snub? She looked at the old man beside her. Snub had turned away. Thank God. She rolled onto her back. Elizabeth needed to think.

Dawn cheered the room, but her annoyance remained. What's bothering you, Biz? Are you angry at Snub or, as you should be, at yourself? Neither bites you, does it? No, this celebration, this reunion— Santa Reina's city and high school centennial weekend—is stirring you up. You've gone far enough up and away to break free of that old queen city mojo, boosterism, but coming back pinches just as hard as it did to tear out of town. One question: Would Elizabeth Moore fall under the spell of Snub Randall once more?—had already been answered. She could tick that item off her worry list.

She sifted her thoughts. Maybe it was the goddamn speech that had her riled. The speech about Snub Randall she was expected to give. How could she, so publicly, lie so much about one person in so short a time? There was no affection, especially, as cold as it was now, that could warm her to this task. It was just too hard. Or was it? Was it more difficult than the hundred half-true speeches she'd given over the years? But this unrest was not just about the speech.

Elizabeth had forever known how to proffer the public face, sanctuary face her father had called it. Keep Biz out of it, and you'll be fine. Be who they think you are, Elizabeth Moore, PhD, not Snub Randall's middle-aged bimbo, a sycophant to empty sex.

No matter what you do, you know there is only one thing you care about. What she most wanted and most dreaded was to see Finn.

Beautiful Finn. He'd been her lover right out of high school. He'd saved her from Snub. Finn had taught her love. They'd survived two college years apart but drifted away, he to baseball and then Viet Nam, she to less heady loves and career. When they came together again as teachers, Elizabeth had thought it was forever. Until you fingered his prize catcher for murder. And maybe you were mistaken.

To see Finn after all these years, after what had happened, after what she'd done. My God, the letter. Will I tell? Meeting Finn would be her test. He'd always thought that she'd been wrong. Now she would have to admit her doubt. Admit her guilt. The prospect of Finn kept her on edge. The letter made it worse.

A martini or two will fix those jitters, one voice told her. Don't get sloshed, Biz, another warned. Two voices. That worried her; it had worried Sarah Petroski.

What a garbled mess. She brooded. I can't keep my mind on one thing. Weather this weekend, Biz, and get back to work. That's been your salvation. Yes, she agreed, it will always be my answer. Still she wanted Finn.

Snub was stirring beside her. She closed her eyes. Oh the wonderful world of work, my barrage of duty, emergency, deadline, and prep. Lovely labor eats the time, fills the empty cup, pushes me out of bed, props my life, gives it meaning. She sighed aloud. And at the end, "There's blissful repose at martini time, the drier the better."

Snub broke in. "Are you pushing martinis this early?" He raised his legs and vaulted from bed with a groan. He tottered stiff-jointed, to the toilet. Elizabeth watched his deflated buttocks pulse and pucker across the room as he went. As soon as he shut the bathroom door, she whipped off the sheet and began dressing.

She had already hooked her bra and was slipping into the slacks she had worn last night when he returned, immediately it seemed, moving more fluidly, yet still a shock of white hair stood straight out above his ear. He came around the bed and stood, naked. "Aw, you're not leaving already. Stay a minute."

She patted his bare chest and pushed him to the mattress. "I've a thousand things to do. I'm not the retired one." He rebounded from the bed, stood closer. "Please, Snub." She pushed again, a bit harder. "You go back to bed." She brushed his offending hair into place.

"Ah, the woman's scorn," he said. "I can drive you to your hotel."

She shook her head. "It's not far. I'll enjoy the walk." It was the last thing she wanted: to be seen getting out of Snub's Z 4 at eight in the morning.

"Breakfast?"

"I don't take it."

"Coffee?"

"I'll get some on the way," she said. "Really, Snub, I need to be going."

"And we were just getting to be such friends," he said.

Elizabeth frowned down his quizzical smile. "Funny. I'm not sure you should call it that." He had helped her. That was true. Her career was in part due to his influence, direct and hidden, but friends they had never really been. You're his patsy, not his friend. She corrected herself. You're one of his patsies.

"Liz, Liz, Liz," Snub said. "Whatever we have been, you have done so much for me. I adore you, don't you know?"

She knew how to get out of this. "And you are a married man still."

"Not much of a marriage. One without love." It was his ancient mantra.

She had to say it, or he would make her stay. "Father figure, I think, is the right term." She eyed his saggy gut, and her tacky ploy worked. She pulled her tee over her head and put an arm through the vest. Snub guided her other through and straightened the garment at her shoulders.

"Yes, my daughter, I have to let you go." He mixed defeat with his self-pity.

Always gaming, she thought, and always playing the sad-sack lover. "You'll be fine, Snub. I'll see you at the Board dinner Friday. It should be fun."

He pulled on his shorts. "You call that fun? I know what fun is." Elizabeth twisted to avoid his grasp.

"Here, read this while I do makeup." She handed him the red envelope containing the note and clipping.

She went to the bathroom to fix her face and hair. When she came back, he was fooling with the coffeemaker. He held the cue card to the light, tipping his head back to bifocal the directions. She approached. He didn't turn.

"I put your poison pen letter on the desk," he said.

Elizabeth waited. "And what do you make of it?"

"It's your letter, dear."

She watched him spill water on the table. "Goddamn," he said.

"Do you think I was wrong?"

He finished spilling and turned to her. "Are you not sure?"

"No. Now I'm not certain I ever was. It seemed so reasonable, believable at the time. Then the sheriff brought . . ."

"Sheriff! What's he got to do with anything?"

"Snub, I may have sent the wrong man to prison! How can I live with that?"

He turned again to the coffeemaker. Snub shook his

16

head. "Oh, I'm sure you'll find a way. You're an expert at rationalizing."

"Ouch," she said.

"Weren't you on your way out?"

She pecked the side of his neck. The wayward shock of hair came free again. "Bye."

She thought he said goodbye just as she shut the door. It didn't matter. Sulky old cuss, she thought. Whew. That was not fun. Not really. She glanced out each of the corridor windows as she advanced down the lobby hall. At each pane she thought of a separate era in her affair with Snub.

You were so foolish, Biz. You walked right into that darkroom knowing what was going to happen once the red light went on, once he locked the door. "We don't want anyone coming in," he'd said. "Light will spoil the negatives."

Snub was all he ever cared about. Negatives? She asked herself. You fell for that line.

Of course, Snub had practiced his come-on for years. The rumors at school had been both rife and long-lived. Later, she'd discovered just what a roll of lies Snub had uncoiled over twenty years before she was his assistant. If lies had been film, he'd have kept Kodak in business. Then again, she should give herself some credit. She didn't let it happen right off, anyway. No, she had resisted, passively but stood it nonetheless. Snub's tales of married life, listless sex, overreliance on masturbation, and an oblivious, uncaring wife—that one led right into him pleading, how many years ago, for that first hand job. Looking back on it, Elizabeth saw just how smooth Snub had become and how stupidly she had gone along.

And she went along again. After college, she felt grateful for him ushering her into teaching. Somehow, he'd gotten her the job without a certificate in the middle of California's credentialing muddle. She showed him her thanks in the only way he would accept it, but his had always been the same piteous story. He was "a loving, sensuous soul trapped in a frigid marriage." How wrong he was. Snub was the cold one, the calculating lecher. He was the best and very worst teacher, and eventually he made her over in his own image.

Elizabeth Moore stopped at the final window, now approaching the hotel lobby proper, and fussed with her belt and hair in that last reflection. "Forget it, Biz," she said to her own image. "Put him out of your mind." She walked briskly into the hotel café and ordered coffee to go.

The California morning was fresh and promised the kind of leafy splendor she had loved as a girl. Bright sun and cool breeze. Now this is joy, she thought. The buzz of the coffee pushed her mind flat against the crisp, thin air. It was a day for being.

"No thinking allowed," she said.

A man on his way up the post office steps turned, thinking, perhaps, she had spoken to him.

"Top o' t'a mornin', Dr. Moore," he said.

"Good morning. Monsignor Phelan isn't it?" It was, and she couldn't avoid him. "You are on the program this Saturday. We share the podium."

"'T'is true Doctor, and I'll invoke t'a saints at luncheon and dinner on Friday as well. I haven't seen you at confession lately."

Though annoyed, Elizabeth laughed. "I'm Presbyterian, remember?"

"Yes, yes. It's the coming festivities, you know, have addled my old brain."

She nodded and truly agreed, as well. "Reunions have a way of doing that, Monsignor. Take care."

Elizabeth Moore left the priest on the post office steps,

walked down the block, sipping her coffee, and felt the tingle of the morning trail down her arms, thrilling her fingertips. She drew her shoulders back and drove the air up her nostrils to meet the caffeine vibrating behind her eyes.

"Heavenly day," she said and strode down the walk through warming sun and shady coolness toward her hotel.

Would Finn stay at The Stanford? That might be too much to hope. Elizabeth ticked through an inventory of memory. Where would he go? She had not seen him since June of '67 but knew him, she thought, through and through. No, The Stanford is too fancy for Finn. God, not the Holiday Inn, Snub's hotel, though something told her Snub would be checking out and going back home to his wife, Bobbie. That room had been for his one-night stand with her. Snub knew she wouldn't repeat the mistake so soon. No, Holiday Inn was not for Finn.

She thought about the string of mom-and-pop motels out on 101. That's a maybe. Does he still have that shack his father built? She wondered. Yes, Elizabeth felt suddenly sure. That's where he'll be. Finn was not shoddy or a woodsman anymore, but she knew he drew strength from solitude and avoided the scramble of small talk and social duty. He'd avoid town as long as he could.

He had invited her to the cabin only twice. One time they'd made love in the narrow bunk by firelight. The cabin was far from squalid but carried a homemade, immigrant-like foreignness that made her feel out of place. The low-door, rough-board interior and homemade furniture had framed in her imagination waiting spiders hiding in dark, woody corners. She had stood puzzled, after unhooking her skirt and lowering her zipper, looking for a place to lay clothes. Finn had dusted a chair, carefully folded her skirt on its seat, and hung the blouse she held out to him over the chair back. She'd said nothing, but her strangeness there flickered in firelight.

She'd snuggled to his chest, caressing his taut forearms, tickling him under his chin with her bouffant curls (now long gone, thank God). Finn's body was flowing and smooth. Fine blond hair, barely visible, coated his round arms and powerful legs, inviting a silky touch. Though carefully avoiding his scarred hand, a burn she hated to think of, she loved to run her lips along his arm, feeling delicate skin and mild down. She remembered him tan, always tan, and beneath the softness, living brawn. His body was not bold, just solid. His strength spoke not power but action. A baseball player's physique, muscled and pliant, fluid and strong. What made Finn so special, though, was another softness beneath his skin and muscle. It was as if gentle layers wound around a resilient core all stitched over with a durable glowing warmth. Manly, Finn beamed health, a plain honesty, a bashful prominence that set him apart. He's not mean, she thought. That's the difference between us.

Finn is—or at least, was— a man of good will.

What would he say to her uncertainty now, her doubts about who had killed Denise Hagerty?

She paused in the shade of a wide, spreading palm. She felt her cheek. Chagrin and more, the onset of a deepening guilt flushed there. She felt more strongly she'd been mistaken, stupidly wrong. I've been the hard-hearted one. The dream from that morning startled her again, right in the middle of the street. She teetered on her heels, crossing quickly to the corner, and plunked down hard on the bus-stop bench.

Elizabeth had seen Finn with Doug Brandling before the boy's arrest. Finn with the young catcher—whose brother, Warren, she had taught (more than taught like Snub had done for, rather to her). As she watched from the doorway, the boy leaned against the huge table in Finn's classroom. Sitting on the oak-table edge, Finn hugged the boy with one big arm, his burned hand dangling over the young man's shoulder. He bent his head to the boy's ear. Was he saying something tender? They seemed, instead of being at the center of a murder inquiry, as if they were having a coach and player conference at the dugout railing as she had seen many times during the games she'd attended.

And then had come the moment that had split her and Finn apart. She'd entered his classroom with two detectives and the chief of police. Finn did not, could not, look at her. The catcher stared wide-eyed in terror, but Finn kept talking, counseling. With that bad hand, the only ugliness about him, he patted the boy's back gently.

Now, sitting at the bus stop, Elizabeth pressed her fingers to her cheeks, probed for any softness or warmth. She slumped back on the bench.

Twenty-four years ago, that morning in Finn's classroom, her face had felt like cold stone. It must have looked that way, too. She'd nodded to the chief. "That's the one. The catcher." At that moment, she'd known for sure. Now, her certainty was a thing of the past.

Finn had cared. He'd been tender. He had protected her against her father, against Snub, sometimes against herself. And then he'd protected the boy, against her. Finn had held up his hand without looking away from the boy. He'd stayed the police.

"Let me bring him around, would you?" He'd squeezed the boy's shoulder and shook it. Finn nodded to him. "It'll be all right, Doug." The boy had just cried, unable to speak.

A bus pulling up to her bench shook Elizabeth from her thoughts. The driver watched her expectantly. She shook her head and moved quickly away, began walking again, forgetting her coffee on the bench. Her thoughts followed her.

Again, Elizabeth Moore, the accuser, had stood stiffly by the door as the police advanced. "Let me bring him around, would you?" That was what Finn had said. And he moved with his catcher held close. He passed by her still bending over the boy, still talking to Doug in the same assuring voice, still hugging his shoulder with that scarred hand of his. He did not look at her.

She'd felt like ice. Finn hadn't ignored her. He just passed her by, patting the boy's shoulder and talking gently, reassuringly to him.

After that day, she and Finn had talked twice. Neither encounter had been sweet.

"I'm the hard one," she said aloud.

She had passed the Stanford Hotel entrance.

Elizabeth Moore was annoyed.

Don't ruin this day, Biz, she told herself. Let the muck lie on the bottom. Don't let the past play so heavily on you. She thought about the interview Finn had asked for. See Finn, even as a journalist, and be happy. She turned around, tugged her vest down, and strode into the hotel.

4

Monsignor Phelan

"Reunions have a way of doing that," she'd said, and I knew I'd slighted the truth. How could she, of all people, know the burden of confessions, the weight of guilt piled heavy on my shoulders? It was not the reunion that addled my mind, so much as fifty years of the contrition and penance of others, a burden too hard to bear. It is not something to discuss with a non-believer.

"Presbyterian?" Atheist more likely.

The truth be told, it was that red letter and what happened before mass that had muddled my mind, those and seeing her, of all people, so soon after.

I had not slept well and had cursed God's creatures:

How I hate these summer mornings! Stuff a pillow over my head. Those confounded birds still stir up a racket. Silence. In the name of the Lord, I say, silence!

"Let there be light," He said, but not this much, please dear Lord, humbly I pray. It's an uncivil twilight. Please, don't wake me with dawn at 5:15, with mass to be said in just a few hours. Dear Lord, your humble servant, I beseech thee. Those starlings! Agh!

Where did that cursed pillow go? Off the bed? On the floor again. And slippers? I need my slippers and robe. Oh, gird me, O Lord, at least with the girdle of warmth. With the girdle of . . . , yes, snugness . . . that I might extinguish . . . I may put down this chill.

Oh, Phelan, wake up. Don't break the lamp. Aha!, My slippers. You vile pillow, good at hiding my comforts but useless against a June morning's rudeness. Let me lay my hands on you, now! Back there. Untangle my robe. My alb for mass. No, my robe.

Five-twenty and wide awake. No paper. No sun to warm me. Shrieking, hiding birds. Dash them. Consider, yea. They need no robes. They neither toil nor spin. No, that's lilies, Phelan. At least flowers are silent, robed or not.

Then up and sorting through the mail, a few paltry contributions for the building fund, only enough to require a letter of thanks, I come across that red envelope, an out-of-season Christmas greeting, I thought. Tore it and tossed it into the trash. No, no, it might be a tithe or gift for the fund. Now I wish I'd let it be.

First I saw that news photo, Mrs. Hagerty and I hugging Dennis between us. Oh, sweet Dennis I tell you, the one Jesus loved reclined beside him. I loved you Dennis, and they sent you off anyway:

Who saved that clipping all this time? So like in my memory. Oh, sweet Dennis. Let me comfort you. Come to me, lovely boy. God will comfort thee. "No," I told him, "your sister didn't deserve to die."

That is what I thought this morning. Someone saved

that picture to torture me. I comforted that boy on the death of his sister. He felt that weight, felt responsible. He did not need to be sent away.

The torn note I read next like a horror after dread:

Who but 'D'
knows, but she?

Beside myself, I swore:

Damn this envelope. No, nothing on it. Who? Who is this man sending the good Father this? A sinner. A brute. An enemy? So the note, "Who but 'D'" Who? I hammered it with my fist. I'll kill this red letter man. "She?" A woman. Even so, I can do it. I have it in me . . . , but pray, Phelan, pray, "'nevermore to offend Thee.'" And "D" is Dennis, or is it Denise? All typewritten. Could be anyone. My God. Salvation. The mass. My sweet Dennis, forgive me. The mass.

Addled? I'd nearly forgotten the early mass. Somebody knows something. But why did they send it to me?

Had a parishioner seen me dash out the back door of my residence in my silken robe this morning, he'd likely have shaken his head and thought to call the Bishop. I knew they talked of me and dementia in the same breath. They worry about my drinking. Early mass, though, is sparsely attended in summer, and I slipped into the church unseen.

Unseen and thoroughly confounded, but joy, my altar boys, bless them, were waiting. I have a new Dennis to love:

Bless you, Dennis. You remembered the door. Still time.

"A blessed morning to you boys."

"Good morning, Father."

"Even with the Lord's early light, we are running late. William, see to the missal and ordo, please. Dennis, please assist me in the sacristy."

"All is ready, Father."

"Good boy, but today I need help." His hair is so soft, a delicate neck like my first Dennis. Don't fondle, Phelan. "Good, good."

"I'll get the door, Father."

Yes, yes. Go ahead. Let me splash my cheeks here. "I'm coming, Dennis."

"William, light the two candles. Hold the door, Dennis."

"Oh my boy, you have done well. Look! Everything is so orderly."

"Thank you, Father. William did most of it."

Of course. So modest. "You are too generous, my boy." And so pure. Give virtue, O Lord unto my hands that every stain may be wiped away . . . . Always fumbling with the knots. "Help tie this, please, Dennis. Bring the stool. That's it." See how supply his fingers move. The work of the Lord. "Well done, my boy. Thank you. "Place, O Lord, the helmet of salvation"—say it quickly, Phelan—"upon my head that I may overcome . . ."

"'. . . the assaults of the Devil?' Is that it, Father?"

"Yes, yes. That's it, Dennis."

"Your alb, Father."

The stool. Yes, up on the stool. "Step up, Dennis. That's good. Does it hang well behind? Just brush the cloth a bit, thank you."

"Father?"

"Oh, yes. Why don't you say it? For practice."

His voice is sweet, an angel. "Yes, 'everlasting joy.' Fetch a longer cincture."

"Around me. A bit lower. Good. You tie it. Now, let's us pray together: 'Gird me, O Lord, with the girdle of purity and extinguish in my—our—loins the desires of lust so that the virtue of continence and chastity may ever abide within us.' Well done."

"Thank you, sir."

"No, no, you must not call me 'sir' but 'Father,' Dennis." Oh, his cheeks are smooth. So warm. "Listen to me." Such sweet breath. "Don't fear. You never harmed your sister."

"Father?"

No, no don't pull away. "Listen, my boy. Still. I know, Dennis. You've always felt it was your fault. But it wasn't."

"Father Phelan."

"You must not let guilt kill innocence. You are so pure." Such a face. All right, let him loose. Such a face.

"Yes, Father. You only think me pure, but I don't know what you mean. I have no sister."

"No, of course, not now, she is gone, but

once . . ." Watch the stool, don't fall.

"I'm sorry, Father Phelan, I do not have a sister, only a brother. Do we need the stool more? Are you all right, Father?"

"Your sister. . . what? You had no sister? No Denise?"

"Denise?"

Phelan. Wake up. This is wrong. "No, no, of course, Dennis. I was . . . I was thinking of someone else. I'm sorry."

"I should check on William."

"Yes. Yes. But bring me the maniple." He moves so delicately. "Thank you. Go, now. Go." Let me latch that door.

"'May I be worthy, O Lord . . .' That Christmas letter. That red curse. Sweet Dennis. It was not your doing. You were innocent, so innocent." A sip of wine. Just a sip. First the birds. The newsclip. The letter. Who? And late for mass, then a fool before Dennis. Hurry.

The violet stole! My penance burns me. It should be red. Red? Red for love. That letter is not love. Penance? Hurry Phelan, the mass. Violet, violent, violet. The chasuble, too. "'My burden is light' make me able to bear it . . .'" do the Lord's bidding. All else must wait. But "she?" Who is "she?"

And later that morning, when I recognized Dr. Moore from the post office steps, I considered an answer to that question. Though she'd never admitted anything, others in town who confess regularly had, no names attached, painted me a portrait of Elizabeth Moore.

28

5

Farley Pike

And why shouldn't I? Farley Pike said to himself. He had never been caught at it.

After all he lived alone now, and wasn't it entirely a private affair? And Elizabeth—he always insisted on thinking of her as Elizabeth, not Biz, which some seemed to prefer—was certainly on his mind, provoking him. She had been his greatest conquest.

Pike rubbed his shoulders with the Lux towel, moving the plush down his hairy back, buffing hard. He rasped his buttocks with the towel and buffed upwards again, then dropped one end, swung it up and through his legs, running the towel rapidly through his crotch, back and forth vigorously. He felt that familiar tingle. Well, no time now. He whipped the towel up and wiped the mirror.

The truth was that his drive was flagging already at fifty-five. He glanced sideways at his profile. Still handsome as ever, though. Distinguished, he mused. That gray splash across my sideburns and all.

Pike pushed his little potbelly and what hung below it against the sink, gyrating in one, then in the other direction. He thought again of Elizabeth Moore. Farley dried his glasses, and when he put them on, applied the shaving cream, starting as usual at the right ear, working around the chin and up the left cheek.

Elizabeth Moore. Pike gestured to the mirror with his razor. Now there was a woman. A sexy walk without the voluptuous come-on, ample breasts—here he rubbed his pelvis up and down against the sink—and a nice protrusion at the pubis. She was not like those fat-thighed girls who insisted nowadays on wearing jeans over all too-ample bellies. Elizabeth knew how to walk.

For years—three, starting in 1958 when Elizabeth came up a sophomore, and two more when she taught at Santa Reina High—Farley had stood outside his classroom and later in front of the office between the passing bells, watching her pubic bone, pressing against her taut skirt, shift against it (more circling of hips at the sink, here) as she'd swung down the hall to the student lunchroom or, later, the teacher's lounge.

The single time he had prevailed (Elizabeth had been a teacher then. He, Farley Pike, was no sleazy, coed-chasing Snub Randall) her guard had been down. Perhaps she had been a bit drunk, though he liked to think that was not a factor. Even so the encounter still gave him more than satisfaction. Yes, gave him hope, that was it. Hope for what? For more? Perhaps, but certainly a sense of pride, a feeling of well-being. Yes, a new beginning, the sense of a life well lived. He wiped the cream residue from his neck and flicked a spot from his earlobe. He leaned over the sink.

They looked long, those ear lobes. Didn't the ear and nose keep growing throughout life? He took his glasses off to splash his face over the basin, removing the towel from his waist to shine the spigot, and then put the glasses back on, leaning close to the mirror, preening the little David Niven moustache he had worn since the mid-fifties. Yes, he thought, I would have her again. He cocked an eyebrow.

And that idea might not be so far-fetched. He stroked his paunch. There were events all around town, late dinners at the conference, and parties some of the professors from State were hosting. There were luncheons and a breakfast too—he was most fond of breakfast—though late parties seemed more appropriate to an interlude.

"Interlude," he said and rolled the idea around his mind. Yes, Elizabeth would be an interlude. Nothing permanent. That was not her nature, not in the cards for her, especially after Finn Pyykönen. Elizabeth was now a professional woman, not the spouse type, not a wife. He could not visualize her in an apron, with curlers, or draping lingerie over the shower curtain rod. Well, she must do those things, he decided, but he could not imagine her existing, drudging through the daily tasks of life, any more than he could conceive of living each day with her, or, for that matter, with any woman now that his mother was gone. Elizabeth belonged in the halls of schools dressed in her tight skirts and tailored blouses, balanced on heels, wearing a pearl necklace and matching earrings, jaunty flips and curls at that slender carefully coifed nape of neck that he wanted to kiss again.

Pike clipped an errant moustache hair jutting over the lip. He closed his eyes and pursed his lips to the air.

Elizabeth was on the program. She would be there. They all would be there, the class of '67 everyone called them. None of them graduated that year, of course, but that was the year that changed their lives, their pivotal year, the fall that he had had Elizabeth, the year that had ushered him into school administration, that had sent Finn Pyykönen packing so soon after arriving, that had pointed Elizabeth on her path to stardom as Dr. Elizabeth Moore. Then again, 1967 hadn't changed Snub at all. But then Snub didn't "need" to change. He had everything he wanted, and nothing touched Snub Randall.

Pike combed his hair over, then back, then lifted the receding peak up with the comb, pressing the ends down and forward to create a wave.

Stephen Randall had already been a legend by the time Pike had arrived to teach junior English right across the hall. Anyone else would have been notorious rather than legendary. Snub should have been in jail, if the rumors were true. Well, Mr. Pike was there to teach, not to fool around. Leave that to gadabouts like Stephen Randall.

Yes, Mr. Randall—Pike always addressed him formally while everyone else, even, most inappropriately, students called him Snub—taught with the door open. Always there was laughter in Snub's room. Snub was always leaning on that windowsill, talking in that conversational, friendly tone, authoritative but always as if he imparted something the students already knew, a secret they shared before, that Snub was now reluming. The students loved him, but for Farley Pike there was too much levity. And always music. Mr. Randall leaned on the radiator and jingled change in the pockets of his creased trousers, always playing with something in his pocket. And the innuendos. Pike had to shut his door. He couldn't stand it.

"Hello, FP," Snub had greeted him his very first day. "You mind if I call you FP? S. William Randall." He flashed that damnably genuine smile. It was the kind of smile that said, "We have a little confidence here, you and I, and can laugh about it together, but, please"—the smile said at the same time—"don't forget that I am laughing at something entirely different, something unknown to you, something that I will not tell you about."

"Mr. Randall," Pike had said extending his hand, "I've heard so much about you. Farley Pike." Randall had not joined the handshake. That hand remained in his pocket, jiggling change or something. Snub just smiled. "My pleasure."

That's why they called him Snub, Farley thought. He was

able to demean one gracefully.

In his bathroom, Pike squeezed a dab of Brylcreem on his index finger, swirled it in his palm, and plastered the ends of his wave to the rear of his bald spot. He ran the comb over the ends and slid his palm softly over the few hairs once more.

He spoke to the mirror. "I never agreed to FP. FP! Whoever heard of it?" No one had, but that is what Snub and afterward all of them called him, FP. He knew the students, too, used it behind his back. They made up meanings for the acronym, "Farty Pants," and "Fucking Pansy" were two he knew about.

"Oh, thanks so very much, Mr. Randall," he said to the mirror. He did not look forward to seeing his former colleague.

Farley Pike grimaced at his reflection. You are ruining a perfectly good mood by thinking about what? Mr. Sneaky-Smile, Stephen William Randall. Snub to all the world. Just stop it. Think of Elizabeth. He tried to conjure the scene, Elizabeth reaching to slip her panties off from up under her skirt, how she tugged and worked the skirt and slip up and leaned back on the desk. It was no use. He couldn't bring it up. The scene shied elusively away, faded. Thoughts of Snub Randall had swept it entirely out of his mind.

Anyway, he must hurry. He must not skip breakfast. Farley Pike never missed breakfast.

6

Snub Speaks

I don't mean to complain so much, but let me say a few words about the inconsistency of words. When I was learning English, at the beginning of this century, I often wondered why words sounded exactly the same but meant different things. Then I learned that some words look nearly alike but also represent divergent ideas. Then there are a small number, like "let," which in fact stand for opposites. Look it up sometime.

So when I wrote, "Clear your sight!/ Who's Mr. Right?" Who did I mean? "Mr. Right," as I should have known, could be anybody. Biz jumped to the conclusion that it was our convicted murderer, Doug Brandling. Wrong! Snub is "Mr. Right!" I meant me over Finn Pyykönen, that's for sure. After all, who is still sounding the depths of Elizabeth Moore, PhD? Him or me?

Take it for what it's worth. Even misunderstood, my mischievous missive will be fun to watch.

If you've been keeping up with fashions in the book business, you may know that I am what they call an unreliable narrator, though I assure you that I am telling the truth perhaps for the very first time in my life. At least for the first time since swiping apples off the Dollard's tree at age five: I stepped forward saying, "It was me. I did it." Mr. Dollard's hands-on-his-hips question was answered.

Please. I know I've been going on about myself, but don't get the idea that this is a story about me or that it is a defense of my activities. Far from it.

First, if there were an excuse for my life as I've lived it, believe me, I would use it. Since there are no good reasons, I'll stick to telling it as plainly as I can.

Secondly, I am not even the main character in the story. I don't tell most of it (more about the main characters later). The story is about the "class of '67" as I've mentioned before—not the graduating class of 1967, though one or two of them are in the story, but that small group of people whose lives were altered, some derailed, by what happened at Santa Reina High School starting a day before the 1967 Memorial Day break, which, for us, began, by contract and tradition, the Thursday afternoon prior to the actual holiday, May 25th that year.

"The event," was one of those senseless, sickening, and brutal crimes—yes, sick: it takes a long while to stab a person nearly twenty times (even working quickly), and I would hate to tell you the thoughts that likely run through the mind during that interval. That kind of crime, it seems, only the very young, the very desperate, or the very crazy can commit. I am not spoiling the narrative here, so this is not a point at which to put the story down. For this tale is about much more than who committed the crime. Actually, for over twenty years most people in town that year thought they knew "whodunit," so not many wondered about that one. I had a special reason to be interested in that aspect, but I was actually more intrigued by what happened to the people closest to the crime after it ceased to be news. I was intimate with more than one of them.

Now I did say I don't tell most of this story? I'm in it, as you've seen, but someone else tells most of it. You might call that someone the reliable narrator. It stands to reason that if there is an unreliable storyteller—an early example is Nelly Dean, the housekeeper, in *Wuthering Heights*, one of my favorites—there must be a reliable one. That might be Lockwood, the tenant in Emily Bronte's book. If you can believe anything anyone tells you, especially when she changes her mind, then you can, supposedly, believe the reliable one. That, you can determine.

I have a lot to say, so if I can't shut up, I hope you don't mind; after all, I'm the one who is dying.

Like I said at the beginning, I can't help yakking, but remember I'm not telling you your business. As far as I can see, you are all agents free to make up your own minds. Take what I say for what it's worth.

7

Doug

He makes a sound that wakes him. His first thoughts: Gray. Early. The bells haven't been rung. Early and gray before the bells.

He does not open his eyes. His cell is drab, but the light through the slit must also be faint, early ashen light through fog. What there is of vented air is still cool, but it is day, very early morning. No sun, no heat, yet. And what was the sound?

He rolls onto his back. He pulls the blue wool blanket high, thrusts his pillow over his forehead, cramming it against his eyelids. He lies flat like he's on a gurney. What had that sound been?

In sleep, he had found himself on a ball diamond. He saw skeletons of bleachers but no stadium. The field was huge, open, unfenced. That expanse worried him. But the sound? No, not yet.

He was clothed. Wildcats uniform? No. Prison-thin blue cotton, that kind of pajama. But on a diamond. He crouched behind home plate. The world flew outwards before him, chalk lines diverging, running out forever. It was wide as prairie. The infinite spread of the field sickened him.

The grass of the infield was grizzled, a light silvery gray. Out beyond second base it was dark, wolf-gray. The acreage beyond swirled in excess. The outfield flowed for miles, and he could see to the right and left of the foul lines, through the tiers of short bleachers and over the top seat boards, the land expanding. Now it breathed. Ponderously, the prairie inhaled

39

as if to suck him out there to the horizon. Breath was let go, heaving the faraway hills in undulating rises, alive.

Horrified, he backed off, came out of his squat, scurried backward, facing the grisly scene, unable to tear his eyes away.

Get to the dugout, behind walls, sheltered by concrete and fences. Never turn your back on a hitter, but he must flee from the mushrooming hills. He kept his catcher's mask on. He stared out at the dreadful field through the visor's protective bars, yet he was afraid. He stepped back toward safety, tripped on the step's curb, and fell into the dugout.

Deep into it, he had fallen. And flat on his back, landed. He made a sound. As in a collision at home plate, his breath burst forth, punched by the shoulder of the flying runner, then slammed by the fall to the ground, his lungs completely emptied in a guttural ugh.

That sound woke him.

Doug Brandling lies on his back, a pillow pushed over his eyes, waiting for bells to stir the prison.

From outside, through the narrowness of the slit that serves as a window, he feels the air stir. The faintest freshness moves, a cool feather tickling his nose below the pillow, signaling the beginning of the day.

Wednesday? Doug asks himself. No, Thursday. This is Finn's day. Finn will be here at lunchtime. He thought. Doug ordered his activities. It's workout day. It's shower day. It's Finn's day. Then reading day. Malamud day.

He tosses the pillow off. The faint sound of radio music, a Sacramento station, country music, filters through the slit, echoes, too, in the corridor.

Finn, he thinks. His heart skips, misses a beat and hurts his chest. Did he hurt himself in the fall? He breathes. No, he says to himself, it was a dream. You dream. Finn visits. The day begins leaden, always gray. Doug rubs his chest, moving his hand in a slow rhythm circling his ribs, breathing out and in, sinking and rising on the thin mattress. It is something he has learned here.

Malamud day. He thinks of Malamud's character, Roy. Had Roy Hobbs done time? Roy can't be free, but Doug will be some day. Doug opens his eyes.

The cell is dun. The bunk above is painted gray, boxed in and bolted. No one can sleep there now. The wall, the door, the floor and ceiling beyond the upper bunk are gray. Only the book jackets he's taped to the wall over his narrow desk have color. Now before dawn, they must be dark, too, lifeless in a light so dim itself seems incarcerated. But when the morning bells ring and his light illumines the cell or in evening with his desk lamp on, the book covers are brilliant. Greens warm and blues glisten, intense as a baseball field under morning skies. When the light comes, the writers' names stand out: Harris, Malamud, Kinsella. Now though, his towel hangs between, hiding the book covers above the desk. The towel is ashen like everything else.

Doug thinks of Roy—Roy Hobbs. He is reading *The Natural,* recording it on a tape for the blind. Doug will send the tape out into a night, black not gray. Someone, another kind of inmate, will behold what he cannot see, will glimpse through Doug's voice how Roy cannot be free. What will it mean to him, his customer, his Braille reader, his listener? Will that one hear in his voice that Doug will be free? Will they still share, he and his sightless readers, what there is to learn in here? How to do time? How to live in mist or darkness? That gray or black is for thinking? Doug wonders if blackness, if blindness, is the same as prison.

He thinks of Finn again. Doug rubs his chest. There is nothing to fear. Doug feels for Finn's goodness. He knows his friend's kindness.

Years later now, he still sees Finn on his first day teaching, January 9, 1967, standing at the door of the classroom. Doug feels Finn's goodness. The wood of the door trim frames a warm expectation. Finn smiles. Doug understands.

He had known Finn was to be his coach, that he had led the Wildcats through the glory years, '59-'61. This is good luck, Doug had thought, to follow a former champion, and to have the coach as your history teacher couldn't hurt. Doug, already good in history, would become much better even in that half year under Finn. It hadn't been quite a full semester, but Doug counted it as a completed term anyway. Near its end, he felt he had really begun to understand history.

Then his life had ended.

Don't go there, he orders himself. "Don't go there," Doug says aloud. "You don't remember, anyway." He flips the pillow over his head. Undercover, he sees his brother, Warren, dressed in his Wildcats uniform, saying as he always had, "Watch my back, Dougie." Doug tosses the pillow to the floor. He opens his eyes. He rubs his chest.

Feelings, he reminds himself. They are feelings, only feelings. It is something he has learned here: Let feelings pass. Warren, who has never visited, who has never written, is gone. I can think of Finn without remembering Warren. I can take the good and leave the bad.

He knows it is nearly six. It has been years since he had a clock. No need here. He knows the time. Doug swings his feet to the floor. This time, when Finn gets here, I will tell him. I know what he'll say, but this time I'll tell him. He stands, and as he has every day for nearly twenty-four years, he makes his bed.

Bells clatter in sudden alarm. Stop. Again clamor. His cell lights flicker. The day begins.

Doug is up. Dressed, he stands before his door, ready

for it to open. He can wash at the kitchen before serving. Thursday: grits, scrambled eggs, grapefruit. Some call it gray-fruit. Serving was his privilege. Steal and if caught, you're out. And they are always caught. Again, stubbornly, Warren comes to mind. Someone inside says, "Warren wasn't caught." The door opens, the day moves, and routine squelches Doug's memory.

"Serving detail. State your name."

"Douglas Brandling, C-63." He moves toward the cafeteria.

The forced habit of Doug's days follows him like a faithful dog. If he didn't embrace the rut, he would become the dog, the animal. His hug of routine, today's plan and tomorrow, Friday's, puts him in charge. Even though his route would be bent by Finn's visit, Doug's regimen will stand. Finn sweetened the day. A special break, a visit on Thursday. It was a privilege.

That old fear that it would not happen needled Doug's mind. He touched his chest. No, Finn comes. Still, Doug never waits. That was something he'd learned here. Don't wait. Never wait.

In the kitchen, at the deep stainless steel sink, Doug splashes his face, washes, and then scrubs his hands twice. Teammates, watch out, he thought. If anyone noted his care, he shrugged. It is his choice, his plan. Doug keeps clean, he'd decided. And no one suffers.

Doug adheres to the ration. Workout day means eat light. Eggs, milk, bread and butter. Plenty for a busy day.

He and Kettner will practice in the bull pen. Special dispensation for the championship battery. Kettner had pitched baseball in college for a year. Though he's young, he knows some stuff. He hasn't studied the game as Doug has, so it is instruction as well as practice. Kettner's eager.

Stretch, warm up, call one-hundred pitches, cool. Working with one pitcher is not perfect. New ideas are hard to come by, but it is what Block C, the C-Cats team has. K-B, Kettner and Brandling, Killer-Ball. It keeps him in shape. And they mix the two—pitching one day and weights and stretching the next. No one could touch them. Doug can play.

In the afternoon, he will read. It had been unusual and difficult to promote the titles he wanted. Inmates do not get to choose. He'd lobbied without suggesting. The success of the films had helped. "Should we try to include the blind in the wider, popular culture?" That was his strongest urging. The popularity of the films, especially *The Natural* and, later, *Field of Dreams*, proved influential. And it happened.

The order had come through. After brailling the book, he'd recorded *Bang the Drum Slowly* four years ago. The "shit deal" (Hodgkin's disease) the fictional catcher, Bruce Pearson, was handed, flooded Doug's reading with feeling. Then he recorded the pitcher's story, *The Southpaw*. Doug loved this battery of books. His recordings had been very well received. They were ordered often.

Then it had been Malamud's turn.

He'd not known the book then, just the movie. He'd already set a laurel on Roy Hobbs, his cinematic hero. So once he read far enough into Malamud's book for the horror of Roy's character to grip him, it was too late to shake Hobbs-as-hero and much too late to abandon the reading. That time, he had recommended the book outright.

Doug hoped, as he read, that the redemption of Roy Hobbs could still lead Doug Brandling and his listeners to their own cure. This close to his release, Doug couldn't say it wasn't so. He still hoped.

Page by page, as he read into the machine, those hopes had dwindled. What he laid down on tape for The Blind

Project was not the deliverance of his hero—Roy's crimes and gluttony sickened Doug—but became sure damnation, self-wasting delusion, and spiritual corruption. Yet Doug waded through the text determined to finish.

He wants it to be at an end. He has more time, though it might be close.

Don't wait, he tells himself.

8

Finn

And here is Inga. "At last," Finn says under his breath. Always worth the wait. So tall, so sophisticated. She's grown her hair again.

Tense blond curls crowd at her broad tanned forehead and cascade behind her round brown cheeks. The color of Mexico, Finn thinks.

Inga Pyykönen scans the room, spots her father grinning broadly, rising from his chair by the window overlooking the garden of Henry's Café. She strides to him, weaving through the tables and waiters, waving and shining her smile over his face.

"My lovely girl," Finn says, opening his arms. He hugs her, then pushes away to offer his cheek. "A peck for Pekka?" he says, using a family pun on his given name. Inga kisses her father.

"Smart and lovely," she says, correcting him, flashing her smile, and looking into his eyes. "How are you, *mon père*? Did you sleep?"

"With fraternities across the street? Hardly. Sit. How was Mexico? I can see it in your face."

"There is nothing more splendid than building straw-bale houses for people living in ragged tents, *mon père*." She hugs him again, tightly, "But look at you. Here at Henry's, whoo-whoo, staying at the Durant, my-my."

Finn colors and squirms at his extravagance. "I wanted it to be convenient for you. Better to meet you at the Claremont?

47

That's out of my league. This is fine for a night. Hucci-Gucci but fine." He pulls out a French Provençal chair for Inga. "Sit," he says. She swishes with élan into her place.

"*Merci, mon père.*"

Still with the French even after Mexico. So like your mother. Not just the hair, the button nose, the punky chin. The voice, the edgy twists, the politic sass are Ellie's but sharper in you. He takes her hand. "I have missed you, Sweetie," he tells her. "Berkeley is a long way from home. I miss you in Pasadena."

"This is home, Dad, at least for the next four years or so. You won't be at the house much anyway. Won't you be working on something in New York with Pers at Columbia, now? Besides, you really have to make a life of your own, *mon père.*"

"Hey, order something other than me carved and served on a platter. I'm having a waffle, but order anything you want." He fingers the water goblet and fiddles with the brocaded napkin, the coat of arms of the Durant Hotel emblazoned on it. Gauche.

Inga is right, of course. He should have stayed with David, his high school teammate, or even with Inga's aunt, Millie, though either would have proved complicated. Especially Millie, who had never approved of her sister, Ellie, marrying beneath her. Millie did not understand the term "love of my life," and she had thrown it in his face at Ellie's funeral: "How's the love of her very short life?" It was bad enough losing his wife after only fourteen years, worse being blamed for her death. Still, he forgave Millie. Ellie was her loss too.

Even so, Finn could not see sharing toast and coffee with Inga and Millie. Not oil and water; potassium strips and acid. Ridiculous as the hotel was, and noisy with youthful bluster and brag, it was better than Millie's Orinda ranch. It was not as entangled with the past as David reliving his locker room lust in his tiny Berkeley apartment.

Finn's cheeks flush. Inga is right about New York, too, and about getting his own life, his life as a single man rather than a single parent. Inga obviously did not need a father mooning about now. Her brother, too, would likely tolerate only infrequent visits. Finn thought of his own freshman year, how seldom he had been mindful of home, of his elders. So, of course, that's as it should be.

"I have an interview in New York with Derek Walcott the end of the month," he admits. "There are rumors he'll be up for the Nobel Prize next year."

Inga nods. "He is deserving. Of course, you'll introduce him to Pers."

"Other way round, but yes," Finn says.

"I'll wait for the article. Is it the *La-La Times*?"

"Where else?" he says. "What are you having?"

"*Huevos rancheros, mon père*." Inga smiles at her *idioma-mixte*. "What I'm really after are the rice and beans." She sits straight and tall, purses her lips, glazes her eyes and sways to and fro like a windup doll. Then she laughs. "I'm so glad you stopped to see me. How was Vacaville?"

"The investigative reporter still," Finn says. Her questions are fine. Inga is unafraid and courageous, qualities that made her a great editor on the *Daily Bruin*. For her, truth lived in the open. When Ellie died—barely thirteen? Inga was, yes, just turned—her first words, "We have to pull together even more, Dad," set the tone. "Especially," she said out of her brother's hearing, "for Pers."

Inga had cried, maybe more than any of them, he recalled, but she led them, forming a tighter, yes, smaller, family that lifted each of them. Finn had wondered if she did it more for herself than her two men, Pers and him. With Inga there was no suffering in silence, no isolation, no running away.

No wonder I love her so much, Finn thinks. She's not Ellie, but for Pers and for him, too, Inga pegged the family tent to the ground. She kept Ellie alive in many ways. Brandishing a book or taking a cardamom-laced loaf of *pulla* from the oven, Inga included her mother. "Mom would have liked this," she'd often said.

Now Inga leans in, levels her gaze at his eyes. "Did you see Doug?"

From far away Finn hears himself say, "I'm driving out there this afternoon."

"Dad?" Inga shakes his arm.

"I was thinking of you, baking bread, ten years ago," Finn says, coming back from that past. "I guess this is the beginning of a new era, isn't it?"

"For you and for us all," Inga says. And Finn notes that Inga blushes as she says so.

They order.

Inga straightens in her chair. "You'll drive to Vacaville and then all the way back to Santa Reina? That's a chore. Where are you staying?"

"At the shack," he says.

Inga lifts an eyebrow. "Will that be comfortable?"

"I thought coming a day early I could make it work, you know, gussy it up a bit. I have my sleeping bag just in case."

"It's going to need more than a sweeping, *mon père*." Inga guesses his reasons, but she must protest the obvious deprivation, the monastic taint, and the solemn history.

Her father had always thrived on an ascetic sturdiness. All these years, for one thing, he'd denied himself companions. Since her mother died there, at the cabin, he'd been alone. Of course, he would stay at the ramshackle retreat her grandpa left. Perhaps it is a farewell. No good to complain, she thinks,

Dad would just laugh. "Shacking it," as he'd say, prevents intrusion from the hoity-toity quarter of Santa Reina. She more than understands but disapproves mildly, "Why?"

Finn does laugh. "I know, I know. A hotel would be more comfortable . . . for someone else. For me it's a hard bunk, *wasabröd*, and black coffee." He knows Inga would worry about him, not worry, really, but express concern, still keeping her great confidence in the rectitude of his choice. She would do the same in his place, that he knows.

"Actually," she says stirring a spoon around an empty cup, "I was thinking of staying up there after summer session."

"You know where the key is."

This time Inga's cheeks flush crimson beneath her tan. She starts to speak, then stops. Finn's waffle and her eggs arrive.

Finn butters his waffle, studying the flow of the melting pats, then looks slyly askance at his daughter. Inga's face is salsa-red and deepens under his gaze. "What are you up to now, *Tytär*?"

She lowers her hands to her lap, sits tall in the chair, eyeing Henry's lofty dining room ceiling, then smiles widely, and lets seep out a joyful sounding sigh. "Dad," she says reaching for his hand, "I'm in love." Inga rushes on before her father can speak. "He's Mexican. Mexican-American, really. An adjunct professor in Latino studies. A poet. A sweet, sweet man. We built together outside La Paz."

"And does this dream boat have a name?"

"José María Antonio de la Cruz Hidalgo," she says rolling each syllable over her tongue like a mint candy. "I call him Jamie, using the American 'J.'" She squeezes her father's hand. "This is the one, *mon père*." She presses her lips firmly together and nods. "He is coming to meet us after his class so I can introduce you." Her impish smile taunts Finn.

He studies her. Is this sudden? Not more than his meeting and marrying Ellie at twenty-four. Inga's twenty-three. Don't be old-fashioned.

"You seem very sure, *Tytär*."

"I am sure, Dad. I waited until I was sure."

"Waited?"

"To tell you, *mon père*," Inga says, "but let Jamie and me announce it together, okay?"

"Anything you wish, my lovely daughter."

She shifts in her chair and forks her eggs. "Smart and lovely, Dad." Inga shifts. "So tell me about Doug."

What can I say about Doug? Finn wonders. What do I know, really?

Doug Brandling, his student over two decades ago. The catcher on the Wildcats varsity team Finn had coached his half-year of teaching had been, for the last twenty-four years, all of Inga's life, an inmate of the California Medical Facility in Vacaville, though he had long been off the psychiatric ward.

Doug became a ghost-brother to his kids, someone Finn was raising as if in another household far off. His presence, though, was felt at home. Doug resided in Finn's life. Inga's mother, too, had talked of the boy, now a man, as if he were living at the Pasadena house. Afterward, when Ellie died, Inga, insisting on openness, demanding to be clear, chatted on with her father about Doug just as her mother had. She urged Finn to keep in touch, to bring back news about Doug.

"He's due for release at the end of this year. I'm looking for a place for him, a job."

"That's scary, I bet." She bites her lip. "It scares me."

Doug had grown nearer, more tangible after her mother's death, and though Inga had never met him, she'd made a point to ask about him just as she would about Pers, her younger brother, even when she was living in Westwood at UCLA.

Doug, though, had not been a physical presence. Now that would change. "What can he do?"

"We're talking about it. He is an expert braillist and machine repairman, but I'm not sure he wants to do that anymore. It's a prison thing. He may not feel he can continue it. He's very hard to read."

"You think he's all right?"

Finn answers grimly. "After a quarter century of prison, who can be all right? He has been seriously wronged."

Inga curiosity flares immediately. "Have you found something?"

"Not exactly. I just have stronger suspicions. I'm working a new angle."

Inga is suddenly like a child sensing a secret. "Tell me."

Finn half smiles. "Next time, *Tytär*. Let me talk to him first. I will say, though, I've talked with his mother."

Inga waits but knows her father well. He'll talk when he's ready.

Now it is his turn to change the subject.

"When is Jamie due?" Finn asks.

"Actually, class is over now. It's a ten-minute walk," Inga says, "enough time to grill you about the reunion."

"It's really a commemoration-slash-reunion."

Inga leans in on him. She is interviewing him now. "And will Dr. Elizabeth be part of this commemoration?"

Finn frowns. Sneaky little devil. Inga has a way of pinning her subject down early in her interviews. It made her the sound journalist she had already become.

"All right," he says, "I'll play your game." There was no avoiding Inga's investigation. She'd become even a better journalist than he, but he'd make her work for every bit.

"I expect her to be there."

"How much will you see her?"

"Quite a bit. I'm planning to interview her for the retro. We are on the same program."

"Tell me about that, could you?"

"We are speaking together."

"Nothing more?"

"Not that I know of."

"What about off-platform? What are your plans with Doctor M, no, with Miss Elizabeth?" Inga is through playing. Now she wants to know.

Finn evades her probe. "'Frankly, my dear, I don't give a damn.'" He smiles broadly. It's been too many years, he thinks, too much difficult past to sort out, and too much had changed.

"Really, *mon père*, you can tell me," she coaxes. "I know you want to see her. Don't you?"

Did he? Elizabeth the proud and the wayward. Elizabeth so hardened. She had never been easy to be with—not like Ellie at all—tightly wound, taut with unspoken, ambitious dreams. Liz had always been tuned to appearance. To see and be seen might sum her up, but she was secretive, too. She had to be if appearances were so important. More than anything, though, she was responsible for Doug's incarceration. Finn was sure she had sent an innocent man to prison.

"I'm not sure. Complicated relationships are not much fun," he says.

Inga will not rest. "You are always full of praise for her, so I thought you would be glad she is coming. It's her advent."

"Advent? You make it sound religious." And glad? He knew it would be unavoidable. They were both free, he had been widowed for almost eleven years and had raised his children. Elizabeth, since college, was married only to her career. They did have history, though a troubled one. Finn was unsure just how he felt about Liz and had little idea how she now felt about him. He guessed that was what he would find out. He also wanted to see if she'd reconsidered her accusation of Doug Brandling.

"Yes, Inga, it will be nice to see Biz again," he says. "But this isn't a beginning, an advent, and please don't start ringing bells or pinning hopes for dear old dad on this old romance."

It had been more than a romance—they had dated after high school and were lovers by late that summer. Though she went out of state, they stayed together in college—at least he had stayed true to her. And until he left college for his crazy ride with the Giants organization that led only to a stint in Viet Nam, they had been an item. After he returned from the war and completed his degree, they reunited as teachers at Santa Reina High. Their future seemed certain then, but murder intervened.

"Sometimes it's better to leave well enough alone," he says.

"So not the advent of Elizabeth. Let the past lie?"

Is Inga leading again? Impossible girl. "I'm playing it by ear. I'm not ruling anything out, but I don't expect this event to spell romance."

"Well," Inga says, "at least you're keeping options open."

Her father looks sternly at her. "You are smart, lovely, and irritating."

"*Mais oui, mon père,*" she says, "but of course. I'm your daughter."

Inga stands. "Here comes Jamie. *Aquí, Enamorado.*"

9

Snub Speaks

This is also a story of a town. The boosters here would call it a city. Maybe it has become that. Really, though, by virtue of its smallish behavior, it is a town, and its story is the same one you could tell about a thousand towns in the country.

Except here, this place is thought of as "Wherever particular people congregate . . . ." That Pall Mall cigarette theme, from back when I was a smoker in my teens, hits it right. The rest of that fragment, I might add, should read "there will be trouble." That is how towns like Santa Reina operate, fuming like a pressure-cooker time bomb.

This is how they start: Let's say that when this part of California was inhabited only by the Miwok, a couple of groups of intruders arrive. Someone says, *sin dudo hablando en español*, "See that man (any non-Miwok) over there? Let's go see what he's up to." One thing leads to another, and pretty soon you have a town where everyone is saying, in effect, let's go see what the others are up to. Civic leaders say this is cooperation, building together, being good neighbors. Just as much, though, it is about idle curiosity, a lack of gumption to do something on one's own, or pure interference. Again, though I'm not telling the whole story, and I could be wrong. Ask yourself sometime: "If people were always being so cooperative, would we need civic leaders like Monsignor Phelan and newspapermen like Finn Pyykönen?"

How a California town grows is much like how any other

town in a newly settled area of America grows. The people who get there first, especially if they have powerful friends, buy up land or start making something everyone needs. They usually get the upper hand. A couple of examples not too far from our area are W. R. Hearst and L. Strauss, probably as different as two men who became prominent could be. It was for good reason. They were enterprising, but the most important was that they got there first, to San Francisco, that is.

Santa Reina is a smaller pond than Frisco—I like to call it that because it grates on the sensibilities of people who think highly of that city—so SR's big fish were minnows compared to Frisco's. That, however, did not make them, in their minds in particular, any less important. An exception close by was L. Burbank, of course, who might have been more plant than person and was known to be humble and kindly. And being such, he established no dynasty, though he certainly left his mark on horticulture.

A town couldn't be a town with just first comers, landowners, or bankers. There have to be Johnny-come-latelies: people to rent from landlords, workers to do the dirty jobs, and to be the small depositors at the bank, who might not even be up for a loan because they don't own much of anything.

To me this is where it gets interesting, because these two groups—you could call them the rich and the poor, but I think that is narrow and misleading (note, for example, what happens to a rich man if you take his money away, or to a poor man who finds a fabulous treasure buried in his backyard). These early birds and late comers do not mix very much. Yet since they depend on one another to make the town run, they look at and talk about each other quite a lot.

Some very-latecomers in our area were Finns—Sonoma

was really the focus for this group—a few of whom after a time trickled down to Santa Reina. As you know by now, one, Pekka "Finn" Pyykönen, is in this story. Finns were noted around here for being hardworking, thrifty, clannish, incomprehensible, and certainly not the right match for, say, the well-to-do descendants of the first arrived, in the present case the now Elizabeth Moore, PhD. Another mismatched pair was poor Denise Hagerty and the Brandling boy. You'll see about that as their stories unfold.

As Santa Reina moved from its beginnings—when the Miwok, then the Spanish, then the Russians were displaced and gold opened this area to eastern interests—toward the so called modern times, the social order flattened. It became more middle class and easier to move up or, I suppose, down the social and financial ladder. That is my era, post-World War II on right up to 1967, when all hell at Santa Reina High and in the town, too, broke loose—it was the murder, you know—though not everything came into the public eye so much as lingered like the smell of cooked fish on drawn drapes and murmurs behind closed doors. That "not everything" I mention lurks here even as folk gather now for the high school centennial and gives me the chance to stir things up a bit.

Taken for what it's worth, even considering the source, it's intriguing.

10

Warren

Sixty-seven was scrawled large in his own hand on the tab of the manila folder. I started this file in the kitchen. The silent, heavily draped house crept back into Warren's mind. He turned the file cover carefully. Folded in quarters was the front page of the *Santa Reina Republic*, Friday, May 26, 1967.

He spread the first fold out to read the headline:

Gruesome Stabbing Stuns SR High

He read, tracing the lines as he went with a slender, almost delicate finger. When he reached the second fold, he spread the page out fully and sat down on the lid of the trunk where he had found his file. One photo showed an ambulance and police cars at the brick-gothic façade of the school, and another picture, the sad stunned face of his madrigals conductor.

"Oh, yes, Elizabeth Moore, good old Bizzy. She was so sure." His narrow shoulders slumped away from his slim neck and shook slightly. He touched his groin, left his hand there. He said, "She never really knew which end was up." Warren Brandling read the first two paragraphs of the article below the subhead:

Music Teacher Discovers Body on Stage

A Santa Reina High School freshman was found stabbed to death yesterday morning on the school's music room stage.

> Denise Hagerty, 14, was found by music teacher, Elizabeth Moore, who reported interrupting a masked assailant stabbing the victim before fleeing the room. Hagerty was declared dead at the scene from multiple stab wounds. Authorities have yet to identify or apprehend the alleged assailant. Hagerty was known at the school for being the orchestra's clarinet soloist and had played junior varsity tennis.

The article made Moore sound heroic. There was no mention of her activities in the practice room just prior or that she had fainted directly at seeing the body, knocking herself unconscious for several minutes. "Thinking on her feet," he mused, always resourceful. Warren smirked.

"Warren?" his mother called up the attic stair, "is that you up there?"

"Yes, Mother," he said. Who else would it be?

"What are you doing? Warren?"

"I'm looking for a tie," he said. "A school tie to bring."

She called up from below. "I ironed it and packed it already, dear. Come down. It's dusty up there."

"Thank you, Mother. I'll be down in a minute." He heard her shuffle at the threshold. Go away. Here I am a full professor, a gynecologist, the department chair, being nagged to death by my mother. Leave me be, woman, for God's sake. He folded the *Republic* page and set it aside. He picked through other clippings. He heard his mother clump down to the kitchen.

Classmate Arrest in Hagerty Killing

> Police arrested a Santa Reina High School junior, a Wildcats baseball team player, for the murder of

Denise Hagerty, 14, a freshman who played in the school orchestra.

The suspect remains unidentified because of his age. "We have positive ID from the teacher who interrupted the attack," said Police Chief William Rehnquist. "The motive is still under investigation."

God bless you, Bizzy Bee. You were always so certain. Well, good. He turned the cover of the manila file and carried it with him downstairs to his room. He slipped the file of clippings into a sleeve of his brief case, shut it, and twirled the combination tumblers. Must keep nosey mothers out.

Warren took up the Southwest ticket his mother had laid atop the neatly folded clothes in his suitcase and slid it into his blazer pocket. In the suitcase beneath the ticket lay the tie she had ironed. When was the last time he'd worn it? At graduation? No, at the trial? Maybe at the sentencing the last time he had seen Doug. The last time any of us had seen Doug, he thought. Yes, he wore the tie that time and not since. She had thought of it, his mother had, before he said anything. The tie was his lie. It was the file from the attic that he wanted. Though he had not thought of his cravat until he needed a fib, he knew it had never been up there. A weak untruth, but you always need a lie around Mother. Warren shut and zipped the suitcase.

His mother called from the kitchen. "Warren, time to eat. Don't let your breakfast get cold."

You are over forty years old and on the faculty of UCLA, and your mother is still cooking your meals. "Coming," he shouted. Warren took up the suitcase, draped the blazer over his left arm and grabbed the briefcase with the other hand. His shoulders slumped further as he bumped downstairs to breakfast. I hate breakfast, he thought.

Warren had last seen Elizabeth Moore on the steps of the school. She sprang to his mind as he descended to the foyer with his luggage. Always his memories of Bizzy were laced with longing, mixed with both contempt and gratitude. I'll be seeing her again. It's been over twenty years. At the end, he couldn't talk to her. The family had drawn the drapes, retreated in seclusion. And Bizzy Moore had been his brother Doug's accuser, at least she had identified him. Warren wondered. Is that why he confessed, because he had my back? Thought I was there?

In the weeks after the murder, with the inquest, indictment, court appearances, and sentencing, talking with Bizzy Body would not have been appropriate or, after their meeting in the practice room, smart, either. He could not talk with her, much less touch her, and definitely not caress her. So much happening then made life unseemly. When Warren announced that he wanted to walk the commencement stage and get his diploma, it had exploded into a knock-down-drag-out battle with his father.

"Warren, though I understand, it is not decorous," his father said. "In fact, it would be scandalous. For God's sake, your brother has murdered a girl at that school, and you want to flaunt our name there? I cannot allow it." His father towered over him as high and mighty as their supposed Lincoln ancestry allowed. At that point, Warren was not afraid of him anymore nor would he obey. His father dismissed the issue. "I know you're an honor student, nearly the valedictorian, but your presence would be a distraction. You're not going."

"You act as if I murdered Denise. No, I've missed everything else, Father," he said, "the tournament we would have won, the senior picnic, the awards banquet, but I am not missing my graduation, no matter what Doug did." It was true. Memorial Day should have been a glorious highlight to a brilliant season and a notable high school pitching career that had made him a hot commodity for college recruiters. After the murder, even before the weekend had begun, he'd been confined, had not seen the outside of the family's rambling Tudor house once. The Wildcats would have won the tournament even without Doug behind the plate, but never without Warren on the mound. Anyway, Pyykönen had cancelled their participation. It would have been "unseemly," he imagined the coach saying, though Finn Pyykönen would not have used that word. Ha, Finn Pyykönen. His brother's keeper, defender of the oppressed. What a chump he was.

Now, dreading breakfast with his mother, Warren set his suitcases by the front door and went into the kitchen. "I'm not very hungry this morning, Mother," he said. Warren draped his jacket over the chair and sat looking at the sausage-and-eggs breakfast set before his place. His mother joined him, drinking her morning coffee.

"You have to eat, Honey," she said. "It will be a long day for you."

"I'll just have some juice."

"Eggs are your favorite, dear. Please?"

She won't let up. Impossible woman. A real bother. He tried to hide a glare behind a sympathetic smile.

"Oh, don't look at me like that, Warren. You remind me of your father."

He broke the egg yolks with the toast and ate. Warren imagined on his return finding his mother broken-necked at the bottom of the stairs. Perhaps she would be underwater in the tub. He looked at her coldly.

"Now stop that, Warren," she said. Her voice quavered in a skittish plea.

"Of course, Mother," he said. "And what's this?" He held up a red envelope she'd placed under the newspaper.

Mrs. Brandling, who like any good mother read her son's personal mail, fibbed sweetly. "I believe you would know better than I."

He slipped the letter into his coat pocket, hiding it from her stare, and cut the sausage savagely with the steak knife. He swirled a forked piece in the yolk. I swear I'll never eat eggs after she is gone. Never.

His mother stirred more sugar into her coffee. "Are you nervous, Warren?"

"What should I be nervous about, Mother?"

"Oh, flying. You never fly. Perhaps you have jitters about going back to Santa Reina."

"And maybe it is the constant nagging and picking I get around here that puts me on edge." Warren's mother looked away, biting her lip.

He relented, "Yes, Mother, I am nervous. It's natural. It has nothing to do with what happened." They always referred to Denise Hagerty's murder as "what happened" and (honoring his father's dying wish) did not speak Doug's name, neither in connection with the murder nor in any other association. For the family, Doug did not exist.

His mother looked into the whirl of her coffee as she stirred. "I just hope no one tries to talk about it, at least to you."

"Don't worry. I can handle it. It is a celebration of one hundred years of Santa Reina High School, not of the class of '67."

She pursed her lips crookedly like she always did, furrowed her brows, and crinkled sad eyes at him. "You know best, Warren."

He smiled kindly. Drop dead, Mother.

Later that morning on the plane, Warren leafed through

the clipping file.

Sexual Assault Unlikely

Santa Reina Police Chief William Rehnquist, announcing the preliminary autopsy results, said the girl died of multiple stab wounds to her chest and abdomen. He would not comment on whether she had been sexually assaulted but noted that the victim was fully clothed after the attack.

Warren shook his head at the article. She was not the one assaulted in that way. It was not part of the motive.

He noticed the woman on the aisle seat looking across the empty seat between them, and he lifted the folder cover to obscure the clipping.

"Newspaper files?" she said.

"Yes, old clippings. I'm on my way to a reunion, of sorts." He closed the file and placed his hand on it.

"Do I see a late valentine in your pocket?" The woman tittered over Warren's jacket that had slipped open on the seat between them.

You are a bag just like Mother. He smiled and glared. He refolded the blazer.

His neighbor persisted. "High school or college?"

"My high school, Santa Reina," he said, and when the woman puzzled over it he added, "It's about fifty miles north of San Francisco."

"I haven't heard of it," she said.

"It's an old town, but not that well known outside Northern California. Mostly orchards and vineyards."

"Oh, wine country. I'm visiting Napa this trip."

"That's nice," he said, "have fun." Warren moved his coat to his lap and returned to his file. He was not in the mood for a conversation. She kept talking, but he ignored her. He reviewed the article from the day following the murder:

> Several dozen people, including fellow Santa Reina High School students and family friends of 14 year-old murder victim Denise Hagerty, gathered Friday on the front lawn of her family's home, set back from Cabot Street.

> "She was her father's favorite, the heart of the family," said Father Berach Phelan of Sacred Heart Catholic Church, of which the Hagertys are longtime members.

After the day of the murder, Warren had hidden from sight, watching through the parted drapes of his parents' bedroom windows, standing back in the shadowy room away from the cut of sunshine he'd let in, and watched cars filled with classmates park down the block. No one parked at the Brandling curb. Mostly they were the kids who had gone to Sacred Heart. Some came with their parents. They milled around on the street in front of the Hagerty house and filed through the gate to stand in knots in the big front yard.

I wouldn't have gone anyway. His crowd was mostly Presbyterian. Not that there was any religious animosity in town, just different schools and different paths, at least until high school. He watched the priest arrive, then some of the teachers. Later he saw Bizzy Body come.

She had pulled up with Snub Randall. Warren watched her unfurl her body from Snub's Mustang convertible, twisting, swiveling, and straightening at the curb. She tugged her tight skirt down and smoothed her hand over the front of it—Warren ran his own hand down as Elizabeth Moore did—then arranged her vest over her breasts, just so, and secured a second button beneath the swell of her chest.

Did she look over here? Warren pulled back from the

window. Now he wanted to be over there. With her. She might have hugged him for comfort, teary-eyed, her breasts heaving against him. He cursed his brother. "Stupid jerk," he said under his breath. "Who would confess to something like that?"

He parted the drapes again, this time looking for the coach. If Snub Randall was escorting Bizzy, though, Finn Pyykönen would not be there. Finn and Snub did not get along, and most of it, everyone said, was about his dear Miss Moore. She and Finn had been an item, both as high school students and now as teachers. Somehow, though, Snub figured in, a spoiler, playing second fiddle, the rumors said. Warren knew the delectable and seductive Miss Moore well enough to believe it. Snub was playing third chair but didn't know it.

Warren turned from the window then and went downstairs. His parents' voices mixed with another. Someone had broken the dreary silence that had turned the house into a tomb. He listened.

"I'm not at all certain that Doug did this," the man said.

"He's confessed," his father said. "You think he's lying?"

"I think he is scared and confused." It was coach. Finn Pyykönen.

Warren moved into the living room where they talked.

"Warren," his mother said.

His father turned to him. "This is a private conversation, Warren."

"Wait," Finn said, "I think Warren needs to be here. Hi, Warren."

"Hey, Coach," Warren said. "What's this about?" He thought it was an idiotic thing to say, but it had popped out. Everything was about the murder and about the two families that lived on the same block and about Doug and about death.

"Mr. Pyykönen is telling us he doesn't believe Doug did this," his father said.

Warren looked from one to the other. "Well, then, who did?"

Coach asked, "What do you think, Warren?" The unexpected question had jarred him.

He heard himself like a tinny echo in a long hall, "I don't know. Dougey gets really crazy sometimes."

"You mean he loses his temper?" Finn asked. "This was done by a desperate person. Doug isn't desperate."

"Why would he confess? I do not understand." His father was torn. He wanted to believe Pyykönen.

Finn put a big hand on his father's shoulder, it seemed like he was coaching him, consoling, and instructing like he always did. "Maybe Doug is protecting someone," Finn said.

It was his mother who spoke now, "Whom? Who do you mean?"

Finn had turned to him, Warren. The coach stood there with his hand on Father's shoulder. They both looked straight at him. "What do you think, Warren?" Finn said.

His mother rushed between them and stood in front of Warren. "Oh, no you don't. How dare you come in here casting doubt and suspicion. We are mourning here. We've lost a son. You won't come here accusing anyone. Get out, Mr. Pyykönen."

"Doris, the man is simply asking," his father said. "What do you think, son?"

Warren felt like he was on the mound, in a game that meant the title, facing a hitter who had homered off him three innings back. The bases were loaded, with two out. This was the pay-off pitch. Warren could read the signs. He knew what to do.

"If you mean, Mr. Pyykönen, that I had something to do

with Denise's death, that Doug had my back on a crime, you are wrong. I don't know a thing. I only hope that Doug wasn't involved, but now we would have to prove it. "

His mother shot her arm out at Finn. "You heard. Now get going, mister. I don't want to see you again."

His father had walked the coach to the door. For that one time, Warren held his sobbing mother in his arms.

The pilot was announcing something. Warren lifted the shade. Out there, dry and golden, was the northern California coastal range. They would land in San Francisco shortly.

Warren twisted in his seat, slipping on his blazer. He felt the card in its pocket. He flopped it out atop the file. This, whatever it is, can wait. He returned to the last clipping:

Confession in High School Murder

A 17 year-old Santa Reina High School junior confessed yesterday to the murder of 14 year-old schoolmate and neighbor Denise Hagerty, according to assistant district attorney, Jeffry Blauman, who cited the assailant's anger at the victim's rejection of his advances as a motive.

"Have a happy reunion," the woman next to him said.

"Oh, yes. I hope you enjoy Napa."

"I'm sure I will."

11

Farley Pike

Farley Pike, kneeling gingerly in a tightly bound apron—bending down would loosen his comb-over—swept the *Republic* from the welcome mat in the hall. Without looking at it, he carried the paper to his breakfast table. He'd already wiped the table, and now, before setting the paper down, checked to see that the top had dried. Yes, he admitted to himself, a laminate top, not really oak. He defended it. Very practical.

It's nice eating in the kitchen, he thought. Sensible. Better morning light. He untied the apron and sat, unfolded the paper, and carefully poured his milk over the banana and Grape Nuts he'd prepared. Pike lifted a spoon, hesitated. Just a touch of sugar. A little won't hurt. He sprinkled the cereal.

There alone in his apartment's kitchen, he munched, leafing one-handed through the paper, pressing his tongue into the slurry of banana and syrupy, masticated wheat filling his mouth. He accompanied his reading with a throaty, melodic hum in harmony with the sweetness of the cereal.

This morning's *Republic* was thick with coverage of what it called "The Great Event," the 100th Anniversary Celebration, the centenary of Santa Reina High School. The front page carried that headline and three pictures: the school as it appeared when just completed in 1891, a not-too-current photo of Dr. Elizabeth Moore, and a definitely out-of-date head shot of Snub Randall. Pike imagined a headline for the Randall piece: Sycophant Lauded. He read about Elizabeth, graveling a love ballad as he chewed, his larynx bobbing with the tune.

Page two presented a calendar of events for the next three days and the first paragraphs of Santa Reina's "'First Hundred, a Retrospective' by Finn Pyykönen of the *Los Angeles Times*," beside the beginnings of two other related articles, one on the architect of the school, the other on its first superintendent. The facing page listed contributors to the Santa Reina Education Foundation, most of the businesses in town—the banks, of course—and individual philanthropists, topped by longtime, prominent families in the area, the Moores (Elizabeth's brothers) and the Randalls (second cousins of Snub) being among the first listed. Far down the page in the smaller print of the under $100 column, the bronze level contributors, he found his own name. Farley Pike considered. I could have given more. No. You can't buy your way to the top. Not here.

The emboldened names listed under "Platinum Donors," were mostly pioneer families, first comers—that inbred, snooty bunch, Farley snorted, like the inimitable Mr. Randall (Who would want to imitate Snub?)—that formed the in-crowd, the givers-of-names and slurs like FP, but, just as infuriating to him, familiar, pet names, like Biz and Snub. Those were unearned, public endearments. Farley Pike had no need, no desire to be among those. You're from the outside, he soothed himself. Never to be accepted. Take a slur for what it's worth, he thought, then cast his spoon into the residual milk in his breakfast bowl.

He fanned the *Republic*'s pages and snapped the paper to a new section. Well, let them, he brooded, make fun of old Farty Pants if that is how they play it. Society always rots from the inside.

Farley Pike thumbed quickly through the *Republic*'s

news and community sections, then the sports pages. He read the retrospectives carefully, like a fact checker on staff. Even in the sports section, the paper avoided mention of the '67 Wildcats baseball team. Any article about what might have been the best team since the 1920 'cats would demand a reminder of "the event," the murder. Nothing was said, not in sports, not in news, not in human interest stories, not anywhere. I suppose it's just as well, he thought, but reviewed the tragic event, clinking the empty bowl every now and then with his spoon, the event even now so very clear that his heart thumped hard, pulsing against his narrow, sunken chest.

How long does it take to stab someone nineteen times? He tapped the spoon, now on the place mat. When he had reached the fifteenth tap, he said, "Stop it! Don't be a ghoul."

He closed the paper, left it folded neatly at his place, and brought his dishes to the sink. He tied the apron around his waist. As he rinsed his bowl and spoon, his juice glass, placing them carefully in the dishwasher, Farley Pike watched out his kitchen window to see the cars passing the school across the street. Below, Mrs. Baxter next door moved about her garden, over which he had for nearly thirty years kept a close eye on the Santa Reina High School campus. Now, in summer with nothing much to examine, he idly scanned the grounds, the facing end of Old Main, where he had his office, the humanities building behind, where he had taught English, and the gymnasium further down the block. Farley Pike had lived around the corner from Santa Reina High School all that time. A great location. Very practical.

Back in '67, of course, he had seen nothing. The music room was on the other side of the campus.

Mr. Pike rinsed his spoon under the faucet. He closed the dishwasher, wiped the counter, and polished the faucet with his dish towel, which he then hung on its bar. He took another look toward the school. Below, Mrs. Baxter was bending down, tying tomato plants to her chicken-wire panels. Farley Pike leaned over the counter to watch. A car passed, then pulled to the curb down by the gym. He forgot his neighbor and studied the woman driving the car. Opening her door, this woman dangled a slim stockinged leg over the pavement, then stood between the door and car as she tugged down her short, tight skirt. She faced the gym building. He fancied he knew her. Then as his jaw dropped, his lips parted with a distinct flapping sound. No, this is too fortunate.

Farley Pike rushed to the hall. He threw on a jacket. Even in summer, he always wore a coat, a blazer or suit coat. He smiled at the hall mirror. Smoothing his thin moustache with his fingertips, Pike took his keys off the hook there, and turned the knob. In two steps down the hallway, he pivoted and returned to his apartment. Farley Pike grumbled all the way to the kitchen, tugging at the apron that would not come loose. Finally, he tossed his keys on the folded *Republic*, tugged at his jacket, throwing it over the chair, and extricated himself from the tangle of the apron strings. He went to the window. She was just clicking heels up the steps. He threw the apron on the table, grabbed the blazer, and ran.

With his jacket over his arm, he rushed from the apartment, slamming the door behind him—though he did not realize it right away—locking his keys inside. He strode from the apartment building and around the corner to intercept Dr. Elizabeth Moore, watching her as she stood before the glass doors of the gym and once again adjusted her skirt. She let herself into the gymnasium lobby.

Farley caught just a glint of sun off the glass as the door swung shut behind her.

12

Snub Speaks

Let an old man have his vanity, even if he doesn't deserve it. I suppose I should say "dignity," but that is less important. And I suppose I could have booked a room at The Stanford, your hotel. As it turns out, it wouldn't have been worth the extra fifty dollars, not that I would miss the dough.

Was it you, Biz, or me? The hotel? The martinis? Something was off. My tooth ached like a son-of-a-gun. That didn't help. The little blue pill worked wonders, but that alone cannot do it all. Some finale. And you took my little letter all wrong as well.

To stew about last night, my final night with my beautiful work of art, Dr. Elizabeth Moore, PhD, at the not-so-cheap cheap hotel, the Holiday Inn, saddens me. Yes, even now I can feel melancholy. At seventy-six (you are misinformed about that, too), what should I expect? Dreariness. A dispirited performance. An occasion for ennui. Our last, and we both knew it.

I didn't even say good-bye.

Is it vanity to think I was your best, Biz?

I knew about that time with Farley Pike. God! How could you? "The piker" is what I should have called him. Anyway, I more than one-upped that old fart, didn't I?

Then you had to fall for Finn. Youth. No surprise. Next to me, he was the man all the senior girls of '61 talked about. Of course, Finn made himself known, but no one could miss a *Väinämöinen* like him. Straight out of the *Kalevala*. That I could understand. I take it as a point of pride that I outlasted him.

That's what I would want to know, though, if I were stupid enough to ask you, "Will I outlast Finn Pyykönen after all?" I hardly think you'll waste the entire centennial weekend on me.

And another thing troubles me.

Were you emulating my own behavior when you were balling that baseball pitcher? I've known about that one for years, even about your trysts in the practice cubicles. Maybe you were trying to prove something to me or to his coach. Perhaps you yourself don't know the reason for such racy behavior.

Now here is where I prove my point.

None of those boys knows you like I have, and none has really helped you along.

"Your first and last," I said that day in the darkroom. Certainly, I was joking—not to you, but, I thought, to myself—yet it was true in some sense: I was your first. You were my last.

I say it without regret: "It could've been better, but I don't mind." I took you for all you were worth.

13

Finn

Glory and splendor of the California morning framed Inga and Jamie as Finn bent down behind the windshield to wave goodbye to the young couple. Those two stood haloed in sunshine at the curb, hand in hand, watching him depart. He pulled away, moved into traffic. He would see them at the centennial, they'd told him.

"We wouldn't miss your speech for anything," Inga had said.

Finn glanced back at them in the mirror, their image distinct and sharply bright. They were kissing.

Good, Finn thought. Inga deserves an attentive partner.

He'd found the young man intriguing. Jamie was as handsome as he was brilliant. Inga would go for nothing less, yet Finn had detected little professorial hauteur, no young man's bravado. Jamie proved genuine: political and personable. His Mexican heritage spelled distance someday, but Inga's man was here now and had family in the States. Brushing the rust off his Spanish Finn had said, "*Voy a tener que visitarlos a Mexico.*" No matter where they lived, though, Inga would never be far off.

An image of Inga in white, on his arm in a Pasadena cathedral surged, brimming his eyes with tears. Finn considered the possibility, crooked a finger to wipe each eye. Sentimental fool. He knew what she would do. Elope. Cohabit forever—after all, who marries these days? She might partake of a simple civil ceremony, without family.

Jamie's background, though, veered toward tradition, and Finn's sudden vision of Inga as bride-in-nave coupled with what he knew of the Mexicans' love for fiestas resurrected the pomp of the bridal march in his ear. It swelled into a lofty transept, marching him and his sweet daughter toward her new best love at the altar. Come on, man, you're not even religious. Jamie might be, though, and was definitely Catholic. "*No pasa nada.*"

He drove, jingling inside, happy and bright.

Finn had planned a wide, looping swing on back roads, allowing him to take photos for the newspaper stories that made the drive north a business trip. The freeway to Vacaville was hours shorter, but he'd get good shots of the Rio Vista bridge and railway museum by going out of his way. Besides that, Finn loved the countryside. "Now this is California," he said.

He sucked in the fresh northern air from the ocean-clean sky. Dawn had turned every detail crisp and clear. Thin outlines clung with fine sharp lines to buildings distinct against the sky. It seemed to Finn that the sunshine lighted every leaf, every line, every surface with radiant warmth. Shafts of light warmed leaf, line, his face and arms but left the air cool, brisk, and trim. "I love it here," he said. When he shouted out the window, "It's glorious," two summery girls jogging in shorts waved from the sidewalk.

He turned up Stadium Way. Take as little highway as possible. Go past the ball fields. Just breathe in the green. His years in Los Angeles made Finn ripe for rural roads, the woodsier the better. Check the diamonds first, he decided.

The university baseball field hid behind an ivy-covered chain-link fence, but Strawberry Canyon softball stadium he could see from the road. Good enough, Finn thought. He pulled over. The diamond appeared a miniature—sixty-foot-long bases and only 252 deep to the center field fence. Yet the perfect edges of lawn, chalk lines angling in from right and left to home, and the solid balance of the stands and dugouts overjoyed him, tingled his senses. The little field brought his playing days to the plate.

Though dust on the fields had stuffed his nostrils most of the time, it was the smell of the grass that had marked his mind. No matter how hot, how powdery and dirty, how dry the mound actually was, at each delivery, throwing himself with the ball toward home plate, the whiff of fresh mown infield grass welled up to soothe his spirits and his thoughts. That was how he remembered high school and college ball, how he recalled his short sortie with the Giants in San Jose: snappy, fresh, and clean.

The expectations the hopes of youth leave the image so distinct in the memory. The dream and excitement churn with the fragrant, groomed outfield to sprout ecstasies in the heads of boys. To the players there was not just fielding-green but desire and faith in the grass.

Finn left the car and leaned against the rail overlooking the field. The fancies of youth and reveries of boys stretched across the lot before him in the insistent morning. The grassy ambrosia and fragile scent of yearning boyhood bruised his contentment. Against his will, Doug Brandling came to Finn's mind.

Doug could have played up there, at Cal. Like disappointment climbing from the dugout over a manager's downcast head, Finn felt baseball being lifted from his pitching fingers in a kindly remove, completed by a gentle pat on the shoulder.

You've made your peace with baseball, he reminded himself. Don't let what's done shadow today.

His choppy career had been enough for him. Finn was a high school champion. He had played into sophomore year at Stanford University, had then gone to the minor league Giants for a wonderful run before Viet Nam snared and wounded him. A few years after his discharge, he'd coached his old Wildcat team, but that season ended foully at tournament time with the murder halting play. He'd let go bit by bit, as if checking the wind to left field with a strewn handful of grass: his facile dreams sailing off a blade at a time, as life moved on faster at each interruption of his play, finally, colliding with Doug Brandling's confession and conviction. Finn had known that baseball was over for him. He relegated it to his past, off to the showers. "Doug, Doug, Doug," he whispered to the field.

Finn would break his heart over Doug's lost dreams more than his own, which seemed now as tiny as this field next to the behemoth of Candlestick Park. Finn was content to sniff the grass and leave it at that. What Doug wanted was another matter. Finn sensed this trip to see his ballplayer would tell him what that was. That reveal shadowed his thoughts.

Still, the sun heated the railing and warmed Finn's forearms. He turned his wrist and checked. There was still time to dawdle, but he knew he had to go.

He drove.

It was a pleasant winding road, nosing uphill by the university's botanical gardens, passing beneath oak, hillside-huckleberry, Monterey pine, and eucalyptus that shaded and scented the road like soothing medicine. He climbed past the science hall to the mirador of Grizzly Peak Boulevard. He slowed but did not stop.

It had certainly grown. Finn looked beyond the burgeoning cities and land to the Farallons. The islands dotted the Pacific with conical specks far out of the Golden Gate. For a moment Finn considered moving back. No. Give Inga some space. Maybe later. You're having a holiday. Take it for what it's worth. He turned the phrase over in his mind like something he'd stumbled on dumbly, a thing found at the bottom of a seldom-opened drawer. He turned from the bay below and its restless towns.

He drove on.

Looking up and down the road crossing, Finn edged out and turned, swooping down the steep, narrow grade to his left, down to the freeway. It was the only way through, a pleasant highway compared to home.

The hills towered green over the road he drove atop freeway tunnels. The hills fell to the ravine narrowly at Caldecott, then farther on widened into the Reliez Valley. Those far-off hills had browned already in the valley's June heat. "Heigh-ho Ygnacio," Finn said. Kirker Pass toward the delta would bring him through the best that was out there. Before that though, California 24 wound below him through hills that danced steeply in sunlight. Finn whistled.

His thoughts sped ahead to the delta, still thirty minutes away. Ellie and he had stood on the narrow shoulder of a levee road there once, the river below on one side and pear orchards beneath on the other. They'd brought Inga and Pers, still a baby. Ellie loved it, as she did all things.

"Such a strange mix of river, farm, and wind," she'd said. The blustery air had tangled her hair, and she took to wearing a beanie all through the trip. "It's cultivated and wild all at once," she snuggled up to him. "Like you, my dear."

He had grasped her shoulders holding her in his gaze and smiled at her. "Wonder and love," he'd said, "that's you, Ellie." She kissed his lips and went whirling away, arms spread above her head, spinning like a leaf blown off a twig. She twirled around him twice then fell into his arms. Inga danced with her. They all three went laughing to the ground.

"Ellen Gamble Pyykönen," Finn said now, "I love you." Her fiery ebullience reached across his ten years a widower, broadening his heart. How can you miss someone who's still with you? Ellie's spirit by his side, Finn topped a rise on Ygnacio to see the river spread in the flat distance below. "Look, Ellie," he yelled and raced down the incline. In fifteen minutes he'd crossed Antioch toll bridge to Brannan Island he'd roamed as a Boy Scout, a college student, with the family; he'd even brought Liz down here once. Ellie's warmth faded. Oh, God. Elizabeth.

That dismal evening and night spent with Liz at Brannan Island opened darkly. She'd delayed their start by two hours, dragging her feet, fussing with makeup. She'd ignored his plea, "It's camping, sweetheart," but he'd been patient. He'd unpacked and then restowed the gear in the station wagon while she was upstairs filling a large suitcase. "A suitcase," Finn chuckled, "for one night of camping." That had been a sign. One he'd not heeded.

They'd arrived after sunset. The wind howled and blew steadily through the evening and night. Liz confined herself to the car for her hair's sake. Later in the tent, her first time ever, having teetered from the car in dress shoes, she shivered, awake most of the night. She hated that place and Rio Vista, too.

I was—I am—too rough for Elizabeth. It was not her refinement. Ellie had, too, come from a mannered, classy family. But what? The way Liz regarded that highbrow (a word she used, but Ellie would never) heritage as a platform, a stage from which to survey the world, made it impossible for her to come down to earth, to come down to him. Perhaps what Liz thought so natural about herself was her worst trait: disdain. It blinded Elizabeth to pain, her own and the glut of it she found in others. Class that lent Ellie grace hardened Liz. Though not at all in the same way he had loved Ellie, hadn't he loved Elizabeth once? Hadn't he worked to protect her, even from herself?

It would be better to leave well enough alone, but he wondered. He'd told Inga that, but didn't he also admit it would be nice to see Liz again? Too true. He was curious. She did mean something to him, but the sunshine of Ellie's love for each thing he cared about cast shadows beyond Elizabeth's aversion to all things plain, many of them his favorites. Pay attention, he told himself, don't rush.

And moving slowly, leaving Brannan, Finn drove.

The drawbridge was up. Different, wasn't it? Finn scanned the structure for an answer. The drawbridge towers stood like sentinels guarding each bank. The bridge was the same. "It's a little Tower of London Bridge way out here," Ellie had said. Finn had laughed at her crazy comparison, though seen from their campsite on the river at night it had looked that way. Come daylight she had said, "Where are the cables and walkways? And who stole the stones, the peaks, and finials?" She had to explain to Inga what she meant. Then Inga started in too.

The truss construction was intricate enough to satisfy the bridge watchers, and their little family was treated twice to the raising of the center span, once from the campsite when a ship churned up the river. That seafaring boat seemed fitter to cut waves abreast a wide ocean than to squeeze down the channel and duck beneath the raised roadbed. The second bridge raising interrupted their drive, and they had to wait in line to cross to Rio Vista. Inga jumped out of the back seat and, towing her mother, ran around in stopped traffic, looking over the railing at the sailboat passing, until the bridge lowered and the crossing bells clamored. Then Ellie shooed her back to the car.

Finn set up a photo of himself with the bridge in the background. He'd telephone it to the photo agency and send a copy to Inga later on. Will she remember? She had been only four.

The agency, which owned the fancy camera, would convert his picture for the *Santa Reina Republic*, where Finn had a deal for three stories over the long weekend. A local history had run that morning. The bridge story he'd already submitted, a personal and public memoir, would run Friday with his picture of the bridge. He would cover the centennial finale at the gym, more as a pictorial than anything else. Another story, on the Electric Railway Museum for which he'd come out to take new pictures, was for the *Times*.

Finn basked in the pleasure of his journalistic work. His stomach rumbled in response. "Donuts next stop."

He drove across the bridge to Rio Vista. At Front Street he veered off the highway toward town. The burg had changed little since his last visit fifteen years ago. It had a fisherman's feel to it still, a bit uncouth.

He was looking for a landmark on Main Street. What was the cafe called? He tried to remember. Perhaps it was gone. Finn searched for a name but came up only with a fish. He watched the buildings as he drove slowly up the street. "The Striper," he read. The neon-trimmed awning sign: a striped bass leaping up to a martini glass arced over the restaurant name. The symbol of Rio Vista, which each year hosted a huge bass-fishing derby. Had it been October, he could have written a story on that.

The hotel façade housing the bar and cafe had changed, was now sided in wide, white clapboard. Not a great job, Finn thought. This was the place Ellie had liked. Bass were mounted along the walls above the tables. She liked the booths toward the window. He could still see Inga and Ellie sliding along one side, Inga's nose barely reaching table height. She'd curled up, sitting on her knees.

The first place they had stopped in town was a restaurant-bar and big game museum lined with deer, moose, and gazelle heads over the counter and tables, both sides. They'd peeked in, but Ellie had not wanted to stay. "I prefer American bass to veldt-fare," she'd said.

Finn parked in front of The Striper. The locals, he remembered, pronounced it more like "stripper." It stuck with Finn. He entered the restaurant section.

Despite the lure of its famous donuts the place was empty. Music was turned up too loud. Across the huge dining room a waitress was cleaning the glass shelves inside the pastry case. She sang along with the radio, a bit shrilly, slightly off-key, but following the melody, though consistently flat. Finn tapped his keys on the case top in time to the beat.

The girl sprang up like she was taking a jump shot. "Welcome to The Striper (she was local)," she said. "How can I help you?"

Finn felt ready for a little conversation. "Not too busy today?" he said looking around.

She was young, maybe still in high school, thin and smiley, waving a ponytail around her shoulders. She was chewing gum. "It was jammed for breakfast," she said. "We'll have a lunch crowd soon."

"You could probably use the break and maybe less volume."

"Oh, for sure," she said. She dialed the radio down and snapped her gum.

She was at liberty to talk. "School must be out by now," he said.

"Yeah, for me," she said pushing her shoulders back, strutting in place. "I just graduated last week."

"Congratulations, Kelly," Finn said, reading her tag. "What's next for you, Miss Graduate?" He flirted in a fatherly way.

She looked suddenly lost, hunched her shoulders, and looked at the cash register. "Well," she said finally, "I'd like to stay in town, but there isn't much to do here. I don't want to wait tables forever." She flashed an alarmed look at him. "Don't get me wrong, this job is great, I've been part-time for two years, but full-time is really boring, if you know what I mean."

"You have a good fix on small-town life," he said, "maybe you could try something different for a while."

"You mean Sacramento?" she said. "I don't know about a big city like that."

She was local. Probably hadn't been even to San Francisco. "You look intelligent," Finn said. "Why not go to a nearby college?"

"I'm thinking on it," she said. "The counselor at school said I should. It kind of depends on my boyfriend, what he does."

The freshness and foolish ideas of youth. Finn could challenge them. "Let me order some of those donuts," he said. She'd listen better if she were busy.

"Oh, sure. What would you like?"

"You still do a baker's dozen?"

"Sure," she said, "same price as twelve."

"Okay, give me a two-box assortment. Put the two extra

in a bag."

"So you can eat them before you get there?" Kelly smiled and started assembling the pink boxes.

"I guess I'm not the only one, am I?" he said. "A donut sneaker."

She laughed.

Finn talked over the pastry case. "Well, Kelly, if your boyfriend is smart enough to choose you, he should go to college and take you with him."

She glanced up to give him an apologetic shrug. "He didn't do too well in school. I don't know." She counted donuts, placing them carefully in rows.

Finn flipped through the menu. "I don't know either. I used to teach high school, and if you were my student, I'd tell you to take care of yourself. Anymore, even the best relationships don't always last."

"That's for sure," she said. "Bert and I had a big fight just last night." She laid in more donuts. "Would you like some Old Fashioned?" He nodded. "Where did you teach?"

"A small town by Sonoma. Over at Santa Reina High."

"I know where that is," she said, "and it's not so small."

"It was small back then."

"You don't teach now?"

"No, that was over twenty years ago."

Kelly turned the tables. "What was next for you?"

"Writing. I'm a journalist. Mostly freelance; I write for the *Los Angeles Times* and a few others down that way."

She snapped her gum. "That's exciting. I worked on the newspaper in school."

"See, there you go," Finn said. "You have skills and talent. You just need to develop them a bit more." Kelly perked up. "You know, give yourself a chance," he said.

She finished filling donut-boxes. "I might do that. You

suppose they have journalism classes over at Solano?"

Finn echoed her enthusiasm. Nothing like youth to pep you up. "I am sure they do," he said. "Usually, a community college publishes at least a monthly paper, might be weekly. Believe me, they're always looking for talent."

Someone came in the front door. "Oops, another customer," Kelly said. "Can I get you something else? Coffee?"

"A small one to go," he said. "You know those donuts are not all for me."

She shot him a skeptical look but said, "I knew that. You're in good shape." Now Kelly was flirting like a daughter.

She tied the boxes with string and set the donut bag and coffee on top.

"It's been nice meeting you, Kelly," he said. "Take care of yourself." He pointed a finger at her. "You know what I mean."

He paid, and she said, "I do. Thanks for the tips."

She was about to turn to the new arrival, but Finn interrupted. "Say, pick up a copy of *Santa Reina Republic* any day this week. I have a series of articles starting today. Name's Finn."

Kelly snapped her gum and bobbed her ponytail. "Thanks, Finn. I will."

He left feeling good. Young people. They have so much. He shook his head. They need so much.

There was an outside chance Kelly would look into Solano, but small towns were skeptical and hard on anyone who prepared herself to leave.

The boyfriend would object. "What do you want to go to college for?" he'd say. "Where you getting these crazy ideas?" The magnetic pull of family and friends, despite the economic difficulties of staying close, were strong in a place like Rio Vista. Well, he said to himself, there is compensation: A continuous thread of history in place made knowing who

90

you were a bit easier. Yet was knowing who you were more important than knowing who you could be? He thought back to his small-town beginnings and fit the question to the people he knew. The trouble was that he had lost touch with those who stayed. One of the few he was sure to know was Snub Randall. He stopped himself. Half thought and half said, "Bastard."

In the car Finn took up the bag and set the two boxes on the floor. One was for the guards, the other for Doug.

In some ways Doug was like Kelly, about to begin the rest of his life. He'll have a lot more baggage, though perhaps not so much more of a burden than the new high school grad from a remote town. Doug would leave a forced isolation, a twenty-four year confinement, and would exit with the mark of Cain on him.

Finn finished one donut on that note, cramming the last bits into his already full mouth. He wrenched the car into gear.

Ten miles up Highway 12 he was to stop at the rail museum to take photos and interview Jess Pritcher, the museum historian. Buy something for Doug there, he told himself. Then Doug drifted to the back of his mind.

He drove.

Finn had been looking for out-of-the-way places to feature on this trip. Most Santa Reina stories had been written by locals. Only the local history, a Jack London appreciation, and the pictorial finale story would be his. So the Rio Vista bridge story might be an outlier just to fulfill a contract. The stories wouldn't be interesting without photos. Particularly, the museum was better known than the bridge and would stir interest down south. Still, pictures were needed.

What tied bridge and rails together in his mind, Finn knew, weren't the trips with Ellie and family. It was that ill-fated trip with Elizabeth. Having taught only two weeks at Santa Reina, he cajoled Elizabeth to drive with him to the opening of the museum.

"They just completed the car barn," he told her, "and they want to show it off."

"A car barn?" she said. "It does not sound exciting."

"Free trolley rides on vintage Key System cars," he said, "that will be fun."

Elizabeth was not impressed. "I rode them as a child."

"Yes, it'll be nostalgic."

"I have tons of papers to correct," she said. "Don't you?"

"No, nothing has come in yet. Bring yours along. You can work in the car."

He prevailed, and Liz seemed to enjoy the ride if not the museum. "I'll admit the trolley rides were interesting."

At the end of their museum visit a docent told Finn that the Rio Vista Bridge had been destroyed.

"A ship plowed right into it," the docent said. "Knocked the whole thing right over."

He'd grabbed Liz's wrist, saying, "Let's go see." They were on their way. Elizabeth had no time to object. "I've got my camera and notebook," he said.

Toward the river, a thick fog slowed the drive. Finn crept along doing twenty. It was too dark to correct papers by then. Liz fretted and peered out into the fog. They couldn't get near the bridge. The road was packed with cars. They pulled into town a half a mile from the span.

"I am not walking down there in these shoes." She brandished a heel at him. "You go. I'll stay here."

"It's not that far. You can walk."

"Not on your life, Finn," she said. "You dragged me out

to that stupid train museum in the middle of a brush heap and then to this podunk town, even further into the boonies, but I am not going to walk a mile to that broken-down bridge that used to connect nowhere with nowhere."

"I get your point. Sorry," he said. "But I really want to get this story."

She opened a book she had brought, found it too dim to read, and slammed it shut. "I'm going over there for a drink," she said, pointing to the Buckhorn a block from the roadside.

"I'll meet you there in thirty minutes," he said.

It was not half an hour or an hour. By the time Finn returned Elizabeth was gassed and sharing a cozy time with a couple of fishermen in the back booth. He sidestepped her insults and the jeers of her companions simply, apologizing and reminding Elizabeth that her students would be waiting in Santa Reina the next morning. She looked a bit surprised but rose unsteadily saying, "Sorry, guys, duty calls."

They crept back to the highway in thick fog, Liz quietly drifting off into a private, gloomy haze. His photos had been good, the earliest of the scene, and he'd sent two of those just last week to support his *Republic* story. Still, the memory of that dour day with Elizabeth drove Finn toward a funk that a visit to the California Medical Facility, Doug's prison, would do nothing to sweeten. The museum might spark some luster, but once that dimmed, only the jail loomed ahead.

In the bright sunshine, Finn Pyykönen drove toward that.

14

Farley Pike

Farley Pike skipped up the gymnasium steps, breathing hard from his jaunt around the corner and down the street. He grasped the door handle. The door was fixed solidly in its steel frame. It did not budge. Locked, he thought, of course. He reached into his pocket for his keys, already feeling the queasy rage of forgetfulness stirring his Grape Nuts. Suddenly, his breakfast wadded into a choleric lump in his gut. "Geoffrey Chaucer!" he shouted.

Farley Pike raised a fist to the thick, wire-enforced window. No. No. Don't pound, you idiot. Be a gentleman. He turned away and jogged back to his apartment. Yes, the door was locked, the keys inside.

He had already broken a sweat. Get a grip on yourself, Farley, he coaxed. He stood for a moment outside his apartment door, letting his breathing smooth out, subside. He would have to, he knew, deal with the Widow Baxter. She kept a spare key for him, and though he liked her well enough—they were the same age, and she had known his mother—Farley always felt uncomfortable alone with her.

"Good morning, Mr. Pike," Mrs. Baxter said. "Doing a bit of jogging this morning I see." She stood amongst her peonies holding a bouquet she had clipped. "Aren't these just lovely?" she asked holding the bunch out to him.

Though he was rushing, Farley knew it did no good to hurry this woman. He did his best to smile, while feeling wary of the ants he watched crawling on the big blooms.

"Wonderful. Do they keep?"

"Oh a day or two. I shouldn't cut them, but I just love a bouquet on my dining room table. How are you, Mr. Pike? You seem flushed." Always the nurse, she made a move to feel his forehead.

He backed away. "I'm fine, Mrs. Baxter. I was hurrying to my appointment at the gymnasium, and I've locked my keys in my apartment." He pulled the shade of whimsy over his irritation with his neighbor. Please, he thought, let's get on with it.

"I'm glad I can help. Come inside. I'll fetch the spare. Perhaps you would like a lemonade? It would cool you."

Good Geoffrey, lady, can't we just . . . well, never mind. "Yes, that would be nice. Perhaps you have a paper cup for me, I really do have to be going."

They had entered Mrs. Baxter's glassed-in porch leading to the kitchen. "I think I have those cups somewhere."

Inside, Mrs. Baxter laid the peonies in the sink, where she rinsed her hands and the stems before sliding the bouquet into a vase she kept there. "Now where's that key? She sifted through a drawer and came up with the spare dangling from a fob, a replica of the Wildcat medallion. "*Quaere scientiam, veritate, et virtues,*" Mrs. Baxter said. "I need a little more *scientiam* right now. Where are those paper cups?" She pocketed the key. Farley Pike had nearly grabbed at it. Is she absent-minded or consciously delaying me. I can't miss Elizabeth. "Oh here they are." Mrs. Baxter took a cup from a stack in her pantry, set it next to the sink, then went to the refrigerator. Farley watched helplessly as she fumbled with the lemonade, looking for a large spoon first, then for a small strainer. Finally, she poured and extended the cup. "Here you are, Mr. Pike."

"Thank you so much, Mrs. Baxter," he replied.

She watched intently as he took a sip. "Mr. Baxter always took lemonade in the heat."

"Delicious."

His neighbor smiled. She was pretty when she smiled. Mrs. Baxter began fussing with her flowers. "There was something else you came for, wasn't there?"

"Yes, Mrs. Baxter, the key to my apartment. You have it in your pocket."

"Oh, so I do." She fished it out and proffered it to him.

"I will return it on the way to the gymnasium. Thank you very much."

This time he ran. Next door, up the stairs, through the door, grabbing the keys atop, he noted with a sigh, a picture of the high school on *The Republic*'s front page. With keys in hand he leapt the stairs, ran along his building's driveway, took the side gate to her garden, and slipped the spare into Mrs. Baxter's hand as he passed through.

"Again, thank you, Mrs. Baxter."

"Any time, Mr. Pike," she said, following him as he let himself out the far gate onto School Street.

He knew that Mrs. Baxter would be smiling behind him all the while he whizzed down the block. I don't care, he told himself, and broke into a faster jog, racing all the way to the gym.

Inside, Farley calmed his breathing and mopped his streaming face, watching Dr. Elizabeth Moore, through the glass slit in the balcony door.

She sat alone in the huge expanse of folding chairs to be used for the centennial presentations set in three files across the gym floor. She studied the stage. Farley Pike admired her straight-backed, almost rigid posture. She faced away from him. Looking up, she rolled her shoulders back. He admired the swell of her breasts rising below her shoulders. Ah, he sensed, she's looking for inspiration. He grew excited. Then, Dr. Elizabeth Moore tapped her fountain pen on the legal pad she held on her lap. Oh, Farley thought, to be that pad. She wrote some. She stopped, held the pad out to read it nearly at arm's length, then tossed the notebook down on the chair beside her. He grasped the door handle but did not release the latch.

He stopped. Now this was curious. As he watched, Elizabeth draped her arm over the chair next to her and leaned left a bit. He watched her vest slip away from her breast. She raised and crooked her arm, caressing the air above that chair as if tousling her neighbor's hair. Farley stirred against the door. Did she shut her eyes? He slid noiselessly through the door to get a better view. Yes, he thought, my little conquest. How sweet.

She sat a long time, it seemed, first fondling the air then draping her arm around the back of the chair and listing further left. Farley Pike imagined himself seated in that chair, Dr. Moore fingering his hair—not too roughly, my dear, he would be thinking, please don't muss it—and laying her arm across his shoulder, ah so softly. Oh, to be wrapped in such alluring scent.

She took up the pad again. He sighed very quietly and watched her write a sentence or two. When she suddenly slapped the pad down without reading it, he just as quickly stepped to the railing of the balcony, and the door slammed shut behind him.

Good Geoffrey. Elizabeth jerked around toward the sound. Does she recognize me? He smiled and waved. Before she could respond in any way, Farley Pike marched across the balcony, strode along the aisle before the padded seats, and, once out of sight, sped two stairs at a time down the stairwell that led to the gymnasium floor.

Ah, he thought, at last a moment alone with Elizabeth. He could barely contain his excitement or his imagination.

He sidled down the row to the fifth seat just left of Dr. Elizabeth Moore and, with a clank of the keys in his pocket against the metal of the chair, sat down.

"I thought that was you," he said. Her cold, professional look evoked a thought: What a fool.

15

Doug

It's nearly lunchtime. Doug Brandling sits in his cell. He is not waiting for Finn.

He has served breakfast, eaten, stretched and caught one hundred of Kettner's pitches—mostly heat and curves with a few screwballs here and there—has showered and dressed. He sits in his cell.

He thumbs through *The Natural* to find, he hopes, deliverance. He hopes for Roy Hobbs who, Doug already knows, having read the book twice through, will not redeem himself. Doug has again found Hobbs guilty of manslaughter, though the bum was too drunk to know even if it really happened. Now the prisoner thins his lips and shakes his head as Roy stuffs himself on platters of rich food that his sexy girl, Memo, plies him with. Hobbs will ruin his big game tomorrow, Doug is sure. Even though he understands the outcome, Doug hopes against what he knows. He yearns for Hobbs to purify himself.

Doug reviews the reading he will record this afternoon when Finn leaves. He does not wait for Finn. He reads. Through the fiction, the real world, the world he left twenty-four years before, creeps over him, sticking to him like pine tar on a bat handle. Doug has no other way to know that world. He broods: I won't be a Hobbs. I'm stronger than he was. I'm going to play well. I have paid the piper. Now I'm going to tell Finn. He can help. Roy Hobbs had spurned aid. Doug would not make that mistake.

The enormity of his desire buoys his shoulders, and through that levity his dreams breathe into his hope. Even so, Doug hunches beneath what he cannot know, a future as featureless as his cell's walls. He tosses the book on his desk and pitches himself on his cot. The envelope crinkles below the blanket. Doug turns on a hip and lifts; he retrieves the letter. The inmate rubs his chest. He breathes deliberately and pries up the flap. Doug doesn't wait for the approaching footsteps in the hallway to stop at his door, but when they do, he stows the letter again and rises.

It's Ransdorf. "Off-day visitor. State your name."

"Doug Brandling, C-63."

The metal slab door swings open.

Ransdorf follows protocol. He wouldn't be one to deliver illicit letters. "This way." He holds out his arm like an usher. Ransdorf will follow him, weapon at ready. Even though Doug knows Officer Ransdorf does not approve of this visiting privilege, he appreciates the discipline his keeper expends to hide the fact.

Finn Pyykönen, Doug Brandling's his visitor, had been a special friend to more than this one prisoner. In his writing Finn had touted the institution of the California Medical Facility (CMF). Doug had copies of the articles Finn had written about the prison for the *Los Angeles Times* and *The Chronicle*: a series on The Blind Project, a careful and correct retrospective of Manson's years at CMF, where Doug had fallen for a time under his spell, and a few general articles like profiles of the warden and human-interest stories on the success of some of CMF's alumni. The positive exposure, especially from the three-part series on the Project, had earned Finn special treatment, and though exemption from search or examination on entry was not part of it, this off-day visit, usually reserved for attorneys, was a perk. The venue, a lone picnic table under an awning overlooking the ball field, was another privilege as was the proximity he and Finn were allowed. The staff blinked at hugs Finn showered on Doug. Finn, as Doug's coach, had always been physical.

Ransdorf escorted Doug to the table where Finn already sat. He'd somehow brought in a thermos of coffee and two cups to compliment the donuts. Even though gifts to the staff were prohibited, Finn had left half the pastries at the entry station for the guard's coffee break. Prison personnel liked Finn.

He rose to greet Doug, but orally stroked his escort first. "Thanks for bringing him, Officer Ransdorf. Donut?"

Ransdorf shook his head. "Not allowed, sir."

When the guard turned to take up his station just out of hearing range, Finn came around the table and hugged Doug heartily. "Oh, man, it's good to see you."

"Thanks for coming, Coach."

"Whew, look at you. You are buff. You've been working out." Finn indicated the bench. "Let's eat some donuts. I'm starving."

"It's not on the training menu, but if the coach says so, all right." They both laughed.

They sat across from each other, and Finn poured the coffee. "A little milk?"

"Black, Coach."

Finn sipped his coffee. He looked carefully at Doug. He scanned him up and down. "What have you been working on?"

Doug assumed Finn meant baseball. "The curve and the screw."

"That pretty serious stuff for amateurs, isn't it?"

Doug showed no offense. Even Finn misjudges. He's on the outside. "It's hard for me to really know, but the competition here is usually pretty stiff. A lot of the teams are young. Everybody's strong."

"Not exactly a recreational league, I guess," Finn said.

Doug shook his head. "All the men can hit, run fast, and field easily. Of course, they don't hit us."

"Who's the pitcher?"

"A lefty. Kettner. KO we call him. The kid's got stuff. Two years of college ball."

Finn knew better than to ask what KO Kettner was in for. "KO as in knock-out?"

"As in strike-out," Doug said. "He pitched for San Diego, the UC."

Finn considered Warren, Doug's brother, who had pitched for the University of Southern California after Stanford rescinded its invitation. Finn would not mention him, at least just yet. He would look for the proper opening.

"You've got games coming up." Finn knew about the games, was covering one at the request of the warden.

"Sunday. A double-header with the best team over there," Doug tossed a glance toward the neighboring Solano State Prison."

"A double-header, that's big."

"A visitor-day special," Doug smiled. "You coming?"

"Thanks for the invitation," he replied. "Actually, I've been asked to cover the second game."

"Good. I could use the publicity." Doug felt this was his chance. "I've wanted you to see us play again. I've got an idea."

Finn lifted an eyebrow.

"Listen, Coach, when I'm released come November, I know what I want to do."

Finn waited and prayed it wasn't baseball Doug wanted.

Doug looked hard into his coffee cup. "I want to try out."

Finn hoped against having to hear what he thought he

would have to hear, but in his patient way he gave Doug time to put it out. He kept smiling yet held his eyes impassive.

"I know it's a long shot, but I've been working hard at it, and even if it is only a season or two, even if it is Class A, I want to play."

"Baseball," Finn said evenly.

"Yeah, baseball."

Finn held firmly to his dispassionate smile. "It's been more than a few years since I wrote for the sports page, but I think I still know a few people with the teams."

Doug shot him an expectant look. "I was hoping you could talk to them, for me, Coach."

Finn held steady. "What about the brailling?"

"I'm not sure, Coach. I know I can do it, but I'm having a hard time with it right now."

"What are you working on?" He could tell Doug would rather not talk about it. "Tell me, Doug," he persisted.

"It's *The Natural*," he said. "Roy Hobbs. It's hard."

Finn studied Doug's face as his catcher swirled his coffee and frowned at the table. He suspected Doug saw himself in Roy Hobbs, the film version, a hero returning from the netherworld. Now, reading the book closely enough to record it, he had grown disillusioned, fearful, likely, or at the very least troubled by the gross imperfections of Roy's character. He likely feared his own imperfections, his anger. Doug was still just a kid. A wonderful and honorable kid, but still a kid. It was not up to Finn to tear the young man down.

"You're not like Roy Hobbs," Finn said.

"You don't think I can play?"

"I think you can, but can you hem in your temper?"

Doug grit his teeth and hardened his face. "All that's in the past, Coach."

Finn shook his head. "I didn't mean it wasn't. You're a

good man, Doug. Roy Hobbs was not like you in that way. As a baseball player, you are probably as good or better." He put his hand on Doug's wrist. Ransdorf standing by the door shifted his stance but kept quiet. "Remember, Doug, it is fiction. Roy Hobbs is not a real person. You are."

"You don't want me to fail."

"I don't want to mislead you. It'd be hard." He held his breath. Finally, he said it. "It might be impossible."

"Take a look at me in the game first," Doug said, "then decide."

"Sure. I'll look, but I'm already committed," Finn told him. "I'm with you all the way."

"The game will show you. I'm making all the calls."

"All?"

"Yeah. No one else has a head for it. I'll call pitches and run the offense from the dugout, too."

"I'll keep that in mind. Make a great headline. 'CATCHER CALLS THE SHOTS.'"

Doug liked that. He grinned widely.

Finn nodded. "All right, but you think about the Braille job, will you? It could be off-season income."

They shook hands. Ransdorf started toward them. Finn held up his hand. "I've ten more minutes, if that's all right, Officer Ransdorf." The man checked the time. "Eight," he said and returned to his post.

"We can talk a bit Sunday, Doug, after the game, but it would be better if I tell you now."

Doug checked Finn with narrowed eyes. "What's it about?" Now he was wary.

Finn broke another donut and dunked it in his coffee. He watched it drain then drip. "I've had some new conversations down south."

"With who?" Doug said, sounding defiant.

Finn drew a deep breath. "First with Warren. Then with your mother." He stopped to watch Doug's face.

"Again?" Doug hunched his massive shoulders and shook his head at the table top. "Why do you want to dig all that up?"

Finn waited until Doug faced him. "Let's say for the sake of justice."

Doug spit the words out quickly like they were hot. "Justice for who?"

"For you, for me, for your family." Finn immediately sensed this last addition was a mistake.

Doug stared at him coolly. He spoke without rancor in a practiced phrase, "Outside you, Coach, I have no family."

Finn knew it was true, at least in Doug's view. Finn Pyykönen himself was Doug's only visitor in all the twenty-four years of his incarceration. Doug's family had receded in horror after his confession to first-degree murder.

Again, Pyykönen put his hand on Doug's arm. He spoke softly, "Doug, I know they were protecting Warren."

Doug didn't shake off his touch. They were friends. Finn was his only friend. "So was I, Coach. At least I thought I was. I've always had his back."

"I know, Doug. I know." Finn clasped his hands before him on the table. "Listen, I know some things now that I didn't at the time. Whereabouts and relationships. But none of it will ever matter if you stand by your confession." He reached across the table with both hands and clasped Doug's. Ransdorf lurched toward them but halted when Finn let go. "I know you didn't do it, Doug," Finn said.

"Time's up Mr. Pyykönen." Ransdorf stiffened in command, "Brandling. Time's up."

Doug started to rise. "Look," he said. "I'd think about it, but first Warren has to come here."

Finn nodded, and even as Ransdorf waited he hugged his catcher long and hard.

The guard ushered Doug back to the building. Doug turned and raised his arm in salute.

Finn thought, I'm in deep this time.

16

Snub Speaks

I want to set the record straight. I've been a bit unfair to Finn Pyykönen, not that he deserves special consideration. Our history can hardly be called anything but spotted. Yet, despite my red-letter meddling, I want to look beyond that.

In many ways, I suppose, he was the kind of fellow I would want to be known as: very decent, kind, handsome, popular, lovable, and well-known. Four out of six isn't bad. Just allow a tinge of notoriety on the "well-known" and I qualify, though decent and kind, I am not. I've never saved a life; I'm no war hero, either.

Our history centers on Elizabeth, of course. I saw their attraction first at the 1961 graduation. I don't think either of them gave the other a passing glance before that. It was the luck of the draw, since the administration matches the seating so when each row of students splits to approach the stage from opposite sides, the shuffling between right and left results in a reading of names in the alphabetical order printed on the program. Thirty years later, it is still done the same way. They faced each other on stage and returned to adjacent seats as if they were destined for each other. In 1961, "Moore" and "Pyykönen" were thrown together. None of the Norrises or O'Connors graduated that year.

I took the picture of Finn hugging Elizabeth. It appeared in the *Republic*: "Star pitcher and scholar celebrate!" Liz held onto Finn too tightly, too closely, and too long for my liking, but the pose and picture became the class icon for a day or two. That hug lasted longer for Elizabeth and her new beau. At first, I thought their attraction was a graduation fancy, a classmate thing, but later on that summer, when she started to feed me excuses, I watched more closely.

She worked part-time in my darkroom, sorting negatives, filing the year's prints, and otherwise, well, acting as my assistant. Then she missed a day, stretched it to a week, and, finally by mid-July, wanted to quit. "I don't really need the money, and this is my last summer to relax," she'd said on the phone. My reconnaissance—late-night cruises in her neighborhood and, I have to admit, following her around town and out of town, too, led me more than once to Pyykönen's shack on the Sonoma Road. Her after-dark cruises out there told me all I needed to know. She had fallen for the guy. I expected as much from Biz. I suppose I taught her well.

I caught up with her, waited outside the hamburger shop she frequented, led her around the delivery entrance for a chat, and made my plea. "Look Liz, I don't mind playing second fiddle," I said, "you have meant too much to me to just end it here." Go ahead, say it: I have no shame.

She couldn't say no. I knew that beforehand. We made a date I knew she'd have to keep, even though I could tell she didn't feel so good about it. The unspoken conflict, Finn Pyykönen versus Snub Randall, confounded both her sense of loyalty and that which no pair of panties could hold.

The double-dipping lasted until August. Then she broke off with me, and after I nearly broke a leg avoiding discovery at his cabin, I was sure she had told the boy about us. No one had done that before.

I've always thought things would end badly for me: at the end of a rifle barrel or a rubbing-out-Snub with a pistol. I preferred that to tire irons or fists. I'd often wondered whether it would be a father, a brother, boyfriend, or husband who would show up at my house at night. I'm not a thankful person, but I am grateful in a sense that it was Finn Pyykönen and not someone else who knocked on my door a mid-August evening just as I was finishing dinner. The timing was good. Bobbie, my wife, you know, had the dishes to tend to. I ushered Finn into the living room.

For a fellow just eighteen years old, he handled himself well. We sat. He got right to the point, though I probably asked to what I owed the honor of his visit. I knew darn well what it was about.

He leaned forward, confidential-like, and said, "I want you to leave Elizabeth alone."

I'm sure I didn't show any surprise. I just wanted to keep the lid on things there in the living room. "I'm not sure I know what you mean." It was an opening, but I had to take the risk that he wasn't sure.

He might have shot me right there. He rifled a look so square and tough—maybe like he was a pitcher again, staring down a big hitter who faced a full count—that I felt like I was shot. "Oh, I think you do. You might be friends, but don't touch her again. Just leave her alone." I must have nodded. I don't remember, but I went down looking. That was for sure.

He didn't threaten, didn't say anything else, didn't make a scene, but as if he had brought by a cake or a misdelivered letter, he stood, nodded a good-bye, and let himself out the door. That was it.

If you can like someone who does what Finn did, then you are a better man than me. I've saved my best writing in hemlock for good old Finn.

Admiration is appropriate. Affection I can't stomach. Just the same, I had nothing much to do with Elizabeth Moore again, until she showed up after college applying to teach at the school. By that time, Finn was out of the picture: he'd left college, was drafted, wounded and honored in Viet Nam. Elizabeth wasn't waiting for him. In any case, she needed help getting the job. At your service, my dear Biz.

All I have to say is thanks for the warning, pal, but remember, all good things come to those who wait. (You'll be hearing from me.) At the last, this was 1965, she was back, and, of course, it was the loitering hand of Snub Randall that opened the door to help her get the job. God be praised.

17

Elizabeth

Elizabeth Moore, PhD sat entirely alone in the Santa Reina High School gymnasium in row eleven, seat six of the four hundred and eighteen folding chairs that had been set up on the gym floor, precisely in the seat she had occupied June 9, 1961, 6:45 to 8:00 p. m., at her high school commencement ceremony, though there had been only about two hundred chairs at that event, not counting the parents' cushioned seats in the balcony above the bleachers where the underclassmen sat.

The somewhat tattered blue and white stage skirting and backdrop before her might have been the same used thirty years earlier. "Time for a facelift," she thought. The wide wood podium centered on the stage, from which she would speak Saturday evening was, she knew, original to the school—one hundred years old this year; that's what this celebration was about. Mounted on its front, the colorfully stained wildcat emblem proclaimed 1890 in numerals hand-carved by a failed prospector-turned-lumber-dealer. The medallion shone now under a recent coat of varnish. A collar around the emblem carried the year MDCCCXC at the bottom and the words *Quaere scientiam, veritate, et virtutes* arced over the top. The translation all Wildcats knew: Search for knowledge, truth, and virtue. Well, thought Dr. Elizabeth Moore two out of three isn't bad.

The podium really is quite nice, she thought. Dr. Moore warmed to decorum and the trappings of tradition. That's how I could start, with something about the medallion. It wasn't the school that dampened her spirits, though it, too, mouldered in difficult memories, but the subject of her speech. She'd agreed to praise one who deserved more a public flogging than what he'd get. She'd agreed, though few understood the extent of her duplicity, to eulogize with lies, or at the very least with omission. And for all she knew now Snub might have been involved even with Denise Hagerty. The poor girl had been too young, but then Snub was Snub.

She found, looking up for inspiration, only steel trusses supporting the high roof. The gymnastic ropes hoisted up and basketball backboards folded against the trusses mocked her search for help. No ideas up there. Why such a hard time with this?

She tapped her fountain pen, a-going-to-college gift from Snub, on the legal pad she held on her lap. Just start, she told herself. Use the tried and true. She wrote: Ladies and gentlemen, the hand-carved symbol of our school that you see before you, made by . . . she stopped. Oh, who was it? Could she call him just an unsuccessful gold prospector? No. Keep it upbeat, entirely positive: by a pillar of our community. Corny, Biz. No. No. No . . . By Owen Marshall (that was his name, or was it Orville Marshall?) the operator, no—she scratched out the word—owner, no, lumber entrepreneur— that's it—who milled the redwood for our first schoolhouse, built one hundred years ago on the site of this gymnasium.

She read what she had written. Fragment, she mused. Dr. Elizabeth Moore lost her train of thought. She slid the pad to the chair to her right and set her pen on top. She closed her eyes.

On her left, she let herself feel Finn. Thirty years before, he had sat row eleven, seat five at her side, whispering jokes during the speeches, kidding her with feigned admiration when she stood for awards—he'd won several himself she remembered, the Scroll and Quill scholarship, the Scholar Athlete honorarium, and The Help-Me-Go-to-Guy designation. He had hugged her long and gently after they received their diplomas. She could still feel his chest against hers. Had she kissed him? Not then. She had hoped Snub had seen the hug. He had. His photo of them appeared in *The Republic* the next morning.

She felt Finn's big-shouldered warmth beside her.

He'd whispered to her. "And now, ladies and gentlemen, T. Schantz-Halleran, Secretary of the Board of Education, will lead the graduates in a four-minute nap."

Elizabeth had not even smiled. She swatted his knee with her program. "Shush."

Later he poked her side. She jumped.

When the principal was about to speak he mumbled lowly, "Now Principal Scientissimus Virtutem will impart his truth." Finn made a snoring noise.

When she stood, recognized as a National Merit Scholar finalist, he, too, stood and shook her hand, then quickly sat again.

"Don't steal my thunder, boy," she'd said though he had acted sincerely, and she was actually touched. She returned the favor when he was announced as S & Q Scholar. After that they sat, faces forward, smiling devilishly.

You knew right then, Biz told herself, that you and Finn would be an item.

She had felt then and confirmed her attraction four days later on an evening in June. With her best friend, Marlis, she drove Daddy's car up the Sonoma Road, where they passed Finn, hiking along the shoulder.

He didn't turn or try to hitch as they approached and

passed. She breezed right by him. "Is that Finn Pyykönen?" Marlis asked. Elizabeth was already braking.

Marlis hung out the window. "It's him, Elizabeth, but you're not going to pick him up are you?" Her friend was giggling at the thought. Marlis was a bit shy and very straight-laced at home, though she transformed once out of her parents' sight. Her folks watched her carefully, protectively. It was unusual for them to let her ride with "that Moore girl," as they called her.

"You're sweet on him, aren't you?" Marlis said.

Elizabeth had stopped. Finn kept his former pace. She shifted into reverse. Marlis hung out the window chanting, "Ooh, ooh, he's for you, pick him up, and see what's new." She'd waved and yelled back at him. "Hi, Finn."

"Get your body in this car, Marlis," Biz had said, grabbing her friend's belt loop as she turned around to watch the road behind. "I can't take you anywhere." They were both laughing hard.

When they pulled up next to him, Finn stepped off the road. Standing in the grass below the shoulder of the road, he came to eye level with the girls. "You know why I pulled you over?" he said.

"Why is that, officer?" Biz replied.

"Reckless driving, Miss Moore. May I see your license and registration?" he asked.

Marlis was still excited. "But officer, she always drives like that."

"Backwards? That's what I am afraid of," Finn replied. Then he dropped the gagging. "Hi, Marlis. Miss Moore."

"Where you going?" Biz had asked. "Want a ride?"

"Oh, not too far. Toward Glen Ellen."

"Hop in," Biz said.

Marlis pulled up the lock button. "In the back, Officer."

Finn slung his bag on the seat and slid in beside it. "Thanks."

Biz talked to him, watching his face in the rear-view mirror. "We're going to the A & W in Sonoma. Want to come? We'll drop you off on the way back."

She could tell he was puzzling it out.

"I'd love to, but I have a lot to do before dark. Another time, maybe."

"Do?" she said. "We're on vacation. What do you have to do?"

"Oh, get things in order, build a fire. Sweep out the cabin. That kind of stuff."

"You have a cabin up here?"

He met her eyes in the mirror and smiled. "My dad's. It's really just a shack. It's on the creek."

She recalled the accident there a couple of years back, and thought of Finn's burned hand. That sent a shiver down her spine, so she dropped the memory out of mind.

"You're staying up there?" Now, he was watching her in the mirror.

"Keep your eyes on the road, Miss Moore."

"Yes, Officer."

Finn leaned forward and folded his arms across the back of the bench seat, poking his head between the girls. "I'm staying for a week at the shack. Then off to baseball camp."

Marlis turned on the seat and rested her hand on Finn's forearm. "What are you going to do there all by yourself?" Biz threw a scowl at her.

"I've got some reading to do. They have a summer reading list."

"Who?" Marlis asked.

Biz pushed Marlis off Finn's arm. "Stanford University, silly."

Finn sat back. "Slow around this curve ahead, it's just beyond that."

"Already?" Biz said. She'd pouted.

"Duty calls, Miss Moore."

She slowed and Finn guided her to the shoulder where a two-track lane ran into the woods. "It's just down this path, across the bridge."

He got out of the car on Elizabeth's side, hoisting his bag to his shoulder, and leaned into the driver's window. "Congratulations, Class of 1961. Be good. Bye, Marlis." He rested his hand on Biz's shoulder. "Thank you, Miss Moore, and, please, drive more carefully."

"See you around, Officer," said Marlis.

Biz blew Finn a kiss, and after he'd rounded the car, stepped on the gas.

"What a sweetie pie," Marlis had said.

Biz glared. "Get your own pie, Marly. *Laissez faire, ma cherie.*"

"Oh, I was just flirting, Bizzy," her friend said. "You know. Get me out of the house, and I go wild. You're not serious about this guy are you?"

"Why not?"

Marlis thought. "He isn't exactly from a high-class family, you know."

"What difference does that make?"

"Listen to you," Marlis said. "You've lectured me plenty of times. 'Choose well, Marly. The best apples are at the top of the tree.'"

Elizabeth colored. "I said that?"

"You did. And, hey, Finn is Finnish. I seem to remember your dad having a thing about that."

"Shut up, Marlis. My father has nothing to do with what I think or what I do." Elizabeth tromped the gas pedal of the car in defiance of her father's authority. As a matter of fact, in the bosom of his family, Arthur Moore regularly berated the latest immigrant families. He'd disowned Elizabeth's older brother, older by twelve years, when he fell in love with and married a Finnish Swede. Robert had to elope. After that news broke, her father acted like Robert never existed. He wouldn't talk about him. Well, she thought, I've earned my independence. I am not Robert.

Biz slowed down. "Sorry, Marlis. I got carried away. You know, the daddy thing."

"I couldn't forget. Yuck! But they say, 'All's fair in love and war.'"

Elizabeth growled at Marly. "No, fathers aren't ever fair."

They drove on to Sonoma, but Biz wasn't in the mood for a drive-in. She watched Marlis suck down a root beer float and flirt with the Sonoma boys in the neighboring cars. Marly had sprung from the car like a Jill-in-the-box. She hopped around like a nuthatch, pecking first here, then there. Biz finally honked her to the car. The horn brought the carhop as well. Elizabeth drove home, dropping Marlis off early.

"Are you all right, Biz?" Marlis had asked.

"I just feel a little off. See you tomorrow."

Dr. Elizabeth Moore, sitting in the gym, did feel a little off. It was that awful depressing letter and this speech, unimportant except to city boosters. Neither bode well. She worked on ways to get out of speaking, writing it, or even thinking about it, but she could not see any way to avoid it. She picked up the notepad again.

On the occasion of our Santa Reina High Centennial, I welcome you all . . . she wrote. God, this is dull, she thought, but she continued writing: . . . and invite you to join me in honoring one of our most . . . what? she thought, worthy?

august? famous? No, deserving, yes: one of the most deserving—most certainly deserving of public unmasking, though she couldn't do it—members of our community. Here is a man who . . . who what? That's what is wrong; I cannot do it. I can't tell the truth. I can't bring myself to lie, yet I don't dare reveal anything. She slapped the pad down. She rested her eyes and thought. She avoided thinking about the letter and the guilt it had hung on her heart. Instead, she focused on Finn.

Even after thirty years, she smelled Finn's clean hair and the light cologne he'd splashed on his neck. She listened for his jovial whispers—harmless, really, not quite sarcastic and hardly bitter—funny and full of wit. Across three decades, she felt his gentle strength as he lifted her to him saying, "Congratulations, Elizabeth Moore, graduate-cum-laude." Those had been good days. No, she thought when like a missed step Snub tripped into her mind. No, not good but hopeful, exciting. She knew, during the embrace she and Finn shared on the gymnasium floor that night thirty years ago, that he could save her from her past and from herself. So long ago, she mused, but—she was thinking of the weekend to come—he might yet.

After she'd dropped Marlis at home the evening she had given Officer Pyykönen a ride, Elizabeth had returned to the Sonoma Road. Dark had fallen by that time, and, everything looking different and ghostly, she couldn't find the track that led over the creek to Finn's cabin. She'd turned around three times, cruising slowly but failed to find him. Once she'd thought she found the track, stopped, and walked a few steps into the night. Her open car door pulled by the grade of the shoulder slammed and startled her. Heart racing, Biz had scampered back through her headlights to get into the car and drive off.

Behind her far across the huge room, a metal door banged shut. The gym amplified the sharp report. Dr. Elizabeth Moore jumped in her seat and turned toward the sound from the long rise of the cushioned seats above the bleachers.

She was looking for Finn.

Oh, God in heaven, she almost cried aloud as Farley Pike (the always unwelcome, unlooked-for party guest, who had to be invited but who you wished would not come) slipped in the door of the balcony. He waved to her and moved along the first row of plush seats coming her way. Pike disappeared into the stairwell on the side near Elizabeth. In a minute he would be entering the gym proper.

Knowing full well that they were not, Biz thought, I hope those doors are locked.

18

Farley and Elizabeth

Of all the horribly rotten people to stumble in and at just the wrong time, Dr. Elizabeth Moore griped to herself as Farley Pike sidled down the row. Oh, please don't sit down. Then something heavy in his pocket clanged on the metal seat bottom. He had sat. She forced a polite smile and said, "Of all people," even as she stiffened away from him. Please, she readied for his clammy hand, don't touch me.

She still looks young. He removed the bulging bunch of keys from his trouser pocket. Is she cowering? No reason to be afraid. He set the keys down next to him and touched her hand, grasping it, wanting, but restraining the desire, to kiss it, sensing she would pull it away. "I thought that was you," he said. What a fool, his mind flashed, to admit you followed her.

Good God, was he's stalking me? Let go my hand, you oaf. She cooled her gaze, gave his over-friendly rush a professional's indifferent shoulder. With a sudden tug she extracted her hand from his oozing palm, saying, "I'm working on my speech, Farley." Let a woman do her work, leave her be.

"Oh, yes. I was watching," he said. Fool. Twice a fool. "Having a bit of trouble? Looking for inspiration?" He could not seem to stop his blabbing. This nervous chatter, this foolish blather was nothing of what he wanted to say. What was it that he did want to say? Did he want to confess his longing, his fruitless love, his hidden, recumbent lust for a redux of sex with Elizabeth? No, I simply want to talk, he reassured himself. No, that was not it. What then? What? It was only to break the ice, he told himself. "It will come," he assured her. "Don't you worry." He touched her shoulder. His hand stuck there. "I was hoping to see you here, I mean at the celebration."

Dr. Elizabeth Moore, trying to hide the repugnance at his advance, did her best to shrink away tacitly from the sweaty hand clinging to her blouse. Don't go on, Farley. Say hello and move along.

"I just glanced up from my dishes. You know I still live just around the corner." Oh, why couldn't he stop himself? Mercy, dear Geoffrey, please let me shut it off. "I've been there for over thirty years now" (No, no, don't dangle the time, all those years, out there) "and there you were getting out of your car." He halted before the gym rafters fell on his combed-over pate. He'd nearly mentioned her tugging at her skirt there in the street. She's frowning. Do not say one word more.

Farley Pike shut his mouth so suddenly his lips made a flapping sound that echoed even in the immensity of the gym. He tried a smile and then had to mop his forehead.

God, Dr. Elizabeth Moore thought, that same scented handkerchief I bet. Horrid.

She thought back nearly twenty-five years. It's no wonder you repulse me so. I must have been drunk to do it. The long-ago evening presented itself again: a heavy rain had choked off attendance at Parent's Night and had sent the few teachers who had shown up scurrying home as soon as they could. Elizabeth, whose students ordinarily showered her with forgotten umbrellas, had sent the last one home with a grandparent who had arrived early. Now she would have to wait out the downpour.

Her appetite for trifling, though, had not been dampened

by the storm. Two fathers had visited, one at a time, thank God. They were either single or had come without their wives, she did not know which nor had cared to know at the time. She'd watched them move toward her: suave, hunky, too young to be high school dads. She'd flirted. They grinned shyly and in oddly similar ways ran a firm hand oh so softly down her arm. Each did that electric thing with his hand and, she'd thought, swayed his pelvis. Then, they shook hands at the ends of the abbreviated class periods. True to Snub's training, Elizabeth had been ready to turn out the lights and lock the second dad in with her, but he let go her hand and sauntered out into the rain without looking back.

A few minutes later, when Farley appeared, having seen her light still on, she was musing about tutoring sessions with those boys whose fathers had stoked her desire that night. It could be arranged, she was thinking. On the father's request, of course. She knew how to suggest that he ask. Yes, either would do, Elizabeth thought, or both, but one at a time. A flapping noise wrenched her out of her tumescent romance.

Farley Pike, standing at the open classroom door, had startled her then, too. How could she have given into her lascivious longings? And with Farley. And at school, too. Ha! In the classroom of all places! You've no restraint, she blamed herself. Not true, she argued back. You're fine in public, but alone? She admitted, these arguments had raged in her since she left her virginity in Snub's darkroom. This is your weakness: Unmitigated libido, dear.

Now sitting in the gymnasium, she mused, it was never FP. All those years ago, thought of pressing those dads between her thighs in the classroom had lit the fire that burned her. "Turn off the lights, Farley," she'd said. Finally, she'd closed her eyes, shut out all but FP's florulent odor, which could not be avoided, to finish what twice that night had risen rigid in

125

her desire and had settled there not to be shaken loose.

Now decades later, Dr. Elizabeth Moore sighed over that misquenched thirst. She patted Farley Pike's hand then peeled it from her shoulder.

"No, I hadn't known. You're still at the school?" Making conversation might lead to a graceful out.

"Yes, I'm the assistant principal of the lower division." You can't be proud of that, Farley, he remonstrated. Your miniscule achievements pale before hers. "You've done well." He left off "too."

Thank God we're chatting. Harmless prattle. Now don't bring up the past. Don't mention that night. "Yes. As well as a career in education can be called 'doing well.'" He's inching his hands toward me again. She shifted away, fussing with the notepad and pen. "It's a labor of love." No. Do not use the "el" word now, Biz.

"It is," Farley Pike said as he edged closer. "You realize, don't you, Elizabeth, that I've thought of you often all these years (there, you blathering idiot, "years," again), nearly every day."

Dreadful, she thought. Then again, who, she asked herself, is more wretched, old Farty Pants, here, or me? I certainly feel abysmal. Haven't I, too, mooned, after Finn Pyykönen, all this time? Am I so different from this ungainly, smelly string bean? "Oh, you flatter me Farley. I can't mean anything to you." And why say that? She chided herself. Instead of putting him off, you, old hussy, are leading him on, aren't you?

"No, no. You're wrong there, Elizabeth. I have been looking forward to seeing you for weeks. I hope we can spend some time together." He now clutched her shoulder while thinking you shouldn't be doing this.

He can't be dangerous. He's just an old fool. Please, let go, Farley. "I'm so busy," she said. He continued gripping her, kneading her shoulder.

Was that a sign, Farley wondered? An invitation? He knew it could happen. He released her shoulder. "I'd love to have you to tea." Alone, at tea. Yes, Elizabeth, come alone to tea.

"I'm sure, Farley, but I think we will have to limit ourselves to the parties and events. I am scheduled so tightly."

Now! Farley commands himself, then reaches across Dr. Elizabeth Moore, fastens his hand on her other shoulder, and leans in to kiss her.

"Mr. Pike!" Elizabeth lurches away, pushes his arm down, and staggers to her feet.

Wrong, Farley Pike thought. Wrong, wrong, wrong. "Oh, Elizabeth, I got carried away. I'm just so . . . ecstatic, so overwhelmed to see you."

"Listen, Farley," she said evenly but pointedly, "our tryst is far in the past!" Oh Christ! You brought it up yourself, despite your oath. And now that it's out, you'll have to deal with it.

"Forgive me that one moment of weakness," she said. "Let it go. It is nothing I plan to repeat." She wouldn't tell him that the same plan with Snub had fallen suddenly away.

"Elizabeth," Farley rose and took her unresisting hand, "I cherish that night. The night I learned to love, my dear."

This cannot be happening! It's too horrible to be real. Worse than that night. "No, you must not, Farley, it was a mistake."

He took her other hand now. Oh, please listen to me, Elizabeth, it is real, it is true. "I love you, Elizabeth." Kiss her, kiss her now. He reviled his impertinence and reluctance both.

Stop it, Biz. Take command. You have to club him hard. Get out of this, now.

Dr. Elizabeth Moore stepped backward and pushed Farley Pike's hands away. "Listen, Farley, and please understand," she said—yes I'm saying this thing that is certainly not wholly true but is true enough as far as you, FP, are concerned—taking another step away, sweeping with her leg the legal pad and pen off the chair and to the floor where she ignored them.

She looked directly at Pike. "Since that morning in the music room when I discovered poor dear Denise swimming in her own blood with that murderer stabbing and slashing at her chest, grunting and drooling over her . . ." Elizabeth takes her hands to her face, covers it but does not sob, does not cry . . . "nothing, not one thing that happened here at this school, this cursed school, mattered to me anymore. I left it all behind. Everything. There was no care, no innocence, no camaraderie, no companionship, no love that could make a difference. I've turned my back on this chamber of horrors. I am not coming back to it. Not to the school, not to classes, not to the people, and certainly not to you. It is all dead." There. That should do it. That should chill his ardor.

"Poor dear. Elizabeth, how you have suffered," Farley Pike said. He moved toward her and stepped on the pen atop the pad. "Oh, my. I'm sorry." Now you've broken her pen, you fool. Ink squirted over the pages.

You are too far along to stop now, Biz. "I did a terrible thing," she says aloud but not to Farley.

Farley stooped to pick up the pen. Ink ran on his fingers and unnoticed, a little dripped on his white shirt. He stood facing her with the mess, not knowing what to do with it. "Terrible?" Is she talking to me, about me? The mess I've made? What? "Oh, Elizabeth, I'm sorry."

"I was in shock. My blood had drained. I was sick to my stomach. I had never seen a dead person before, never seen a corpse, much less a murdered one, and a young girl. I heard him run. I didn't see his face. I saw only the mask. Then I passed out. I was falling to the floor." She's gone too far, she knows, but she sees her confession has, anyway, stopped him. "Now, someone here at Santa Reina High knows. I've gotten a letter. Some one knows I made a mistake."

Farley Pike stared open-mouthed. He froze stock still with a yellow pad dripping ink over his clumsy hands. The ink mess held him; the murder mess horrified him. "I thought you saw his face." Had she lied?

"I thought I had. . . at the time I told myself I had. But now that I've received this letter, I doubt it," she says. "I never really knew."

He looked around for some place to put the pad. He found none. It was dripping on the floor. "But you said," he says.

"I was wrong. I did a terrible thing, and everyone encouraged me, was happy to go along. Even the family."

"But if you said . . . but then who . . . ?" Farley blubbered. His lips popped and flapped, again and again.

Give it to him, Biz. Get shut of this idiot. "You've always lived so close, were here so early, always. I think you would know." I am going to escape this baboon, she thought. It's at a cost, but probably not so dear.

Farley nearly dropped the pad. She thinks I know. Does her letter say I murdered that girl? She believes it's me! "No, no. I was here . . . not right here, up in the Department office, at the front." Now he was going on again and couldn't stop. "I came early, as usual, to make copies and get ready. It was near finals. I had a lot . . ." Farley stop, he tells himself. You shouldn't explain. "No. I have no way of knowing."

He looked around the gymnasium, then held the ink-smeared pad out to her.

"There might be a trash just outside that door," Elizabeth

said. She pointed. "Just dump the whole mess."

Yes, let me get rid of this. I've got to wash my hands. "Excuse me. Let me tidy up."

"Of course," she said. And as Farley Pike passes through to the corridor behind the stage, Dr. Elizabeth Moore waited for the lock to click shut. Then, brushing Farley Pike's keys off the seat that Finn had occupied thirty years before, she sidled down the aisle and walked to the other side of the gym, exiting the way she came in.

19

Snub Speaks

When I heard the next day what Elizabeth had slapped on old FP in order to get his grimy paws off her blouse—we were sipping Chardonnay before the principal's luncheon Friday afternoon—I nearly spewed my drink on her like some land-roving Moby Dick. As it was, I spilled a little on my jacket. I couldn't stop laughing. Then the coughing set in. My letter had made a point after all. Pike had been piked. It found its own way; I would never have deigned to send that old Farty Poop even a postage stamp.

Father B came over and started pummeling me on the back.

"I'm all right, Father," I said. "Leave off the thumping."

"'T'ould be a fancy t'ing to have you choke on a glass o' wine," he smiled. Berach was in one of his clear-headed Gaelic phases. "What I'm wonderin' is what in God's name all the laughin's about."

Biz broke in. "Sorry, Monsignor, it's too sinful for your ears."

I thought the good Father would stab Elizabeth with his stare, but he smiled and made light of her refusal. "Oh, save it for the confessional, is that how 't is? So's it won't be repeated." He moved toward the bar. "I best be getting a pint before they run out."

"Does he think everyone's Catholic? He knows very well I'm not."

I straightened up. "My only regret, Biz, is that I wasn't

there to see it."

"What? His flappy lips or the sleazy paw marks on my blouse?" Elizabeth could be crass, especially after tossing back one or two. "What's Phelan got up his?"

"My dearest Elizabeth, I would have challenged either man had you wanted it. I've no wish to watch one maul your clothing or another glare you down. The Monsignor has become, let's be kind, a wee bit unstable."

"There is only a wee difference between tottering and doddering, Snub."

I hope I managed at least a weak smile. Elizabeth was in a mood, one I did not want to spend time with. She turned away. As lovely as she looked, I followed the good Father to replenish my wine. Leave her snit to another.

Had she insinuated that Farley did the stabbing just to stop his advance? Or did she now think he could have done it? Would he have? He had been on campus, of course; he was always creeping around the school.

I had never subscribed to the idea that Brandling, the catcher, did it. Sure, I supported Elizabeth when she fingered him. I'm not the one to be correcting the police, that's for sure, but his confession never made sense. I wondered at the time if Biz was protecting the brother, Warren—he's over there now, talking to her and the principal. That boy had studied more than the piano score in her class. That I knew.

In any case, her Farley Pike accusation tickled me, but it also set me to thinking about '67 again. And more than ever I began to wonder if I'd been wrong. Had Elizabeth protected someone else? Not what's-his-name, Warren?

We all believe what is most convenient for us at the time. I've no corner on truth, that's for sure. Let's just say (due to my misappropriated words?), Biz doesn't seem so sure anymore, and I remember a certain worried look she'd cast around at the Hagerty wake. I thought then that we hadn't got the whole story. Still, I refused to believe anything but what Biz said publicly.

Now, I'm more certain. Not that it matters, but I believe I can whittle it down to three suspects. And as a matter for the record, I think I know which of the three it might be.

See if I can shake anything loose over a glass of wine. I'm off to see how the Monsignor liked my little red missive. Reunions are such fun if you take them for what they're worth.

20

Finn and Warren

Finn ignored the freeway signs. That would be the easiest and fastest way to get to Glen Ellen, but the peace of the countryside and the need to do some thinking after visiting Doug led him the long way, north from Vacaville on Pleasant Valley Road toward the reservoir and the back roads to the cabin. Highway 128, full of twists and turns among golden hills, suited reflection.

After all this time, Doug had as good as admitted his innocence. Finn had always sensed that Doug's confession had been wrong. The boy had flown into rages on the diamond, the police knew, but admitting to murder must have been born of fear and confusion. It had been contrived. The sheriff, who had never handled a murder before, felt the onus to arrest anyone, no one in particular but someone, and when Elizabeth said she saw him wear a catcher's mask, her identification sealed Doug's fate and his future.

Having known her well, Finn figured Elizabeth was unsure even though she spoke and acted with certainty. Had he been able to discuss it before she leveled the charge at his student, Finn might have, he'd always thought, been able to sway her. She saved face too well, though, to be influenced after going public. Now, twenty-four years later, he had suspicion enough, fueled by Mrs. Brandling's words, to at least bring forth questions. Now Doug's tacit admission made that act essential.

For years, as Finn's own life had allowed time and energy,

he had worked on his theory. After Doug's brother, Warren, gained prominence in Los Angeles, eventually earning a place on UCLA's medical faculty, Finn sought him out. He'd interviewed him for the *Times* on two occasions—one at his faculty appointment and later on becoming dean—and on a third meeting had broached the topic of Doug's confession. They'd known each other professionally, and even though they were not friends, Finn thought he had the man's confidence. Warren had not warmed to that conversation. He was civil but spoke, Finn thought, as if he could be hiding something.

Finn's last conversation with Warren, a fourth meeting, this one at the family home, had been two weeks ago. He'd asked to interview Doug's brother in conjunction with the Santa Reina retrospective he was writing. As a prominent alumnus, Warren was on the speakers program.

Finn had called early. Warren was snarled in traffic, but his mother let Finn in. "You're the journalist from Santa Reina," she said. She acted, then, as if they had not met before.

"Class of '61, yes. And I taught there, of course. I coached your sons."

Mrs. Brandling drew her fingertip to her mouth and hung her head heavily. "I guess I knew that at one time," she said. "I've forgotten so much." She looked at him through vacant eyes, then revised her sentence. "I've put so much out of my mind." She invited him in.

It had been twenty-four years since Mrs. Brandling had ordered him out of her Santa Reina house, but it seemed that she did not connect him with that time. Maybe it's easier this way, Finn thought.

"Come into the kitchen, if you don't mind. I'm working on old news clippings at the table." She showed him the way. "I'm sorting things for Warren's trip."

One end of the large kitchen table was set with three cups and bread plates. The rest was covered with aged newspaper clippings arranged in short, neat piles. Mrs. Brandling seated Finn at one of the place settings. "I have coffee and some homemade madeleines."

"Not for me, I hope," Finn said.

"For you and for Warren," she said, "I will join you. I'm proud of my baking, you know, Mr. Pyykönen."

She did remember, Finn concluded. Perhaps she's making up for her angry words.

"Then, of course, I will try some. Just a little milk with the coffee, thank you."

While she busied herself with the serving, Finn scanned the clipping atop each pile. Most were baseball results, all about Warren's pitching, though a few lauded his academic or Boy Scout accomplishments. He had not made the rank of eagle. None of the headlines mentioned Doug. He lifted a couple of the top leaves, checking the clippings below.

She seemed to know what he was doing. "Are you looking for Douglas's clippings?" Mrs. Brandling asked.

She surprised Finn. He had not expected Doug's mother to mention his name. The family had cut him out of their lives. Apparently, though, he was still in her mind.

Finn looked kindly into her face. "Yes, ma'am, I was."

"Even Douglas's existence is upsetting to Warren. We never talk about him. My husband forbade us to mention his name after his conviction, and as Mr. Brandling was dying, Warren promised him to keep that silence."

"I'm sorry. It's painful, I understand," Finn said.

"Speaking and thinking are two different things," Mrs. Brandling said, "and I perhaps think more of Douglas because I do not speak of him." She held Finn's gaze as if waiting for something, then spoke before he was ready to reply. "You see him, don't you?"

How she'd learned of his visits to Vacaville, Finn did not know. He'd thought that Doug had not heard from the family all his time in prison. Had he kept something from Finn?

"Yes, Mrs. Brandling, I do see your son, a couple times a year. I write to him when I cannot visit."

"You'll see him during the Santa Reina celebration then."

Finn nodded. "Yes, I plan to visit. I will watch him play baseball."

Mrs. Brandling held a quiet, quizzical look on her face as if she were forming a question, and not knowing how to ask it, mulled it over deliberately. Finn decided she looked sad.

Finn did not wait. "Is there something you would like me to tell him?"

She surprised him again, placing her hand gently on his. "The past cannot be undone, Mr. Pyykönen. What I have to say to Douglas should have been said long ago. Anything I say now would serve only myself. It could not remove his hurt."

"Don't you think it would mean something to him?"

She smiled thinly and patted his hand, then moved her own to her cheek. "Even though we have been separate forever, I know my son very well. Douglas is as stoic as I. I will not belie that in him now."

She poured more coffee, took up a madeleine, and nibbled on it. "You should know, Mr. Pyykönen, that I do have a scrapbook of all Douglas's news clippings, the complimentary ones." She looked at him and gave a slow nod. "In another I've kept the articles you have written about the prison. I have the *Republic*'s murder coverage with them. You see, after all the horror, after all the time that's past, Douglas is still my son."

"Yes, of course."

She smiled, grimly this time. "To you, Mr. Pyykönen,

however, I will apologize. Last time we met I was unfair. Then I was terrified, scared of losing both my sons. I'm sorry for behaving badly. I made mistakes."

"Mistakes?"

"Yes. I was afraid that you were right."

"About Doug's innocence?"

At the front of the house the door opened. Mrs. Brandling heard her son enter but answered Finn's question anyway. "Yes, and about Warren, too."

She rose from the table and left the kitchen to meet Warren in the front hall. Whatever her fault in Doug's devastation had been, Finn recognized that Mrs. Brandling had paid in full. Her resolute suffering had ground her thin, pressed her rigid, and she knew it. Finn heard her controlled, dispassionate voice greeting her son—her so-very-promising son, the one she had fought to protect at such monumental expense (the loss of another)—speaking dry, cloying words: "Oh, how do you stand that traffic. Let me take your coat, Warren."

Warren barked at her. "Leave me alone, Mother, for God's sake."

Finn could not hear what Mrs. Brandling muttered to Warren.

"In the kitchen? Why in God's name there?" He heard Warren marching toward him through the dining room.

"Mr. Pyykönen. Forgive my mother's foibles. We usually do not receive guests in the kitchen. Please, come to my study."

Finn stood and shook Warren's hand. "I'm fine here."

Warren waved him on. "Mother, bring our coffee to my office. Mr. Pyykönen and I will talk there." He lifted an arm to show Finn the way and nearly pushed him along to the back of the house.

"Sorry, Mother is having a rough spell. Mulling over the past is not good for her, and this centennial is dredging up all sorts of terrors."

Finn decided to defend her. "She seemed fine to me."

"Oh, she puts up a good front. That's her nature," Warren said, "but she'll be pacing until three in the morning. Sorry to have run late." In the office now, he motioned Finn to a chair. "Please, Mr. Pyykönen."

Warren and Finn chatted about their work a while. Mrs. Brandling brought a tray with two fresh coffees and a plate heaped with madeleines. She set the tray down and left without a word. She closed the study door behind her.

Finn offered her a clear "Thank you." Warren said nothing.

Finn confirmed the facts of Warren's career and noted several statements Warren made about the school and town of his birth. Warren had sent Finn a copy of his centennial speech, enough to spin a good story: local boy makes good, gives back to the community. The Brandlings had established a library endowment for the school (before the murder) and Doug's father and then Warren had continued to fund it in the years after his father's death. As far as Warren seemed concerned, Doug was not part of his story.

Finn cleared his throat and shifted uneasily in his chair. "Listen, Warren, as a journalist, it is difficult for me to cover this story without any mention of your brother." He had to wait in uncomfortable silence for Warren to answer.

When he did, Warren looked at him with his mother's vacant, sad eyes. "Doug left our family twenty-four years back. I don't think he should be part of your story."

"Still, in good conscience, can you say something about him, the event, his difficulties?" Finn pressed him. "It lends credibility."

"To you, Mr. Pyykönen, but not to me." He crossed his arms. "I'm not saying another word about my brother, and you may not quote anything I have said about him here or elsewhere."

The journalist in him would not rest. Finn leaned toward Warren, "Don't you wonder about Doug's confession? Why he stood by it?"

"I have very little curiosity about my brother. I don't think about him."

"You can't believe he was the killer, can you?"

"Confession and conviction make belief passé."

Finn came forward on his chair. "Doug was covering for someone. Was it you?"

"Absolutely not, Mr. Pyykönen." Warren spoke stiffly, formally, "I have never spoken to my brother about the event, about his confession, or about his guilt. I didn't then and do not now believe he wants to talk to me."

"If I told you otherwise, would you believe me?"

Warren's voice wavered, "How could that happen? He would not want to talk."

"How can you be so sure?"

"I know my brother well. He is a hothead who carries grudges. Discussion was never his forte."

"Do you think he is guilty?"

Warren returned his cup and saucer to the tray. He stood. Looking just like his mother, Warren smiled thinly at Finn and said, "If I thought about these things at all, would I want to discuss them with you?" Warren extended his hand. "See you at the reunion."

Finn followed his host to the front door.

"I'll not hazard traffic advice. I assume you are heading for Pasadena. You know the area well enough. I hope you have clear sailing."

"Thank you." Finn looked around for Mrs. Brandling. She hovered in the dark dining room, watching calmly but looking gaunt. This is not the time to reopen a talk about Doug, he decided. "Thank you, Mrs. Brandling, for the coffee and cookies. They were delicious."

She bowed slightly in reply but said nothing.

Finn had moved down the walk, filled with strong impressions yet feeling empty-handed and uncertain.

No matter what Warren had said then, now with the reunion just a day away, Doug's mention of his brother this afternoon demanded action. This was the time. Finn knew what he would have to do.

21

Farley Pike

In the gymnasium locker room, Farley rubbed his hands hard under the faucet. The ink had set and stained his fingers.

Look at the mess you've made, he told the mirror. Broke her pen, offended her, and ruined a perfectly good white shirt. Even if it is six years old, it was still wearable. He did not try to wash the ink spill from the shirt front. It would just bleed.

Farley Pike made a scrub pad of folded brown paper towels, wet it, and worked furiously on his hands. The tint lightened slightly. He sighed. That will have to do. But I must make it right with Elizabeth.

He left the washstand and stepped into the waxed hallway. Skewed rectangles of sunshine spilled over the corridor floor where daylight poured through windows at each end. He returned to the gym door, peeked through the window, but could not see past the stage backdrop.

She's waiting for me I bet. He grasped the latch and yanked hard. His wrist shrieked strain, and the door stood as if guarding a bank vault. Locked! Good Geoffrey! He stamped his foot and reached in his pocket for the keys he remembered he had left on the chair. Gone!

Farley Pike scurried to the entry at the far end of the hall. He tested that portal more gently this time. Locked! He pressed his face to the window there, and through that oblong, he saw the curvaceous figure of Dr. Elizabeth Moore slipping through the exit on the other side of the gym.

He resisted the temptation. Don't pound, you fool!

As if his day had again darkened—the sun, now covered by a cloud, sotted the gymnasium corridor in gloom—Farley Pike saw a new, unwelcome brightness rise: the smiling face of his neighbor, Mrs. Baxter, in sincere but patronizing hospitality. His arms went rigid over clenched fists. "Twice in the same day!" he screaked at the ceiling and stamped his foot again.

Resignation was nothing new to Farley Pike. It formed the core of his character and had cradled him through life. He ceded to the locked doors, to the left keys, to the escaped Elizabeth, and to the humiliation that from his gut would jeer him, obsequious at Mrs. Baxter's kitchen door. He sighed.

If I am to act the beggar, I'd best get on with it. Had he read that somewhere? Farley left the hallway by the fire exit of the vestibule then through the courtyard to the street.

Elizabeth's car was gone.

Though the morning was still fair, Farley Pike buttoned his coat, covering the ink stain on his shirt. He turned toward home and Mrs. Baxter's garden gate. Despite his consternation he couldn't ignore his stomach grumbling as he thought of his neighbor's kitchen. She always has something nice to share, he remembered. And she will be glad of the company. He pondered his dilemma. Maybe peach scones and coffee.

Mrs. Baxter's coffee was hot. Farley Pike scalded his palate taking the first sip.

"Oh, Mr. Pike," she said, "you should spill some in the saucer to cool. You'll burn yourself."

"No, I'm fine. I'll just wait a minute." He ran his tongue over the roof of his mouth. The flesh felt sickly and loose.

The scones were cranberry-walnut, and when Farley Pike

chewed his second corner, something hard ground against his tender molar. Farley winced and without thinking, put his fingers into his mouth, drawing out a small, jagged shard.

"Oh, my," Mrs. Baxter said, "a nut shell? I'm so sorry."

Pike held his jaw. What, he wondered, is going on? "I'm fine, Mrs. Baxter, but I think I should go home and lie down."

"I'll get the small thermos and wrap up some scones," she replied.

His faint protests did not deter his neighbor. She still had the key in her apron pocket and wouldn't, he knew, give it up until she was satisfied.

He stood at the door. "Very well. Thank you, Mrs. Baxter."

On his way across the garden to his building, Farley Pike studied his sore wrist, burnt mouth, his pulsing tooth, and the question he'd posed: "What is going on?" He decided he knew. The murder is bothering me. That letter she told me about. Elizabeth as good as accused me of that stabbing she witnessed so long ago. "The event" which was conspicuous for its absence in today's paper, of course, had sprung up again. He dwelt on the subject. I connect Elizabeth and that murder anyway. He muttered as he walked, now taking care at each step, alert for loose stones on the garden path, and fingered Mrs. Baxter's spare key in his pocket. He entered his building and mounted the stair to his apartment.

I need to lie down, he told himself. Leave my keys for later.

Farley Pike spread his mother's throw over the davenport and removed his coat and shoes. He lay down and released a wavering, tired breath.

He'd not been able to sleep that night before Denise Hagerty's death, preparing for finals and with questions about

My Antonia whirling in his mind nonstop. How he loved Willa Cather. He had risen at four—not unusual for him ever since the morning his mother had died—followed his routine, which included, while showering, envisioning himself naked with Elizabeth Moore, and after a light breakfast, trudged across the street to school, lugging his weighty briefcase. It was 5:30 in the morning.

Had he been alone on campus? While Farley rested on the couch, he swept through the recesses of memory, scanning for details that might tell something. It had been Elizabeth's Dodge Charger passing on School Street outside his classroom that had stuck in his mind. Of course, you would be watching out for her. That had been 6:20. He'd looked. Lying still now under the throw, he could bring nothing else important to mind. Still he thought.

He had finished, about fifteen minutes later, a test stencil for his sophomore course and took it to the mimeograph room in the next building. He had seen no one, but was there a car other than Elizabeth's parked near the music building? He'd thought so, but twenty-four years later he felt unsure about whose car it was. In any case, he'd said nothing at the time. He had run forty-nine copies—they'd been perfect, thank Geoffrey and his own proper care—then headed back toward his room. Outside, across the quad, the music room lights came on. Elizabeth is getting ready, he'd reckoned. Having thought of visiting her there before everyone arrived, he'd even taken a dozen steps in that direction, but as he told the police, hearing the call to early Mass from the Sacred Heart bell tower beyond, he went back to his room. It wouldn't have been seven o'clock yet.

Now snuggling in the warmth of his mother's throw as if it were warding off the chill of Dr. Elizabeth Moore's insinuation, Farley Pike once again calculated the minutes between his arrival at school that day twenty-four years ago and the time Elizabeth had driven by. Nearly an hour. And how long until she'd raised the alarm? Another thirty minutes. He could hear the questions: "Who saw you, Mr. Pike? Exactly where were you between quarter past six and seven? Wouldn't you have had time to dispose of the clothes and weapon before Ms. Moore alerted us?" They would interrogate him without mercy. What's that stain on your shirt? Would they ask that?

Farley Pike sprang up like a garden rake Mrs. Baxter had stepped on. The stain! He stood up, spread his mother's throw in outstretched arms and scanned for ink that might have leached from his shirt. Thank Geoffrey Chaucer, he thought, the shirt had dried beforehand. He folded the coverlet onto the davenport again and went to change shirts. He washed away a small ink smudge he found on his belly and selected another shirt from his closet. Closet. China closet. That's it, look in the china cabinet. A word popped into his mind, "Tea." That was it.

He would, after all, invite Dr. Moore to tea. He'd tell her that he'd been thinking about that morning, the murder morning, and wanted to share something with her. That would do to bring her around.

"Prepare for the best, though you expect the worst," he heard his mother say.

"I will, Mother," Farley said. One must forge ahead. Mus'n't one?

Farley Pike whistled a Mozart minuet as he laid out the low table he'd set before the couch. He checked the centennial schedule for Friday. Four o'clock will be perfect, he decided. I'll have her then. He could drop the invitation at her hotel. She was staying, he was sure, at The Stanford. Perfect, he thought.

The gloom he'd fallen under lifted. He moved his prize orchid to the table. Placed his mother's lace doilies on the tablecloth he'd spread and folded two coral napkins that accented the white cover nicely. No need for place cards, of course. He plumped four cushions on the davenport and sniffed his mother's throw. His own scent danced in his nostrils. It was fine.

Mozart. Yes, I'll have Mozart in the background. Very nice. Farley Pike smiled. His mother's china pot and cups looked wonderful there. He placed the sugar bowl and silver. He remembered Mrs. Baxter's scones. Oh, and flowers. Her garden is full now. No, he decided, the orchid is fine. No need to alert, certainly not to invite, his neighbor to Elizabeth's tea.

Farley Pike stood back to look at his handiwork. Yes, this would do it. He thought to change the sheets. Better do that. Just in case. Prepare, you know. He whistled his way to the bedroom.

22

Elizabeth

At times, going out past the Pyykönen property, the Sonoma Mountain Road leaving Santa Reina closely follows a deep-cut stream, the south fork of the Matanzas Creek. Since the early days when high-speed autos became generally available, Roy Pulitz of Santa Reina Auto Salvage, or RIP as many called him, spent early Sunday mornings hoisting one or another wreck from the creek bottom, sometimes having to pull uprooted or snapped trees out before he could haul up the tangled car wreck. He'd never looked at the bodies. He was there for the car, to haul it to the Sonoma County Sheriff's impound lot and, after the investigation, to bring it to the Pulitz's Salvage yard on the west side of town.

Once, though he never looked at them, he had smelled the bodies, the two that young Finn Pyykönen had been unable to save.

On the sharpest curve of the road, a hairpin turn, April 12, 1959 at four in the morning, the odor of burnt flesh had laced itself through the trees and hung there in the fog. Three high school juniors had been pinned inside when the flames erupted. Two were said to be dead or unconscious by the time the leaking gasoline ignited. A third classmate was pulled from back seat of the wreck by a neighbor who'd heard the crash. Had it jumped the creek, the sedan might have landed in the neighbor man's cabin. The girl he'd saved—the neighbor was now the hero, Finn—was horribly burnt up one side of her body but lived, and a year behind her class, graduated from Santa Reina High. When the Boy Scouts of America granted Finn its Honor Medal for lifesaving that year, the *Republic* ran a photo of Finn, his right hand bandaged for the burns he'd sustained, bringing the girl a bouquet of flowers.

Driving to his cabin the summer she'd fallen in love with him at graduation, June 5, 1961, Elizabeth Moore pondered those scars on Finn's right hand. Thank God it wasn't the left, his pitching hand. She wondered. Could he have thrown a curve with a disfigured hand?

As if a chill, fetid breeze suddenly curled over her bare shoulders, Elizabeth shuddered. She did not wish to think of the marred hand. Finn was perfect in her mind. She wanted to keep him that way.

She jabbed at the car's console and dug into her purse. When the lighter popped out, she puffed up a cigarette, drew deeply, and exhaled a cloudy breath out the window. She dangled her arm outside keeping the butt out of the car to defy her father's scrutiny. Daddy, you prude.

She drove slowly, watching for the sharp curve that marked the turn onto Finn's bridge, and though she had driven the route before, even in the dark, she'd occasionally missed the narrow drive, having to double back as she'd done on her very first visit.

Elizabeth smiled to herself, recalling a time that summer, their first time:

She'd made up her mind beforehand.

"Don't you think we should get to know one another first?" he'd said.

"I've been driving and dreaming of you." She'd been thinking about those broad shoulders and the fine white fuzz on his neck that had tickled her cheek during their famous graduation hug. The one that Snub had pushed the *Republic*'s editor to plaster on the front page.

She'd envisioned undressing in front of Finn, then, in her imagination, slowly undressing him, pressing lightly first, then hard against that same blonder-than-blonde hair that she imagined spread over his tanned chest.

She'd been ready even before she got there, but then she was the experienced lover.

Elizabeth brooded on her history. Yes, Snub had shown her the ropes, taught her sex. Did she know about love? Biz was puzzled by it. Are they different? The two confused her. Was that Snub's doing?

Once during their summer of love, Biz drove, reviewing the first few times they'd rendezvoused at the cabin. Finn was not shy, but though he wouldn't admit it, he was principled. He truly had wanted to know her before they dove into that abyss of young love. Still, some of their conversation, mingled with the sweetness of kissing, of holding one another, and of petting each other, led directly to the bed Elizabeth had eyed her first time entering the cabin.

He did get to know her. She'd held little back.

She'd told him about the lascivious looks she imagined her father casting on her, following with his eyes the curves of her breasts and thighs, with what she'd thought was a hungry leer. Some nights he'd lingered at her bedroom door talking casually, sometimes about activities at school or the coming graduation, but always, she'd felt, looking at her body beneath her nighties, waiting for an opportunity or, perhaps, an invitation. Somehow, something she did not right off admit to Finn, her father's lurid looks ended when she'd taken up with Snub. She had told Snub about Daddy's lecherous innuendos and knew that Snub had warned dear old dad off.

She had not told Finn immediately that she had known sexual experience. She alluded to it without being open. Something about an older neighborhood boy years back. She casually mentioned a man in town that had been "nice" to her. Laughing about come-ons by teachers, she'd been careful not to name Snub. Elizabeth would give Finn the idea, she thought, without revealing details.

Finn's caution and willingness to go slowly had charmed her. She had not admired the quality for herself—she was much too bold and impatient for that—but he'd attracted her like foreignness often does with an exotic air, an allure of the uncommon. She marveled at his presence, how as brawny as he was he could move with grace, how intensely blue his eyes were (they burned her like ice when he gazed on her) and how their brilliance was heightened by his fine, nut-meat-white hair itself set off against a baseball player's tanned face, a skin so smooth and unmarked she'd wished it were her own. Even beyond his Scandinavian looks, though, Finn stood apart from every man or boy she'd known.

When she spoke or even was about to speak to him, his attention, his full being focused on her. He listened deeply, thoughtfully, wholly in a way no one had ever done before. (Thirty years later she had yet to encounter that same selfless, entire giving over to another person). Finn's sensitive face and awareness grew so hugely alert that, when he trained his eyes tightly on her, she teetered at the edge of fright. Had he been demon instead of angel, he could have instantly destroyed her. He was, however, kind. Finn Pyykönen had grown up immensely kind.

So though it took her a number of visits to the cabin to "get to know" him, twice that first week, then weathering twelve days at baseball camp, once driving down to Stanford to watch and spend an afternoon with him, finally, on his return from camp, Elizabeth had at last had her way with Finn. She'd arrived after dark at the cabin, unannounced, unexpected, and more prepared than she'd been for anything her whole life long.

She'd found Finn snoozing before the Franklin stove.

"Elizabeth. Did you forget something here?" he'd said. "I didn't know you were coming."

She said nothing, but in the firelight slipped off her shorts and moved to the arm of his chair. She reached for his belt and undid the buckle.

"What are you up to?"

"I'm paying you back for last night." Petting as they often had lately, she'd reached orgasm.

She spoke softly as she worked out of her clothes and alternately tugged his off. "Your little touch did what no one else could."

She'd reversed her T-shirt over her head and gave him an order. "Stand up, Finn." She didn't allow him time to wake fully or get principled. She pushed him back and laid him on the bunk in the alcove. She stripped herself fully and climbed atop him, unbuttoned his shirt. His hands gripped her shoulders with unsparing strength, but he drew her down to his kiss as gently as settling fog.

"And that was the beginning of our eternal summer," she said to the night.

With college still a month and more away, she'd made their romance her sole occupation. Tonight, with Marlis covering for her, she would, for the first time, wake in Finn's morning arms. In her August thoughts his scent wrapped in hers rose in a dream.

Then, before she could shake off musing, she was in the turn. Her practice over the last two months helped her negotiate the curve, just barely—the rear wheel caught the soft shoulder—but she had been driving too fast and had missed Finn's bridge. She'd have to cruise half a mile up the narrow road to double back.

Your rumination could be your ruin, she lectured. Finn's delicate kiss from a week ago evaporated with the warning. Keep your eyes on the road, she reminded herself.

A car coming up behind flashed its lights. Shadows sprung grotesque among the tangle of branches over the creek. Elizabeth sped up.

Half a mile up the road a turnout and a driveway directly across afforded Elizabeth a U-turn. The car that sped past seemed familiar, but intent on getting back to Finn, she made no connection. She wheeled around and tromped the gas.

Elizabeth had just killed her lights, parking behind Finn's '51 Chevy fastback, when a car passed slowly along the curve of the main road. That's right, mister, watch out. It's easy to get rear-ended driving like that. Then Finn opened the cabin door, and Elizabeth, overnight bag in hand, walked across the drive and slipped past him into the cabin.

"I've started the fire. The fog will settle in soon," he said.

"I don't think we'll get cold," she replied. Elizabeth draped an arm around his neck and lifted her lips to his. She leaned against him fully, measuring the hardness of his torso with the plush of her own. They would make love first, she knew, and talk later.

From the bunk they were watching the firelight freckle the wooden walls. "I'm going to miss this at college," she said. She cuddled further into his arms, moving her back against his chest.

"You will be too busy to even think about this," Finn replied. He stroked her hip with one hand and encircled her more tightly with his other arm.

She shook her head and spoke to the room. "No, Finn. I won't. I've never felt this way before. I'll go off to college, but I will think about you every minute."

"We'll see each other, Liz. Don't worry."

"I suppose," she said, "but I will miss this." She wriggled against him.

"Shush." Finn whispered. "Listen," he said.

Leaves rattled in the little yard.

"What's that?"

"Shush," Finn lifted a finger to her lips. "I think someone's outside."

Then that someone sneezed.

Finn released Elizabeth, quietly rolling over her to the edge of the bunk, where he pulled his trousers on. He glided barefoot to the door, unclasped his flashlight there, and dashed out. "Hey! What are you doing?" She heard him say.

Elizabeth heard someone run across the bridge. A car door slammed, and the car started. It squealed onto the pavement. By the time Finn came in, the sound of the engine had died in the distance.

She'd swung her legs over the bunk edge and tucked the sheet around her. "What was that?"

He pressed the flashlight into its bracket again, carefully brushed the bottom of each foot, glanced at Elizabeth in a confused-looking grin. He shook his head. "I have no idea. It couldn't be, but I'd swear it was Snub Randall."

The car that followed her, the car that crawled by as she parked, flashed, fugitive in her mind. Finn was right. "Snub Randall?"

"Yes. It was him," Finn said.

Elizabeth quavered under the totality of Finn's steady gaze. His look was benevolent, but her guilt must have colored his expectant look. She had no innocence to hide her.

"What would Snub Randall be doing out here?" Finn said. "Would he have followed you?"

That was the beginning of her confession. It was not easy, but Finn's gentle insistence, his patience and apparent understanding drew her along toward the truth she had sworn she would never reveal. Finn's kindness and concern wore down the vow she had made to Snub. After several hours of coaxing and soothing Elizabeth's tears, he prevailed. She told Finn everything: how Snub had at first protected her, how he stood up to her father, how he, later, brought her to the high school photo studio darkroom, and, avoiding too much detail, how Snub seduced her.

"Honestly, Finn, when you and I started up, I told him I was through."

"What about him? He doesn't act as if he's finished."

Finn isn't angry, she thought. "He told me he wouldn't mind playing second fiddle, but I told him no. I broke it off. Honestly, Finn." She'd felt she'd told the truth then.

"We should talk to him together."

No, no, Elizabeth thought, I won't do that. "I can't, Finn. I'm too ashamed."

"Someone needs to have a word with Mr. Randall."

"Oh, please, don't Finn. Please?"

Finn took her hand. "Truth makes the strongest bond, Liz."

She let the sheet slide away and breathed in his ear, "Please, Finn, please. . . ."

23

Snub Speaks

Y ou may call me what I've already admitted to, "unreliable,"
but this is the honest truth. Yes, I know how it looks—
bad—but, truly, I had no intention of following Biz that night.
I'm a lot of things, but a peeping Tom is not one of them. I
just needed to find out how serious this Moore-Pyykönen
friendship was.

And that is exactly how Elizabeth had put it.

"We're friends, Snub. Just friends."

She must have believed I had been born the day before
yesterday. Well, maybe just a few years back, anyway.

This had never happened before. Oh, yes, my assistants
usually had boyfriends. They were, after all, very attractive,
so that was natural. Mostly, though, sex was saved for me,
and if it were not, I'd just act like I was their one and only.
They seemed to prefer it that way. So did I.

But Biz was different. She became tortured. If you could
believe it after what we'd done over the semester since she'd
turned eighteen, or how often we did it—once started, her
hunger grew prodigious—now, all of a sudden, she turned
virtuous, virginal indeed. I couldn't even play second fiddle
consistently.

Obviously, I had to find out. Pyykönen wouldn't pitch
a shut-out on Snub Randall. I still had offense (maybe a
squeeze play, you might say). That I knew.

So okay, I followed her. Santa Reina wasn't very large
in those days, and I'd seen her leaving town on the Sonoma

Mountain Road. I make it my business to know pretty much where everyone lives or goes, on the weekends anyway. So, that road, everyone knew, led past the Pyykönen ranch (a hovel, really) and not past much else of interest to someone like Biz.

I was following her at a distance, but still I nearly rear-ended her father's car at that hairpin turn. I hid behind my brights and let her get ahead. She hadn't seen who it was, yet. Then coming around a bend, I spotted her dad's car, pulled over, too late, and before I knew it, I had roared past into her headlights.

Maybe she recognized the car. I don't know, but immediately, she pulled a U-ey. I couldn't turn around to catch up in time. So, I went back, cruising real slow up to Pyykönen's bridge and, sure enough, caught sight of her, already out of the car. She pranced in the porch light. Hell, she carried the little overnight bag I had given her. Slut!

That rankled me. I drove toward Sonoma to cool off, but circled back, turned as Biz had, parked on the shoulder across the road, and waited. It couldn't have been more than fifteen minutes; I walked—all right, crept—over his damn bridge and listened at the window.

They'd gotten down to business, pronto.

Though I didn't see anything, I had heard enough.

I turned to go, rustled a few redwood fronds, I guess, and the dust off the tree made me sneeze. Couldn't help it. Then before I could properly retreat, Pyykönen had me in his flashlight beam.

I knew I hadn't gotten away clean, but, of course, you already knew that.

24

Finn and Elizabeth

On his way to Glen Ellen and the Sonoma Mountain Road cabin, Finn had done more than think. He'd dodged hay wagons, edged to the shoulder past trucks that canted on the tight turns that wound around the mountain over Vacaville. Once he screeched to a halt for a mule deer family on its way to the reservoir for an early evening sip.

After his visit with Doug, thinking was what he had to do. Finn needed to try once again to convince Warren. This would be his last chance. He had to do it right. Maybe the fact that Doug had actually asked for Warren would sway the man, but Finn suspected he would need something more. Moore. Yes, Liz might have an influence where no one else could. She had always seemed to have held sway over Warren. Finn didn't like it, but now after listening to Doug, he decided he would approach Elizabeth. He had two questions to clarify for her bio he was writing for the *Republic*. At the same time, he could talk to her about Warren.

By the time he finished stocking up in Napa for the weekend at the shack, Finn had his plans, or at least his hopes, plotted out. Along slow roads the rest of the way, he thought of Ellie. In Glen Ellen, he stopped by Gary's garage to get the cabin key and to say hello to his neighbor.

"Finn Pyykönen," Gary said. "You're early."

Finn hugged his old friend. "I thought I'd do some work around the ranch."

Gary opened a cabinet above his workbench and

produced the key. "Hasn't moved off the nail since last time. Been pretty quiet out on the road."

"And in town, too, no doubt," Finn said.

Gary was far from a gossip, but the best mechanic for miles around could not avoid news anyone thought proper to pass around. "The big celebration has the hive buzzing, my friend."

Finn bought an orange soda and sat with Gary. "Oh? And what honey are the bees making?"

"No one is saying in so many words, but seems a general expectation that 'the event' is going to rise up somewhere along the parade route. A journalist such as yourself might be interested." Gary was baiting Finn.

Finn shook his head, took a swig of soda, and said nothing.

"And, then, there's this. Came here for you." His friend handed Finn a red envelope. "Merry Christmas."

Gary rose to wait on a customer.

When he came back in he said, "Some say Snub Randall is making a big announcement."

Finn shook his head, "I know nothing about it. I wouldn't be surprised though."

Gary laughed, "We know it won't be a confession." He searched Finn's face, finding no encouragement, he finished, "He's way beyond that. Got to be near eighty."

"Gary, I don't care. I'm here as a writer and speaker, but I'm going to relax and take it as easy as I can. Want to stop by for some chicken and a beer later?"

"I'll have to pass. I'm bunking in Napa tonight."

Finn cast Gary a knowing look and finished his soda. "I'll give you room to play. Coming to the presentation?"

"I wouldn't miss it for the world, class of '67 or not. I'll be there." He shook Finn's hand. "You going to open that?" Gary tapped the letter Finn had left on the counter.

Finn slipped it into his back pocket. "All in due time, pal. See you Saturday."

Once on his property, Finn Pyykönen moved carefully and deliberately. He'd driven slowly over the short wooden bridge across Matanzas Creek, a span he had helped his father build, and parked behind the bramble hedge at the rear of the lot. He left the trunk lid up while he rounded the hedge and walked toward the cabin, fingering the key Gary at Glen Ellen Gas and Motor kept for him.

He lingered in a pool of sunshine. He closed his eyes to draw in the pungent bay and redwood scents and touched one at a time, as he stood there, the channels and saw-toothed ridges of the cabin key. The keyway and code, his locksmith uncle, Raimo, had devised. "Unpickable," he'd said as he fit the lock, "eight pins!" Uncle Ray had been proud. He was right, too. Neither Finn nor his father before had suffered a break-in all these years.

No, not a theft, but a loss just the same. Finn leaned heavily against his car door, eyes still closed, feeling the presence of Ellie who, though gone a bit beyond a decade, inhabited these grounds, the grasses, and trees. Finn had lost the better part of his life there as Ellie lost hers. The redwoods stirred straining the air, singing softly.

He opened his eyes. The cabin, crouching beneath the redwood canopy lining the creek, its walls ruddy as the bark of the hushing trees themselves, proffered a welcome to him in the afternoon sunlight, its eaves spun in glistening webs that Finn would broom away in the hours to come. Each task in its order, he told himself. He'd already greeted Ellie.

The late-day breeze shifted the redwood fronds, showering the cabin roof with the tree's litter of cones, seeds, and dusty fuzz. Ellie would have oohed with the movement that started from skyward tips to cascade along lush green steps down to the long wide sweep of the lowest branches some of which you could reach up and touch standing by the cabin corner. Finn felt her there.

He shut his eyes again. A truck passed on the road, gushing air past the drive through the silence the trees enforced either side of the bridge.

Sheltered there with Finn, abode the effluvium of space he listened to now, the muffled, redolent murmurs Ellie had adored and wanted to stay among. He caught the suggestion of her voice and her scent curling around bay leaf and wild grass stems.

"You've got work to do, Pyykönen," he said. He forced his eyes wide and stepped toward the cabin, walking, yet proceeding as if he were preparing a sacrament at an altar of trees. He slid Raimo's key into its way, jiggling loosely as his uncle taught him to do, and gingerly turned the shaft. The handmade mechanism engaged and slid the bolt back scraping one metallic complaint to its nine-month sleep. It's been that long? Nearly a year. He pushed the door in but did not enter, bringing the screen door back in place without a sound. He hung the key and left the cabin to air while he, not ready to go in yet, ambled off to the tool shed and, then, to the car's open trunk.

After he had swept the roof and eaves, after loosening and strapping open the shutters to bring in more woodsy air, after pitching the tent for Inga on the platform behind the hedges, after stowing his groceries and the clothes he'd brought, Finn Pyykönen entered, unfolded the sheets he'd retrieved from storage, and smoothed them over the bunk mattress. Finn worked like a deacon preparing an Easter table, pious and strong. He paused, then placed his hands on the bed rail and squeezed his eyes shut. He leaned heavily, hunch-shouldered, and deliberately worked to steady his pained breath.

In this bunk, Ellie had died.

A lifetime ago at University Hospital, she'd whispered strained words on painful sighs. Ellie spoke softly, her lips ajar: "Finn, can't rest here." She struggled to form her words. "Won't leave life in hospital," she'd said. "Take me to the woods, Finn . . . happy there."

It took him some doing, but with only weeks, perhaps days left and nothing that could be done, he'd arranged it amicably with the doctors. He was fearful that it would be too much for Inga and Pers. In her soft, breathless way, Ellie overruled him.

"Want them with me," she spoke as firmly as her wavering voice allowed. "My wish, Finn."

Once at the cabin, she'd lasted only three days, mostly in pain, often delirious, but certain in her love for them and theirs for her. As far as he could know, she was happy. "Fling open shutters, Finn," she'd said when they'd arrived. In her last hours, they all four held hands.

They'd stayed with her—the kids sleeping in the platform tent, a refuge from the worst—and Finn, between Ellie's bouts and needs, dozed in the rocking chair next to the bunk, nursing Ellie with Inga and Pers helping. Gary, his auto mechanic neighbor, ran errands, stocked groceries, and stood ready on call for anything.

I would have buried you here, too, Ellie. Had they let me.

That could not be done. Ellie's parents wanted their daughter close—Pasadena was home then to them all, then— and Finn could not deny them that.

This place, though, is really where you are, Ellie.

Had he come one last time to say good-bye? Inga pushed

him to move on, not to forget Ellie, but to live, perhaps, to love again. It seemed absurd to him, but maybe it was time.

Finn moved about the cabin, tidying, feeling, and musing. This is right, he decided. This is good for me. He sat in the rocker and lost himself in thought. He retrieved and opened the red letter that had crinkled all afternoon his back pocket.

Now that Finn had the cabin in good trim, he boiled up potatoes and sliced fillets from the chicken breast he'd bought in Napa. He cut some rosemary and found mustard greens at the shady edge of the field beyond the tool shed. He set a grate over the fire pit where he'd let the split oak logs burn to glowing embers. After rubbing two fillets with salt, pepper, oil, and rosemary, Finn laid them carefully on the grate over the hottest section of the fire. He kept his eye on them while spreading out the canvas on the platform. Jamie and Inga would arrive after classes tomorrow. That he was looking forward to more than any reunion in town.

He slid the chicken off to the side then drained and emptied the potato pot. He turned the pan over, covering the fillets, and sliced and laid spuds in its place over the fire. Just give them some color, he thought. He returned to the platform tent, tethered the side walls, and was inside adjusting the poles when he heard the car come over the bridge. Maybe Gary had changed his mind.

Finn stepped out of the tent and looked over the hedge. It was not Gary. It was Elizabeth.

Liz Moore sat in her convertible, freshening her lipstick in the rear-view mirror.

He jumped down and moved around the bushes toward her. She looked at him, holding the golden lipstick tube in her slender fingers, her lips half colored, then returned her gaze to her reflection despite his approach. He stopped at the fire to turn the potatoes then set a steady pace toward the Chevrolet, hiding, he thought, his consternation. She was blotting her lips when he reached the car and placed his hands over the lowered window, leaning on the door.

"Hello, Finn," Elizabeth said smiling up at him. "I hope I'm not intruding." She hadn't reached for the door handle.

Finn did not move his arms. "Intruding? No, I'm just setting up camp. My daughter is coming up tomorrow." He gave her a solid but quizzical look. "No bother. I'm just surprised."

Elizabeth smiled. "Well, you know I like to do that, Finn." She smiled again and returned the lipstick to her purse, inched away from the door, and swiveled half toward him. She lowered her head, shook it, and as she again trained her eyes on him, gently placed her hands atop his on the car door. "I'm afraid this reunion business has unnerved me, Finn."

He stood stock still. He did not move his hands.

She continued, still locking his eyes. "First, Snub came calling, the creep, then Farley Pike of all people stalked me through the gymnasium, and at the hotel I received a poison-pen letter. I don't know if I can do this." She looked straight into his eyes. "I need to talk to a friend. To you, Finn. Could we sit by the fire?"

Finn followed her nod. He jerked his hands away. "For God's sake," he said, then jumping away said over his shoulder, "I'm burning my potatoes." Flames leapt up through the grill. He ran to the fire to scoop up the mess with his spatula. Nearly incinerated. He uncovered the chicken and poked at it. "Like rubber," he muttered.

Elizabeth had extracted herself from the convertible, straightened her skirt and tugged at her vest. She teetered over the uneven yard in low heels to survey the damage.

"I'm sorry. I distracted you." She was sincere. "Is your dinner ruined?"

Finn stood erect. He laughed. "No, crispy but salvageable. Have you eaten?"

"I did earlier at the hotel, thanks."

"This still might beat the Holiday Inn. At least the salad is fresh." He indicated the picnic table. "I have coffee if you'd like."

She looked toward the cabin, then at the table. So rustic aren't you, Finn.

Even after twenty years he could read her. He wasn't about to invite her inside. Ellie stood at the cabin door. "Here," he said laying a ground cloth over the bench, "I wanted to enjoy the sunset out here." He fixed his plate and poured her a coffee. "Watch the cup, it's hot."

They sat on either side of Finn's picnic table, each waiting for the other to begin. A twenty-four-year silence served their only tablecloth.

Same old Finn. Nothing fancy, tin cup, no napkin, rough-shod all the way, but as handsome and brawny as a twenty-year-old Olympian. She blew across her coffee, studying his features as he cut and chewed his dinner. Who's he got inside? Finn is more polite than he's treating me right now.

From his side of the table Finn read her thoughts while following his own: She's visiting the woods in school administrator's garb. I'd be afraid to touch the table, too. You've always been just so, Liz; the skirt and vest keep you on display.

He finished what was edible, then set his plate aside. Let's start over. "You've been in town," he said.

"Oh, have I."

Though he owed her no explanation, he gave her one. "I arrived late. The cabin's still a mess. I'm getting to it later." He embellished his boorishness. "It's terribly dusty in there."

Elizabeth returned lie for fib, "I don't mind. I'm fine right here."

He knew what she had meant, "Tell me about it." He'd been back hardly four hours and, for one thing, had already heard Snub Randall mentioned twice.

Finn left his complaints unvoiced. "I've come early to mend the place some and finish my interviews, yours among them."

"I came early to write. I haven't been able to."

"Not surprising. Tell me about that letter you mentioned. Is it red?"

Liz bumped her knee below the table. "Ouch!" She knew immediately. "You got one, too."

"It came to Gary's shop yesterday."

"What does it say?"

"You first. Did yours include a clipping?"

Liz brought the envelope out. Finn read the note and glanced at the news photo. "Cryptic. How do you interpret this?"

"You are a newsman, aren't you?" She rubbed her knee. "It made me dream about the murder. Made me think I was mistaken, Finn."

He nodded and produced his letter. "Someone out there is certainly focused on 'the event,' that's for sure: Look." The news clipping detailed Doug Brandling's confession:

Confession in High School Murder

A 17 year-old Santa Reina High School junior confessed yesterday to the murder of 14 year-old schoolmate and neighbor Denise Hagerty . . .

"My note seems less a cypher but seems more a warning:

> 'Without a doubt?
> A killer's out!'"

Liz brought both hands to her mouth. She sucked air and then palmed her temples. "I was wrong. I'm so sorry, Finn."

Finn came around her side to straddle the bench. "Not necessarily. Everything about murder is wrong. I've been so focused on Doug's innocence that I ignored the obvious. If Doug falsely confessed, a murderer is still be out there. The centennial brings people together and not without baggage."

"I've already accused someone today," she admitted.

He looked a question at her.

"Once people get wind you're in town, they just can't leave you alone," she said.

Finn nodded and squirmed on the bench. Don't I know it. "Besides this letter, what?"

"I mentioned Farley Pike." She kept control and wouldn't mention Snub again unless Finn did.

"So you've accused Farley?"

"I hinted at it." She told him about the fiasco in the gym. "I went there to write. I couldn't feel it at the Stanford. My room seemed stuffy."

Elizabeth leaned in on Finn. "Farley was his cheap, pandering self, and I had to push him off somehow." She paused, hesitated. "Oh, I don't want to talk about it." Stop acting, you fool, and don't talk about Farley Pike, for Christ's sake. She shifted on the bench and pressed her knees against Finn's leg.

"The only reason I came . . ." she started, then bit her lip, closed her eyes, and propped her chin on her hands. Compose yourself. You're flushing. Biz spoke willfully. "You, Finn, are the only reason I came to town. To this reunion."

She put her hands on his.

Confessing? Finn wondered. He turned his hands over and cradled her palms. "Thank you, Liz, but I hope that isn't true."

"Oh, it is. Why do you think I came looking for you out here? I'm not ashamed, Finn."

Charming as ever. She's not lost her allure or certainty. He squeezed her hands and withdrew. "A whole life has passed since those days, Liz."

She laughed. "Don't I know it." She pressed her lips together, the corners of her mouth turned up in a suppressed smile.

"I have kept tabs on you: You married. You've had a family. A great career. I know about Ellie, your wife, and I'm so sorry for your loss."

Finn didn't doubt her sincerity. "You sent flowers, didn't you."

"Anonymously. I didn't want to trespass."

"Thank you, Liz. Somehow, I thought that was you. Thanks."

She clasped her hands on her lap. "I'm sure you still love her. That's the man you are."

Finn smiled and shook his head. "Yes, I do, and, you, Elizabeth, are fishing Matanzas Creek, aren't you?" Lovely, warm, and devilish: Elizabeth Moore.

Her hands moved to her hips as she leaned forward. "I have loved you, Finn, for years and years. I'm not going to deny it, and if that means I'm fishing, then I'm fishing. Any reason I shouldn't?"

Lovely, warm, and bold, Finn thought. "No, I guess not. And thanks for being clear. I just, well, I never dated after Ellie died. I was a parent, a writer, a widower. Pretty much that's been it."

She extended her hands again. "I'm not going to rush you, Finn, or maul you, either, but I'm sure not going to miss this chance to see you again. Let it mean what it means."

Finn took her hands up once more. He leaned in and kissed one. "We were friends. Lovers, yes, but friends, too." He pulled back.

Leap that last hurdle, Biz, she told herself. Remove the barrier. Get on his side. "Listen, Finn," she said, "when Farley came into the gym, I'd already had doubts."

Now what. "You lost me."

"I did want to tell you about Farley. Not his come-on, but about what I'd been thinking."

Finn waited.

"I pushed FP back with an accusation. I didn't even think, but after I'd said it, it seemed plausible, real perhaps." Cut it to it, Biz. "Finn. What I'm saying is I'm not sure anymore. About what I saw. Who I saw."

He bent closer. "You mean the murder."

"Yes. I thought I knew. I was sure at the time. I swore it. When that boy confessed . . ."

"Doug."

"Doug. When he confessed, I thought I'd been right."

"And now you've changed your mind?"

"The letter unhinged me. It's probably not Farley, of course, but someone killed Denise, and if it's not Doug Brandling, it is someone we know."

Her brow furrowed deeply. Her mouth crooked and trembled. Elizabeth was going to cry. She brought her fingertips to her forehead and covered her eyes. Then suddenly Liz stood and sidled past the table. She stepped back and turned. She faced away from Finn at the picnic table, looking toward the cabin. She clenched her fists up by her shoulders, about to explode, it seemed, then thrust them down her sides tensing them below her hips. She shook. "I hate what I did," she said.

Finn came to her. He held her shoulders and, as she turned, folded her in his arms.

25

Warren and Elizabeth

The whole room bowed its collective head. Warren Brandling ducked below the gaze of the priest leading the all-too-thankful charge of grace.

"Let us give t'anks for our school t'at has served our children so long," the old man boomed into the microphone. "Let us give t'anks for our teaching staff so diligent and helping." Warren thought, please, good Father, get it over with and cut the phony brogue. "And let us give t'anks for a joyous celebration of education, of our young people, and of our town. 'Bless us, O Lord, and t'se T'y gifts, which we are about to receive from T'y bounty, t'rough Jesus Christ our Lord. Amen.'"

The room rumbled with "Amen," echoing the priest, who, reluctant to cede the limelight, shuffled from the podium, shaking the hand of each person sitting at the head table as he passed.

Warren's mind recounted with habitual impiety his high school friend, Jake, saying "Rub a dub-dub, thanks for the grub, yeah God," an irreverence even as Dr. Brandling he'd carried on privately for years.

The priest was now heading his way. Oh, God in heaven, Warren thought squinting at the place card next to him, he's seated here.

The old man grunted as he plopped down next to Warren.

"Monsignor Phelan, Warren Brandling," Warren said

offering his hand.

"M' pleasure, Doctor Brandling," Phelan said. "I 'member ya from t'e high school."

"As I do you, Monsignor." Lay it on, Warren, he told himself. "Let me say," he intoned his most sincere voice, "though I am not a particularly religious man, that the grace you offered just now was inspiring, certainly ecumenical. Thank you."

Who had seated Warren and Berach Phelan together at the first table for the Principal's Luncheon either had mischievous leanings or did not know Warren at all. He found himself also with the lumber company owner and wife, the latest valedictorian, a retired teacher, and two lawyers, one the district attorney.

The wife agreed loudly with Warren. Phelan waved a dismissive hand and turned to chat with the valedictorian, a pleasant-looking girl who'd announced her intention to attend UCLA. "Doctor Brandling 'ere's a member of t'a medical faculty t'ere, I believe," Phelan told the girl.

Warren had trained himself to smile his displeasure. Spare me the freshman, he thought, and as the oversized priest leaned in on the willowy graduate, Warren continued, she's better for you, Monsignor, than for me. He stole a glance at Elizabeth Moore sitting between the principal and Snub Randall at the head table near the podium. Oh, I bet Mr. Randall had his hand in the seating arrangements. I should have been there instead of next to this beast of a priest. Warren smiled.

Phelan now had his meaty mitt on the valedictorian's shoulder. She wilted beneath his heavy breath. Warren did remember the priest from his playing days, always hanging his head at athletic dinners, droning on and on. He'd said prayers at convocations. His church, Sacred Heart operated a first through eighth grade school which his friend, Jake, had attended. It stood across the street from the ball fields and courts. Apparently, as a much thinner youth, Phelan had been an athlete. Hadn't he coached girls tennis? Yes, '67, of course he had, Warren remembered, though the news clippings he had reviewed did not mention the fact. Well, Warren thought, those skinny days are certainly done. The man flows over his chair seat, for Christ's sake.

The girl leaned forward past Phelan to address Warren. Kimberly was her name. "Dr. Brandling, did you attend UCLA?"

"No. USC," he said. He reached for the bread.

"I'm going to be living in the dorms my first year," she said. "After that I hope to get an apartment with two other girls."

"How nice."

"Where do you live, Dr. Brandling?"

Oh, my. Freshmen are insufferable. He put her off. "Nearby." Into the hands of God, I condemn you, he thought and said, "Father, weren't you educated in Southern California?" The priest took over. Warren didn't listen.

He kept his eyes on Elizabeth Moore, PhD who, he noted, mostly catered to the principal. Snub engaged himself with two younger women to his right. Snub. How he had detested the man. A dandy. A sexual roustabout. A downright bore. He'd agitated to avoid Randall's English class, not a difficult feat since the tide usually flowed in the opposite direction toward Snub. Then Warren took a sudden interest in piano to land in Miss Moore's class. His tactics paid off, he thought, in spades.

During the first semester he'd contented himself with watching. Miss Moore always put on a show, not intentionally

175

meant to arouse, Warren thought, though there were times later that he wondered how much, exactly, she'd staged for the men in class, but just something that came naturally to her.

"You think she wears that vest and those tight skirts to be a better teacher?" Jake laughed. "She's got me leaving practice with my music folio over my crotch."

"When I find out if that's all her, I'll let you know, Jake."

And that was the beginning of it. Warren lingered after class to ask questions. Later he'd asked to be tutored, and when baseball season began, he'd asked to meet after practice. Finally, over Easter vacation, Elizabeth had tutored him at the empty school. That was when "my dear Miss Moore," as he addressed her then, locked them into the women's faculty lounge. When school resumed, he'd meet her at her apartment late in the evenings, and if that didn't work out, in one of the piano practice rooms in the early morning.

"Double D all the way, Jake," he'd said.

Jake looked at him cross-eyed. "You bullshitter."

Warren rued the gaff. He had always considered sex sacrosanct but couldn't help the brag now. "Okay, doubting Jake-us, I'll ask her to a game. If she's comes, that's proof. Ten bucks says she's there."

"I'd put up twenty if I had it," Jake said, "but, yeah, I'll take your ten."

Warren was ready. "Good. We open against the Trojans next week. That's appropriate."

"You bullshitter."

It was the sixth inning, and she hadn't shown. Jake sat at the top of the bleachers cracking peanuts at Warren's every pitch. Nice friend. He was off his form. Doug trotted out to the mound.

"Hey, watch the signs, Warren. We've got a man on second, so it's number two."

"Okay, Dougie, I know what I'm doing." That was sure to rile his brother. Doug hated the diminutive he pronounced akin to "doggie" and couldn't shake it off or return the favor.

"I know you do, bud," was the best he could do. Doug knocked him in the arm with his mitt, jogged back to the plate and crouched.

Warren scanned the stands. He was being stood up. Doug called a fastball on the outside. Warren missed. His curve didn't break. Thank God it didn't hang, but he walked the shortstop on four pitches. Finn Pyykönen came out.

When Doug joined them, Finn said, "Okay, they've got the go-ahead on first and one out. Have we been here before?" They had. "We know what to do?" They did. "Okay, Warren it's you. Go get 'em."

Warren scuffed the rubber. He sneered to himself, "Okay, go get 'em." He spit. He spent two strikes on their pitcher, then came inside and hit the guy. Warren didn't look to the dugout. No one there moved. I guess it is me, he thought.

He toed the rubber but stepped off. Jake caught his eye. He was pointing. There, wearing an orange vest and tight black skirt, Miss Moore sidled conspicuously down the third row to a seat right behind home plate. She sat and then waved, perhaps at Coach rather than at him.

"All right. Ten bucks and mow them down," he said. He struck out the top of the order to finish the sixth and in the seventh caught the meat of the order looking at his curve.

The Wildcat fans cheered. The coach commended the team. Warren collected. And the winning pitcher celebrated his victory late that night wrapped in charms of his music teacher.

Warren heard his name. "Stand up there, Doc." The

priest pulled him up. The principal was introducing his table. "Mr. and Mrs. Orville Marshall III, from whose lumber mill came the timbers that built our school." The Marshalls stood. They actually bowed. Warren suffered the ignominy of the moment, but noticed, too, that Elizabeth Moore was watching him intently. I know that look, Warren thought.

At the head table Dr. Elizabeth Moore fumed. Why wouldn't Finn make this luncheon, she groused. He's left me to do the dirty work with Warren, and I'm not completely sure I want that. It's bound to cost me something.

Not that Finn would worry about that. He didn't think in lewd terms. They'd compared red letters, talked about it all, and better than any hope she'd dared to hold on to, agreed they could work together to try to, at the very least, move Doug toward rescinding his confession. Biz felt she had crossed over to Finn's team again. She liked that.

Though Elizabeth fretted about Finn's absence, she in as natural a way possible made eye contact with Warren. He was sitting between Mrs. Marshall and Berach Phelan. What a combination. Was it Marlis who set up that table? No, she wasn't that cruel.

Warren hasn't changed that much, perhaps thinner, with more delicate mannerisms than when he was a ballplayer. Ball-player. It had been a joke between them. "Can you catch my curve?" he'd asked. "As long as no one slides into home," she'd replied. How juvenile we both were.

She discovered the time that Warren had told his best friend about their carrying on and had sternly warned him to put a cap on it. She repeated to Warren the lecture about consequences that she'd heard from Snub. For all the boy's cunning and deception, he'd stayed good to his word. At least she'd heard no rumors. Still, past the first time in the lounge that Easter break, she'd been reluctant and extremely careful to keep her obsession from Finn. For Warren's part, he wasn't much of a lover. Too inexperienced. Hopefully, I taught him something, at least about female anatomy.

Following the meal and the superintendent's keynote speech, Elizabeth scanned the room for Finn, and not finding him there, wandered over to greet Warren. Snub was at the bar drinking with Phelan again and wouldn't overhear.

"Warren, I'm so pleased you could come," she said instantly regretting her phony tone.

He lifted an eyebrow, looked seriously professorial, and took her hand. "My dear Miss Moore," he said and kissed her hand. "You're the reason I decided to accept."

"I hope that's not true."

He smiled. Coy as ever, Miss Moore. Lying is a lifetime occupation. "I protest," he said, "why else would I be here? It's certainly not to celebrate the Irish."

"Doctor Brandling," Elizabeth replied to his ridiculous banter, "you are one of our shining stars. We all knew you would do great things."

"Shall we stroll the grounds, Miss Moore? Or shall we stay while I call you Doctor Moore?"

"Call me Biz, and yes, I'd like to talk." He ushered her toward the Stanford's garden.

Across the room, Berach Phelan nudged Snub's shoulder, "You've lost your date, Snub."

"Oh, I'm sure we'll see each other again!" Snub laughed.

"T'at sounds a bit hollow, 't does."

Snub turned to the priest. "She thinks she knows it all," he said, "but I've a trick or two left." He swallowed his drink and tipped the glass at the bartender for another.

Monsignor Phelan mumbled to himself, then eyed Elizabeth swaying out the room with Warren. He grunted and did as Snub had.

Elizabeth and Warren took the bench beneath a palm out of sight of the hotel's pool. They talked of their accomplishments of the last twenty years, acknowledged each had eschewed marriage in favor of career, and agreed the celebration's vagaries were vastly droll.

Warren has become genteel, but unctuous, still.

She's up to something, Warren noted, I can tell she's waiting for the right moment. It is not what I thought from that look. Make life easier, he thought, give her an opportunity.

"Miss Moore . . . Biz," he took her hand, "what is it that you want me to know? You need not hold back." How many times had he said that to patients?

Her look told him he'd been right.

"I'm sure you don't want to know."

Of course, I don't, Warren thought, but you're going to tell me no matter what I do. "Try me," he said.

"Perhaps this is happening to you as well, Warren, but since I arrived, I have been dwelling on, well, 'the event.'"

"That's only natural," he said and waited for her.

Biz was slow getting to her point. Feel him out properly. "It's extremely awkward bringing this up to you, but you are the right one to tell."

Warren frowned. "I want to know. What is it?"

"I've encountered doubts."

"Doubts?"

"Yesterday, in the gym I found myself accusing Farley Pike of killing that girl."

Warren smiled demurely as if to say "impossible." He let it pass and said, "How did that happen?"

She explained. "He is not the gentleman you are, Warren." She slipped her hand over and patted his. "But once I'd said it, all seemed plausible. Maybe not exactly right, but truer than me accusing your brother. And since I said it today, I can't stop feeling that I was wrong all those years past. It probably wasn't Farley, but maybe it wasn't Doug. Still, he confessed."

"He was a fool. Doug always was."

"Did he do it? Stab Denise?"

"I don't know."

"You're not sure, either?"

"When I left that morning, he was still at home."

You are cold as blue ice, she thought. "You're sure?"

"He was in his room, asleep."

"Warren!"

Don't "Warren" me!   And don't be shocked. You're the one who accused him. Warren said only, "I suppose I should have come forward, but I wasn't a reliable alibi. And remember, I was the brother who most certainly had visited the school that morning."

She stammered. "I see. I suppose you couldn't say anything."

"I thought the police would discover they'd made a mistake. By the time I realized they were too stupid, Doug was charged and had confessed. Then I didn't know what to do."

Elizabeth smoothed her skirt again. "I had plenty to do with that."

Warren didn't hesitate. "Sure, but even later, I thought they'd release Doug and I wouldn't have to spill our beans."

"This reunion brings it all up again."

Warren thought about the letter he'd received. "You're right. It has a way of stirring the pot, doesn't it?"

Elizabeth nodded, started to speak, then held back. She wouldn't tell Warren about the letter.

"So is that what you wanted me to know? That you now think Farley Pike was the man?"

She pressed her fingertips against her temples. "No. That was a feeling. His slimy pawing brought it out. How could he have?" Elizabeth regrouped. She deliberately moved her hands along her thighs. "I want to know if your brother, Doug, actually believes he stabbed Denise."

Well look at you, he thought. Warren clamped his lips together. When his wave of anger ebbed, he said, "How could I know that? I haven't seen my brother for nearly twenty-four years."

All right Warren, do or die, Biz thought. "Can you find out?"

"Find out what?"

"If Doug still believes he is the murderer?"

He lowered his brows and shifted his eyes side to side.

"All I'm asking you to do is to visit your brother and ask him my question."

What are you really up to? Warren questioned his hearing. All right, what can I get out of this? "Just how important is this to you, my dear Miss Moore?"

Before Warren could distance himself Elizabeth said, "Right now, it seems like the most important thing in the world." She rested her hand lightly on his knee. "I feel it, inside."

Warren stood. He brushed the seat of his trousers and buttoned his jacket. He held his hand out to her, and when she took it, he gently pulled her up. "Biz, I'm going to think about this. I'd planned never to see my brother again. Give me some time. I'll call for you at six o'clock for the Board dinner. I'll let you know then what I decide."

Elizabeth thought of what this might cost her. "Fine, Warren. Then I'll see you at six."

26

Snub Speaks

Tired? Tired of me?

You should be. I'm tired of myself. This whole thing is getting the better of me and, remember, I'm not a well man. In fact, I don't know if I can get through this affair. Affair. That's what it is beginning to feel like. Too many highs and lows for a man in my condition.

When Elizabeth went out the door with Warren Brandling, I could have dropped my teeth—which are, I want you to know, still firmly rooted in my mouth. Not everything is sagging or falling out, you know. Anyway, that boy means trouble, and trouble he will be, though he'll think first of old Finn Pyykönen before he gives me his passing fancy. He'll probably think it was Finn who sent him my best verse:

It's not who knows,
but whom he owes!

That, with the news clipping of the battery flanking Coach Pyykönen, should do the trick. I have no idea what Dr. Brandling, old "fast pitch," might do, but that should at least lead to some deviltry.

I'm not the only one who noticed those two leaving ensemble—Phelan, of course, saw it first and kindly, oh so kindly, brought it to my attention—and I'm not the only one, either, who started and now can't stop thinking about "the event." The monsignor, himself, mentioned it. He asked roundabout what Elizabeth really knows. I'm not surprised, of course. Let him stew. Everybody and his ne'er-do-well brother, too, has yammered about "the event" to me. That, of course, includes Elizabeth.

Yes, I laughed and did think it hilarious at the start. Farley Pike did it! What a joke, though I still wish I could've seen his face when she accused him. He could no more stab a breast of chicken or pork chop on the grill than he could a living, breathing girl. And why? What possible motive could one subscribe to in his case? The man is incompetent. So I laughed.

But later on, after she left with Warren Brandling, I got to thinking, and suddenly it didn't seem so funny or maybe so far-fetched. I'm not always the best judge of character. I'd supported Elizabeth in her trauma (with some self-interest at heart, I have to admit) and thought her right. With her back-pedaling now, where does it leave me? And I was on campus that morning. Even with my departure imminent, I don't want to suffer cross-examination after all this time. I'm not well, you know.

So I've been doing a bit of armchair detective work that I should have done right from the start, compiling a list of possible suspects and figuring out exactly where they were and what kind of person each is—not on the outside, but who each is behind the façade that hides him (or her, to be fair), and I've come up with a fairly short list. After all, the event took place sometime just after sunrise, and not that many folk here wake early.

Don't get me wrong. I'm not sure, not sure at all, so I'm going to be a bit coy about what I think I might know. I've got it down to three men (fair or not, actually, no women made the list) who might have the motive, opportunity, and stamina to have rent the body of Miss Hagerty some twenty times with a kitchen knife. I won't guess which it is, not yet, but take it for what it's worth, and it seems an unlikely coincidence, the initials involved here are F. P.

27

Monsignor Phelan

The mother of Dennis Heany pointed her finger at the good Father. "This isn't the '60s Monsignor Phelan. Catholic parishioners can see the truth and still be steadfast."

"My dear child, I'm having trouble understanding you." She is disturbing the boy. "Dennis, perhaps you'd be more comfortable in the sacristy."

"No, Father, I want him here with me. His days in the sacristy are done."

This woman is evil. You can't take sweet Dennis from me, not from the Church. Not again! "My dear, consider his future." Choler. She'll explode next.

"Father Phelan, listen to me. I won't have Dennis tying your belts, brushing your clothes, reciting your priestly prayers for you"—she points her finger right to his face nearly touching his nose—"or being alone with you in the sacristy, ever again."

"Sweet Den . . . Jesus," I almost said Dennis. Be careful, "what can be wrong?" She's the look of Judas on her. Looking on her son. Oh sweet . . . .

"Nothing right now, Father, but I won't further tempt nature. "

"She sent you, didn't she?" The good Father lurched from his chair.

"She who?"

Now it was Berach Phelan doing the pointing. "Yes, she who? Who was it sent you?"

187

"Please sit down, Father. No one sent me. Listen, though, we know about other cases, not here, of course, and from what Dennis has reported, he is no longer comfortable serving you. He'll still be coming to mass, but with me from this point on."

"If this is about his sister, let me assure you . . ."

"Dennis told me about that one, Father. Are you off your beam? That lunacy scared him more than any of it. Let me say it straight: my son has no sister, never had. I've borne only boys."

Why? She looks so at me.

"Are you off your tick, Father?"

Horrible woman. Liar!

"And don't you look at me that way. We're good Catholics, and I won't have it, even from a priest. We're going, Dennis. Goodbye, Father Phelan."

"Mrs. Hagerty!"

"Heany! The name is Heany. Come, Dennis."

Oh, my that was wrong.

She's whispering. Said "off his tick," didn't she? And now what? All comes from that. Twenty-four years I've been fine. Then comes a bloody envelope. And she, yes "she" it says, "knows." And this sweet Dennis taken from me, again. Under threat, once more. I heard it in her voice. Who sent that liar?

No, no, this is a different woman. Lucifer and confusion. It's said it would be so. Keep it in mind, Berach. The work of Satan. You must pray.

Oh, my sweet Dennis, were you with me, it would be easier. Pray, Berach, confess and pray.

Cushions, they are in the sacristy. Don't go there. Oh, Jesus. Sweet Dennis, fetch Father a cushion to kneel upon. Treachery. He's been sent away, again.

Only stone for you, Berach. Kneel on hard stone. Confess

your sins.

"I beseech you to respond to this offering,"—what can I offer? I'm empty, weak—"with Whom you are so powerful on behalf of the living," and what of the dead? What of that girl? The sister? Dead to me. That's an old list. "I beg both for myself and for my relations and friends and . . ." no, not for my enemies. I can't. I won't pray for her, she who torments me. "Obtain for us—sweet Dennis and Jesus, too—peace of heart." No. I have none. No heart for this. False confession without a confessor.

Ah! Footsteps. Don't look. You cannot turn at prayer. They're gone. You heard. Perhaps it is Dennis again. I must look. The first pew. No, not him, no. Cross yourself. That's it. You've done. Bow now. Don't look. To the sacristy. Don't show a guilty face. Don't look behind.

Can I put a stop on it. The lying, spying, letter writing. I'm not so old a fool. Its danger is clear. Pray? Prayer or no, I've the Church behind me. The Devil will out. Randall nearly enough told me. She thinks she knows it all, but I've a trick or two left. I'll have my sweetest Dennis back. Don't leave me my boy.

28

Farley and Elizabeth

When Dr. Elizabeth Moore woke from her nap, her head was buzzing. With eyes closed, she massaged her temples and forehead, smoothing her scalp and hairline as she worked. She thought back to lunch. Too much wine. Rubbing didn't help.

The buzz continued. She opened her eyes. An orange glow pulsed in her darkened room. The message light flashed again; the phone console buzzed. Elizabeth checked the clock. My God, I've slept over an hour. It's past three. She swept the sheets aside amidst the rustle of paper—she'd worked all of five minutes on her speech before closing her eyes—and swung her legs over the bedside. With the lamp on, she retrieved the message, and while she picked up the nearly blank pages from the floor, listened.

Farley Pike's voice was saying, "Sorry to disturb you, but I wanted to let you know, I've thought about what you said yesterday. I'd like to tell you something I've remembered, something about 'the event.' I left a card at the desk for you."

"For the love of God, Farley. Leave me alone," she swore at the recording. Yet Dr. Elizabeth Moore stumbled to the desk chair and rifled through her purse. Yes, the clerk gave me a note. She stared hatefully at the coral envelope. She moved it toward her nose. It's scented, for God's sake. She pulled the drapery cord, ripped the envelope open, and read Farley Pike's invitation to tea.

My dear Elizabeth,

Please join me for afternoon tea. I have something
to relate to you.

Farley

325 South 2nd Street
Apartment 2
Santa Reina
Friday at 4:00 p.m.

"Jesus," she said, tossing the note on the desk. She stalked
to the bath and slammed the door hard. When she emerged,
Elizabeth was freshened. She changed clothes and primped
before the mirrored closet doors.

All right, Farley, this better be good, and make it
fast 'cause this evening I have bigger fish to fry. She'd have
time enough to return and change into her evening dress.
Warren would pick her up at six. She could pump him for
information, too, then, afterwards, drop in on Finn at the
cabin to report. Elizabeth smiled at her reflection. Yes, a
nightcap. She straightened her vest, smoothed her skirt, and
set off for tea with Farley Pike.

Old FP was nervous. He ran from the living room
windows to the kitchen and from the kitchen back to the
living room windows. Oh, she won't come. I should have
gone personally. No, no, that wouldn't do. The invitation was
the right way. It had style. Of course, his best stationery had
come from the things his mother had left behind in the lower
desk drawer. She'll think you're prissy, but never mind

Farley moved the living room sheers aside and looked
down the street. Fifteen minutes. I'll call her again, then if
she doesn't come by ten to the hour. The yearbook. He went

to his bookshelf, and from the lower compartment, from a neatly arranged line of thin volumes, he removed the 1967 annual. He carried it to the kitchen table, glanced at the stove, and rushed to lower the flame beneath the seething kettle. Pour for tea when she parks at the curb, he instructed himself, hearing his mother's voice in his mind. The aroma will welcome her. Full-bodied, deeply fragrant. He swayed his hips. Farley again took the book up and moved to the bedroom. Turn down the sheets? He asked himself. Gauche. Then, oh why not? "You've got nothing to lose, Mr. Pike," he said aloud. He lay the book on the bed when smoothing the sheets, then took it up before returning to the living room window. Five minutes more. He hugged the yearbook, then, set it on the chair next to the sofa where she would see it, and went to the kitchen.

Farley took from the oven the peach scones he'd charmed from Mrs. Baxter next door. "Oh, those scones were heavenly, Mrs. B," he'd said over the pickets between his walk and her garden. "I nearly said a prayer over them, they were that celestial." He leaned at the fence as if reciting the beatitudes and waited for her to offer.

"Thank you, Mr. Pike. They are my secret recipe. My mother made them from the peach tree Mr. Burbank planted in our yard. Of course, these peaches are fresh, but they are nothing like the Elberta peach we used to grow. You know, my father worked with Mr. Burbank. Father even helped develop some of the flowers that gained Luther his fame."

Please don't go on, Mrs. Baxter, he thought, but said, "Oh, yes, I remember you've told me." She's going to make me ask, isn't she. I'll go to the bakery instead. And that struck an idea. "Do you think they'd have something similar at Bloom's Bakery?" Farley asked.

Mrs. Baxter's chatter impaled itself on the pickets of the

fence. She stood staring, mouth agape. "Mr. Pike! I beg your pardon." She looked at him in wide-eyed alarm, as if she had fallen on the fence tines herself.

"Oh, I didn't mean they could be as good as yours. Just, well, I didn't want to bother you."

She drew a breath and shook a gray curl away from one eye. "Mr. Pike—Farley—you are hinting around aren't you?" Mrs. Baxter—she did look pretty when she smiled—turned to her jolly old self, with his flattery. "Why didn't you say so?"

"I am having a little tea with an old colleague of mine, and thought . . . but you're too busy to fuss."

She studied him. "Is it that Dr. Moore you met with yesterday?" She pinned him to the wall across the walk. "Oh, it is. That's something special then." She scolded him. "You should have told me."

He began to protest, then felt his face redden beneath her gaze. Mother had always done the same thing, he recalled, and his color deepened more.

"Lucky you, Mr. Pike. I just happen to have a half dozen fresh from this morning's oven. I'll wrap half of them for you. Dr. Moore appears to be a light eater." She patted Farley's hand atop one of the fence pales, pushing his palm into the point.

Despite the pain, he said, almost through his teeth, "I hope it's no bother."

"We're neighbors, Mr. Pike. What are neighbors for?"

Yes, Farley Pike thought, he had charmed those scones out of Mrs. Baxter, and now he had the idea that Dr. Elizabeth Moore wasn't going to come. He fretted as he arranged and rearranged the scones in a warming basket and covered them in a coral-colored cloth. The bell rang, and Farley nearly dropped his scones. He ran to the window to see Elizabeth's car parked below. Oh, my, the tea!

At once he set the basket on the tea table and slipped into the kitchen to pour the water. Farley tiptoed back to the peephole of the door. As he set his eye to the lens, the bell rang once more. He nearly leapt from his socks, backtracked to the kitchen and boomed out from there, "Oh, I'm coming. I'm coming." Don't say that, he admonished himself. He wrestled off his apron, and pushed his feet into his house slippers. "Coming," he called as he approached the door. He took a final look into the hall mirror, coaxing his mustache into line, and opened the door.

"Oh, my dear Elizabeth, you came," he said. Stop using that word, you fool! "I'm so glad."

She stood, waiting to be invited in. She tapped her foot and said, "Yes, Farley, I've arrived. May I enter?" She lanced an arm past him and nearly set him off balance.

"Of course, I was just surprised." He turned as she brushed past him. "I can be annoying, I realize," he said. "I'm so happy to have you . . . ." He gulped air and added, "here." And even though she was already in, he said, "Please come in. I've just poured the tea water."

"Hmm. Smells wonderful. Like . . . like peaches," Elizabeth said. Might as well be complimentary. It is aromatic. "Have you baked something?"

"I have. Early Elba peach scones. They've just come from the oven. Please, have a seat, yes, here on the sofa." Farley fussed with the pillows and the tea things as Elizabeth settled into her place. "My apartment isn't much. I'll give you the tour later." He brought out the tea and uncovered the scones. A little subterfuge won't hurt. I didn't say I'd baked them, exactly. "The scones are a recipe of my neighbor, Mrs. Baxter."

"She's still there? I remember when the Baxters moved in," Elizabeth said.

Farley nodded as he poured the tea. "She's a widow of

fifteen years already." He cut the scones in half and served to her plate. "Try one."

He watched her nibble the pastry. I like having her here, Farley thought. She is so warm, not friendly exactly, but, well, exciting. Yes, entrancing. He sat beside her and smiled.

Elizabeth related some of what went on at the luncheon, carefully naming those in attendance, mentioning neither Warren nor drawing attention to Finn's absence. She related a story about the lumberyard owners, the Marshalls bequeathing a thousand year-old redwood trunk to be carved into a wildcat sculpture and mounted inside the school entry. "It's said to weigh a true ton," she said. She told him about Berach Phelan and his drinking problem. "I think he tried to slip the valedictorian a martini," she said laughing.

"Kimberly? Oh, my." Farley had never liked the priest. "Yes, I see the good Father occasionally. He crosses our campus on his walks to the diocese offices, and sends us our best athletes after eighth grade. He's always seemed a fixture at the school, don't you think?" Farley glanced at the yearbook. Not yet, he thought.

Eventually, the small talk diminished along with tea and scones. There seemed to be little besides crumbs. Elizabeth excused herself to the bathroom.

Farley bussed dishes to the kitchen, where he drew a sinkful of sudsy water. He donned the apron, rolled up his sleeves, and when Elizabeth returned, was busy washing his mother's tea things.

She lingered at the kitchen door, watching him work. Farley stopped running the rinse water. He looked over his shoulder at her, noting a puzzled look on her face.

"Do you always turn your sheets down in the middle of the afternoon?" She asked, a wry smile crooking her lips.

Farley felt his face afire. He stammered. "I thought, well,

I wondered, just in case."

"In what case?" She stepped forward, reached out, and pulled on the string of the apron.

He looked down at the bow she had undone. For a moment he stood there, his yellow rubber gloves dripping rinse water on the kitchen floor, but, as if about to introduce a celebrity, drew up his full height. What he said next shocked him more than it did his guest. "I love you, Elizabeth." Farley felt like crying. Have I ever said that to anyone in my life? he wondered. It was beyond belief that he'd uttered the words.

She tugged the string again, turned abruptly, strode to the tea table, and sweeping a crumb off the sofa sat down. He followed, halting at the doorway, where he wiped the gloves on the apron. "I'm sure you do, Farley, but we're not going to do anything about it." She fixed her eyes on the apron, now dangling from his neck as he wavered between rooms. "Is this what you had to tell me?"

"Tell you?" This is a lost cause, he told himself. "I had something to tell you?"

Elizabeth looked at him sternly. "Sit down and stop blubbering nonsense. Remember the invitation you sent?" She took it from her purse and laid it on the tea table.

Farley threw off the gloves and apron. He stepped to the table and picked up the card, looking at it as if he had never seen it before. "I love you, Elizabeth" was still echoing through his noggin. He read the card. "Oh, the annual!" he said. "Yes, yes, I do have something, something else to tell you, show you." He sat down and reached over her to retrieve the yearbook from the chair beside her.

As he thrust his arm past her, Elizabeth caught a faint scent, the same smell the letter carried, and though without wanting to, this time she thrilled at its mild floral allure. She barely thought it, perhaps did not think it at all: He is prissy, but he's is still a man. Biz put in the balance his long-past performance that night in her classroom. Something moved in her, something she immediately instructed herself to ignore, as he brushed past her in a hurry to open the yearbook on his lap. What's in that thing I don't already know about?

Farley was rifling through the book, saying, "There are three pictures, just three that tell the story." He turned pages rapidly, marking the places he wanted with his long, thin fingers. Finally, he said, "These are pictures of Denise. Denise Hagerty. One taken in the fall with the orchestra, another in late October with my class, and the last with the tennis team in the early spring. See?" He pushed the book onto her lap and turned the pages back and forth. Biz held steady, both coiling and recoiling inside.

"I don't know." She felt she would fly off or fight but did not know which. "What is it you want me to see?"

Farley Pike drew a breath. "I get so excited," he said, "forgive me." He flipped back to the earlier photos. "Something happened to her. Of course, not the murder. Before that. Look."

Elizabeth examined the photo. Farley turned to the next.

"This she took with my class. Part of a package, you know. It would not ordinarily have appeared in the senior yearbook, but . . ." Farley shrugged.

"Yes, it's something of a memorial."

"Now, look at this," he said as he again revealed the tennis team photo.

She took up the book. She looked closely. "She's not smiling in this one."

"Exactly! Think back," Farley said. "I didn't remark it after she died—was murdered—but you caused me to think yesterday, and it came to me. Denise was unhappy, actually morose, in class starting just after the Easter break. I spoke to her about it."

The book lay open to the tennis page. "She looks unhappy," she said, looking closer, "very unhappy, almost pained."

"She was. She wouldn't talk to me about it, just shook her head and murmured something about problems at home, trouble with her twin, Dennis. Even so, I thought she might be better off to talk to a woman."

Elizabeth went rigid. The book slid off her knees to the floor. She stared. Farley wondered if she was gazing at the portrait of him and his mother. No, he divined, she's reviewing the past. When she turned to look at him, the haunted look on her face scared Farley. "Yes, she might," Elizabeth said.

Farley guessed. "Did she talk to you?"

Stiffness drained from her posture. "It was in the spring," Elizabeth said. "And, yes, something was bothering her, all right." She bit her lip. "I told her to ignore it, thought it was a puppy love. I might have said, 'Boys will be boys' or something like that." She looked past Farley. "How cruel."

Farley patted her thigh. "Who knew where it would lead?" He fixed earnest eyes on her. "You did nothing wrong, my dear." He reached down to retrieve the book and laid it across her lap. "Please, look again."

Reluctantly, Elizabeth examined the team photo once more. "Do you see it?" he asked. She shook her head.

Farley pointed. "Look at the coach, Phelan."

"He has his hand on her shoulder," she said, "and the other on . . . is that her brother?"

"Yes! Her brother." Farley led her gaze. "Is it my imagination? Or is she cringing?"

"You're not saying Phelan was bothering her, are you?"

"No, of course not. Besides, I always thought it was Snub Randall who chased the girls," Farley said.

His statement shot guilt through Biz like a hot iron rod. Does he know? No, she decided. He doesn't even suspect. Farley is simply repeating old rumors. Go along with him. "He did have that reputation."

Farley felt encouraged. "It could be transference. Perhaps Randall was bothering Denise, and Phelan seemed to her the same, one of those dirty old men."

Farley looked at her in alarm. "You're pale, my dear. Are you all right?"

Farley seemed far away. "I'm sick. I must lie down. Please."

He guided Elizabeth to his mother's room, one he hardly used any more, and sat her on the bed. She leaned on a forearm, testing her brow with the other. Farley gently patted one shoulder, guided her legs and feet up on the bed, and removed her shoes one at a time. He took up the throw from the chair beside the bed and spread it over her. "Would you like a cloth? A cool cloth?"

She nodded, and Farley Pike went to the bathroom to run water on a fresh washcloth. When he returned, he sat by the bedside, alert and attentive, while Elizabeth rested.

I've shocked her, he thought. I should have eased into the story. She found the dead girl. Farley remembered the screams. Elizabeth's screams had echoed through the campus for what seemed forever. Thank Geoffrey I never saw her. People said that Elizabeth Moore had been a bloody mess, had fainted into the girl's blood—perhaps it had seeped on to her while she was out—and she, so they said, was dripping blood all around as she ran. A janitor finally located her by those screams and wrapped her in a gym blanket. Farley rued his delirious demonstration. "I should have been more careful. I'm sorry," he said.

The cool cloth was reviving Dr. Elizabeth Moore. "I had

a fright, Farley," she mumbled, "but it's not your fault." Did I black out? she wondered. She roused herself and looked toward her feet which now felt closer than before. That same provocative floral odor flirted with her nostrils. That smell and the head cloth brought her back. He's taken my shoes off, she thought. Biz felt warm under the fragrant knit cotton. Farley moved his chair closer.

"I have some water here," he said. Carefully, with Farley's help, she rose up to meet the glass he offered. Again, she caught the scent of a garden. It's him. Not putrid at all. That's his smell. Again, something in her moved.

"Thank you so much. How kind you are." She squeezed his hand. "I'm better now, and I must go."

Farley helped Elizabeth rise. She steadied herself holding his shoulder then delivered a kiss to his cheek. "Thank you again," she said and quickly left the apartment.

Once back on South 2nd Street again, Dr. Elizabeth Moore heard her name. It was Mrs. Baxter calling to her and waving. What's she saying? Was it something about the scones? She smiled, waved at the woman, and ducked into the driver's seat. She turned the car around, and as she passed, she waved once more and called out, "Thank you. Delicious."

Biz drove toward the Stanford where Warren would be waiting. That was just fine.

29

Warren and Elizabeth

Warren Brandling had already waited the obligatory fifteen minutes. He had known his dear Miss Moore would be late readying herself, but he could not imagine that she would stand him up. *Well, if she won't keep our date with destiny, I won't have to do her bidding.* He'd asked the concierge for stationery and was penning his salutation on a note to her, when Elizabeth strode across the lobby to the elevator. *Irresponsible as ever.*

He crumpled the sheet into the wastebasket of the writing desk and timed his arrival at the elevator bank to coordinate with the door opening. He followed her into the elevator and said, "Floor, please, Miss Moore." His impromptu bellman act obviously surprised her, but she hesitated only a second.

"Seven, Doctor Brandling. And thank you." She did not apologize for her tardiness but tugged at her vest and smoothed her skirt.

They rode in silence, the hush enforced by breeding as much as by embarrassment, each counting the floors, and did not speak again until she invited him into her room.

"I have to freshen up and change for dinner," she said. "Please, make yourself comfortable." She gathered underwear, a slip and bra, a pair of jeans, and a denim cowgirl shirt, placed them in an overnight bag and sequestered herself in the bathroom.

Warren sat at the desk and watched. *If you think that door, locked or not, will protect you, guess again.* But Warren

Brandling is not now that sort of man, he reminded himself, nor was he ever. Beside that fact, in his practice he had examined enough female genitalia to ipso facto inure his senses to their allure. Miss Moore would be no exception. What will dissolve the barrier to unlocking her charms will be her invitation and her eventual subjection to my domination. He waited, examining the half-moons at his cuticles. Warren Brandling was a patient man.

He picked up an envelope from the desk. Elizabeth's name was printed neatly on the front. The return address label on the back flap was torn in two. Warren examined the envelope, held it momentarily to his nose, and visualized the street the address noted. It was near the school, but he could not identify the place. He tossed the envelope aside, found that he'd uncovered what thus far existed of Elizabeth's speech, and read the first twelve lines. Yes, he thought, we each add a layer to the ludicrous whimsy of this risible reunion. And which sum carries the most irony? He raised his eyes to the ceiling, letting the speech fall to the desk. That scent rose again.

Ha! FP, and as if painted on the ceiling of the room, he saw that corner: South 2nd and School Streets. He'd passed it a thousand times: A clapboard cottage surrounded by gardens, and next door, a two-story brick of flats where Farley Pike had lived, probably still lived. Warren took up the envelope again. Certain now of the place, he wondered, what is this about? A perfumed envelope from old Farty Pants.

In the bathroom Elizabeth Moore was shaving her armpits. She'd first thing brushed her teeth and gargled, rinsing out the taste of temptation that had choked her at Farley's, and after shaving and washing her face, she'd redo her makeup.

She looked at herself and shook her head, a bit sadly. Biz,

Biz, Biz, she thought, when are you going to stop? The narrow, bookish figure of Sarah Petroski flitted through her mind, saying, it seemed, "What if Finn knew?" Yes, in and outside therapy, over the years, Finn had stood a standard of purity in her mind, one she wanted to emulate. He'd been every bit as lusty as she, but the innate reticence that ruled him tempered his desire with affection. Her own raw craving—enticing her again that afternoon—felt like lechery. It's all Snub's doing. Sarah had convinced her of that and rightly so. God, was that a mistake. And now I can hardly seem to stop myself. She turned the hot tap off.

Biz wondered what Warren was doing in the other room. Did I leave my speech out? Farley's letter? No, at least that's in my purse. I can't see how to avoid telling Warren, but he doesn't have to know everything.

She patted her face dry and spread a dab of moisture cream over her forehead and down her cheeks. It might be helpful, though, to mention the visit to Farley. He did shine a light on "the event." Elizabeth leaned toward the mirror, applying concealer below her eye and touching up "that damned spot that wouldn't go away." She tossed the tube down and worked the salve over her skin. Biz lifted the bath towel from the bar and wrapped it around her, snugging it above her cleavage. She took up the ice canister and opened the door enough to pass the bucket to Warren.

"Warren," she said, through the door opening, "could you fetch me a little ice down the hall, please?" She opened the door wider. He was at the desk. Had he read my speech? She saw Farley's envelope on the bureau edge. "Please, just a few pieces, Warren."

He entered the short hall and stood before her, but he did not take the bucket. "For you, dear Miss Moore, I would do anything," he crooned, and when she reached further through the opening, giving him a better view of her shoulder and neck, he grasped the container and bowed.

"Not too much," she said.

He was gone, and Biz, clutching the towel, bounded to the desk to examine what she'd left there. The speech and Farley's envelope were all. She returned to the mirror, leaving the bath door ajar. She applied dabs of foundation above her brows and down each side of her face. Elizabeth examined her work, layered a bit more, and circled her fingers over her face blending, finally, down her jawline, turning one side then the other, evening the color. Warren rapped sharply on the room door.

"Please, Warren," she spoke loudly, "just one minute." She applied blush in two thin layers, rolling her finger tips over her cheeks, checked her work, and stepped into the room's short hall to receive Warren.

Elizabeth took the canister from him with two hands, held it against the towel wrap, and pecked his cheek. "Thank you. That was sweet of you and rude of me." She carried the ice into the bath and left the door open. Warren lounged in the doorway watching her work.

"Isn't that Farley Pike's smelly envelope on your desk?" Warren asked.

She glanced at him leaning on the door jamb. "He invited me to tea, if you can believe that. You remembered his address."

"Once we hid in Mrs. Baxter's garden and tossed pebbles at his windows," he confessed. "His mother spoke to us from her window, 'Mr. Pike is sleeping. Please!' It couldn't have been much past 9:00 p.m., for God's sake." He laughed. "We were meddlesome kids but harmless." He inched the door over. "So after his pawing act, why did you attend his tea?"

Biz had been working below her eye and adding shimmer

to her forehead as well. She was in the middle of brushing her lashes and lifted a finger to stay him. She finished her eyebrows too with an upward flourish and turned to Warren then. "He had pictures of Denise Hagerty he wanted me to see. Yearbook pictures."

"Old Farty Pants. Quite a case."

Something in her wanted to defend Farley, but Warren wouldn't understand. She told him directly: "He insinuated that Snub Randall molested the girl. She was desperately unhappy, quite changed from the fall to spring. I believe something had happened."

"Had you noticed a change?"

Biz stroked her lips with a small cube of ice, calming a sadness rising up her throat. She tossed it into the sink and said, "I did. She'd actually approached me, but I put her off." She dabbed on lipstick and smoothed it over her chilled lips. Change direction, Biz. Toss it back at him. "In the last couple days, Warren, no one I've talked to thinks your brother was guilty."

Warren studied her face. "Stunning," he said.

Biz added a touch of gloss over her lips and turned from the mirror. "Thank you, but are you going to speak to Doug?"

Warren stepped into the bathroom, slipped two fingers beneath the fringe of towel, and unfurled the hitch Biz had fixed.

"You are going to smear my lipstick, Warren." She said, but did not move to save the towel.

"My dear Miss Moore," he said, "I won't even touch those lips."

When Biz reemerged from the bath, Warren still lay across the bed. She stood before the closet in panty hose, slip, and bra and retrieved her evening dress, which she stepped into and zipped along her spine. "Please, Warren, could you finish this and hook it?" She pressed one foot then the other into black heels. "And perhaps you could dress."

Warren complied with her first requests.

She reexamined herself in the mirror, fixed a string of pearls at her neck, and took up her clutch purse. "I know you don't want to see Doug," she said, "but I expect you will." She had paid her price, his price.

Warren Brandling returned the gaze of his dear Miss Moore—had she ever seen him look so sad in her life?—and said, "I am a man of my word."

She handed him her overnight bag. "Could you carry this to my car, please?"

30

Elizabeth and Finn

The Board of Education dinner dragged on, and though understanding in his glib, magisterial way, Warren proved difficult to dislodge at the end. It was nearly ten o'clock before Elizabeth fetched her bag from the trunk and hurriedly changed into her new camp clothes: jeans, short boots, and a plaid western shirt. She roared out of the Stanford's parking lot and across town to the Sonoma Mountain Road, which would take her to Finn.

What is wrong with you, Biz? You've never felt this needy, not for years. Right now, she answered herself, I need to see Finn, and I don't care. I don't care a damn bit who knows it. She tromped on the gas pedal and sped around the first bend in the road that followed the stream. An hour behind, she complained, and each minute with him was precious. She was in high school again, as if driving with Marlis that first time when they'd encountered Finn walking the road.

Why did you ever let him go? She knew. It was the murder, for Christ's sake. How can you prepare for something like that? One moment, on top of the world, everything better than you could ever have planned for, and the next—shit, lying in a pool of blood not even your own. God in heaven, it ruined my life. Of course, I chose it in a way. I two-timed even Finn. Not with Snub, not in '67 but with Warren. I was curious to see things from the teacher's angle as Snub had. That was wrong, and I can never tell Finn. I did it right under his nose.

Elizabeth drove fast, how fast she didn't realize. The past twenty-four years welled up before her, playing across her windshield, as if across the now-abandoned Roxie Drive-In screen on the western outskirts of town. There before her, Biz watched herself acting the role, pointing to Douglas Brandling, accusing him, and what was Finn doing? She saw him on the big screen: He ignores me, right then and from that time on. He shuns me. She sees the next scene play out: Five days later she enters his classroom. He's already packing books and his personals, planning to leave not for the summer but for good. He barely looks up.

"Finn," the woman playing her role on the screen pleads, "please listen. I had no choice."

He glances up, but when she tries to fix his eyes in hers, he looks down into the box. "Liz, I don't think I can talk about it yet."

"But you're leaving, aren't you? When can we talk?" The picture fades to white.

Even now, twenty-four years later, she felt anger at her own begging. Bile drove hot up her chest. Don't debase yourself, Biz had thought back then. He's just a man, like any other man. She knew then that it was a lie but didn't realize how often she would, over the next two decades, repeat it to herself.

Now back in Santa Reina, feelings that sprang up in her, call them love or romance or longing or loss, were so fierce that she hadn't slept well or eaten much. Those emotions knocked her off the professional pedestal she'd stood on solidly for years. She'd now grown unsteady. Rocky. It's too close, the first true feeling I've allowed myself in years. Now it's sweeping me into the creek.

She hit the brakes. The convertible skidded. Elizabeth corrected, let up, and pushed the pedal again. She'd spun around, now facing the way she'd come, her tail lights illuminating the tangled trees of Finn's notorious hairpin turn. She sat dumbly, the engine dead, and cried. She sat in the convertible, convulsing against tears.

A woman called out, "Are you all right?"

"*Dios mío*," a man said, "hold right there, we're coming."

The man loped across the road. Put a firm hand on her shoulder. "That was scary! Here, pull in our driveway. Can you do that?"

Elizabeth exhaled a raw breath and nodded.

"Liz!" It was Finn. He bounded to the car. "Excuse me, Jamie," he said, sweeping the young man forward toward the front fender. Finn opened the door, pulled the hand brake, stabbed the emergency flashers, and guided Elizabeth from behind the wheel. "I'll help Miss Moore to camp, Jamie. Can you bring the car over?"

If Elizabeth Moore had felt unhinged before, the entrance she'd made at the Pyykönen cabin tore her entirely loose from herself. Hopelessness brimmed in her eyes. As Finn and Inga guided her across the wooden bridge to the campfire the couple had left when they heard the screech of tires, Elizabeth shook in a flood of tears. Finn hugged her to his side as they walked.

Inga and Jamie had driven up from Berkeley after Inga's final class of the week. With traffic snarled across the Richmond-San Rafael Bridge, they had arrived late for Finn's dinner of mushroom barley soup and fire-toasted bread. Finn had been bringing the few dishes to the cabin kitchen when Elizabeth's car had flown into his view, then swerved back out of sight of the little window where he worked. Inga and Jamie were up and out in the driveway before Finn could leave the cabin.

Now Finn escorted Elizabeth to the fire, wrapping her in a lap robe she clenched around her shoulders. She brushed it against her cheeks.

Jamie drove Elizabeth's Chevy onto the ranch property and parked it next to Finn's car.

Finn stood beside Elizabeth. He took her in his arms, blanket and all, and held her close. "You scared the life out of me," he said. "That creek-fire accident played through my mind." She started crying again. He rubbed her back and cooed to her as she calmed.

Inga broke in. "Your entrance was grand, Dr. Moore," she said, and, then, made her introductions: "I'm Daddy's little girl, Inga, and this is my fiancé, Jamie."

Finn released his charge to allow their greetings. Inga said, "I have heard so much about you. And I am pleased to finally meet you. So happy you stopped by." Even Elizabeth laughed.

"I'd love to make a habit of it, but I think I'll have to slow down," she said. Finn coaxed her to sit in a wide Adirondack chair close to the fire. He crossed the robe across her knees.

"I imagine you could use a drink, but I'm sorry to say I have nothing. How about some tea or a nice cup of soup?"

Finn knelt by the fire, arranging the pots to heat properly, and he pulled up a camp stool beside Elizabeth's chair. He watched the firelight smooth her fright and dry her tears while Inga chatted up a storm from her other side. It had been years since he'd seen Inga so animated and intimate with an older woman. Like mother and daughter, he thought.

When the water boiled and the soup warmed, her father, Inga found herself thinking, served Elizabeth as if she were his patient. Would he have fed her the soup, spooning it in, had they been alone? After all, he'd hugged her openly, protecting and comforting her as if she were his wife.

"I'm calling the county in the morning," Finn said. "We need a bigger sign announcing that curve."

Now past the intensity of her close call, Elizabeth said, "Signs are good for those who read them."

"What happened?" Inga asked.

If Elizabeth colored, the firelight hid it. "Let's just say I was preoccupied. More like daydreaming." She smiled at Finn, then addressed Inga, "I don't know about your father, but this reunion has certainly overtaken my thoughts. I've been transported to another world."

"One like Mexico?" Jamie asked.

"Even farther off than that," she replied, "*mucho más afuera.*"

She could be personable. Socially, Elizabeth moved easily and though, as Finn thought then, plagued by myopia, she fluidly hid an inborn self-centeredness behind questioning. Recovered now, she zeroed in on Inga: "What do you study? When is the wedding? Where will you live? Jamie, who's your department head? What part of Mexico are your parents from?" She had the young couple entwining their history, habits, and hopes with the campfire flames.

Inga seized a pause in the interrogatory, reached for Elizabeth's blanketed knee, and said, "You know, my mother would have liked you."

Finn narrowed his eyes and thrust a private warning-stare at his daughter.

Inga caressed Jamie's cheek. She winked at him, boldly. Inga stretched her arms over her head and changed the conversation, "It's been an awfully long week in academia. We must turn in." She smiled at her father and Elizabeth. "Now don't you kids stay up too late." With that, Inga came around and kissed Elizabeth's cheek. She pecked Finn's forehead in passing and waved, "Good night." Taking Jamie's open hand,

Inga swept away behind the huckleberry bushes beyond the glow of the fire circle to the platform tent Finn had set up the day before. Finn and Elizabeth listened through Inga's giggling to their rummaging through backpacks and settling into their digs.

"That was a sweet thing to say," Elizabeth said.

Finn stirred the coals with a stick. "Inga can be sweet, surprising, and irritating at the same time."

"You don't think she meant it?"

"She did," he said, "but she has been playing matchmaker since before I arrived for the reunion."

"And that irritates you," Elizabeth said.

Now Finn tossed the stick into the fire. "Come into the cabin. Those two are eavesdropping."

Finn took one last look around the fire pit. He ringed the soup and tea kettle handles between thumb and finger and offered his other hand to Elizabeth. "Watch your footing in the dark."

Inside, Finn lit the lantern. Elizabeth settled under her blanket in the rocking chair as he stirred up the cabin stove. "Nights are chilly here even in summer," he said.

"Yes, I remember."

Finn sat at the tiny kitchen table. In the confines of the cabin, he was barely two feet from her. "In Berkeley, Thursday morning, I had breakfast with Inga. She tried to stir up a romance then."

Elizabeth hid her pleasure with Inga's efforts in questions. "How did that feel?"

"I'm sorry, Liz, I told her I wasn't interested. I knew we'd see each other, but then I felt . . . wary, certainly concerned."

She rocked forward, reaching a hand for his knee. "And now? Still wary?"

"Liz, you know me. I am, let's say cautious, reticent. I've

never been any other way."

Elizabeth rocked back. She said nothing but gathered the blanket around her tightly. She waited for him.

"Last night," Finn continued, "I wasn't ready to invite you in here."

"Changed your mind, I see."

"I feel better about it. Maybe Inga was right to say something." He watched Elizabeth rock a minute. "I feel Ellie's spirit in here. Strongly." Finn added an oak chunk to the stove as if to drive a chill away. "You know . . ."

She finished the sentence for him, "that your wife died here? Yes, Finn, I know."

Finn nodded. As if glad to have opened that door to that past, he spoke faster, more freely. "Even now, I think of her every day. I suppose I didn't want anything to obscure her memory. After I'd seen you, after we'd talked, though, I thought I could stop digging in my heels. And Inga, well, she might be right. I do care. I still care for you, Liz."

She tilted toward him in the rocker, but Finn put a hand up as if to stop her advance. "Liz, I'm still the slow mover I always was."

Elizabeth leaned back, again. She smiled. "That, Mr. Pyykönen, is an understatement and a chief reason I find you so attractive." She watched Finn's face, then said, "I understand, Finn."

"You are more than a desire, Liz. I've always felt that way, but touch comes more easily for you than me. It's your nature. Less so with me." Finn sat with his hands together, dangling between his outspread knees. He looked at them a moment, then again at Elizabeth. "I want to be careful. To me that's important."

"All right, Finn," she said.

Into this impasse, Elizabeth poured all the news she'd

gathered from Farley and Warren. That was safe to discuss. She left out intimate details, but told Finn what he would want to know.

"Farley invited me to tea," Elizabeth said. "I actually enjoyed myself, but he reminded me of something terrible."

"Terrible?"

"Yes, something I'd done." She brought the edge of the blanket to her cheek. "Rather, not done."

Finn puzzled but waited. "Farley asked me if I'd talked to Denise Hagerty about her being so unhappy. She'd seemed depressed."

"I didn't know her," Finn said.

"Both Farley and I had her in class." Elizabeth again moved toward Finn. This time he held steady. "She came to me with problems. I turned her away." She took his arm. He caressed her hand with his. "Farley thinks someone, a boy or maybe an adult, was bothering her."

"That fits with the police theory," Finn said.

"He showed me a picture of Denise. The tennis team. She was flinching beneath Berach Phelan's hand resting on her shoulder."

"Phelan?"

"Oh, it couldn't be him. Anyway, he was thought to prefer the boys. But the photo of the tennis team clearly reveals something about her state of mind."

"No girl likes to be pawed," he said.

Finn believes that, Biz thought but said, "True, but I should have listened to the girl. I could have been her confidante. I was so wrong. About that, about everything."

Finn squeezed her hand. Was this really Elizabeth? He wondered. "Take it easy on yourself. We all have lapses."

"Not you," she said. "'Finn's so steady, so understanding.' Everyone said that." Elizabeth snuggled back into her blanket, wondering if she were worthy of him. "You've never given up on your catcher, on Doug."

"I had a lot of encouragement," he said. "And you, Liz, you are here now, and you're doing what you can, aren't you?"

She thought of Warren. She'd paid, and he'd deliver. She would not confess it all. "I sat with Warren at the Board Dinner. He's agreed to visit his brother."

Finn searched her face. How had she prevailed? He hadn't even gotten to first base with Warren. Maybe it was best not to ask. "Good," he said but couldn't stop the question. "How did you manage that?"

Play with it, at least, Biz thought. "Well, I have my ways," she said, "but he had already hinted that he didn't believe Doug had killed Denise."

"When?"

"Earlier, at the luncheon you skipped."

"I wrote instead," Finn said. "Luncheons aren't my scene."

"Anyway, I'd asked him then, and by dinner he'd thought about it. I had Farley's ideas to add, too. Warren agreed to go on Sunday."

Finn rose. Suddenly he felt tired. He offered Elizabeth his hand and drew her up.

"You need some sleep, and I've got some miles to travel yet," she said.

"Are you all right to drive?"

She nodded. Finn circled his arms around her waist and brought her close. Biz nestled to Finn's chest.

Wait for Finn, she told herself. Wait.

31

Snub Speaks

"The good die young." Now who said that? Even at seventy-six (though most, except Bobbie, the wife, think I'm no more than seventy) I wonder what that says about me? I have definitely not been good, but here we are at a centennial event, after all, and that in itself does not, according to that old saw, bode well for the school, which is very, very old. Santa Reina High may have been good, especially when I began my career, but most of that changed in '67, yes, with "the event."

Hey, I know. 1954. *The Good Die Young* with that dish, Gloria Grahame. She was hot. I suppose I remember the film because of her—*The Bad and the Beautiful, Human Desire,* and *The Big Heat*—get the picture? What a mess *The Good* was. I saw myself as Ravenscourt, luring the poor saps into my scheme. Movies can be very influential. Those ones were able to move a mere thirty-nine-year-old like me. I've done my share of baiting, but no one, really, has been hurt. Not like in the film.

So the good die young. There's truth in it. I guess I'm thinking of Denise Hagerty, the youngest of all the unfortunates, and maybe not anyone else in particular. I guess you're thirteen or fourteen in freshman year. That's too young for me. Maybe it's that you don't have time to turn bad. Life tends to wear on you, and pretty soon you find yourself doing things that you swore you'd never do. Take boozing, for instance. Sure, I said I'd never be like my father, carrying a flask of brandy wherever he went. At one time, I wanted to keep myself pure, maybe to show up the old man. You can go on like that for a very long time, but hate can only bring you so far. And then one evening, especially after the old man's gone to heaven, someone is slapping down a sidecar in front of you and you think, hey, why not? Who am I saving myself for?

The same goes for love. When I met Bobbie at The Music Box, I thought I'd never diddle with any girl other than her. That lasted a while, but a sidecar on two legs walked by me one day and smiled. It wasn't the end of Bobbie—we'd been married at least a year or two, as we are to this day—but it certainly was the end of her fan dance in my eyes. So, maybe it should be said, "Those who die young stay good." Somehow, it doesn't have the same ring. "Stay good: die young." Unwholesome advice.

Biz will outlive all the class of '67. And what keeps old FP alive I don't know. He hides an awful lot. If it isn't evil thoughts, it might be kitchen knives. The Brandling brothers will celebrate ninety at least. Warren will outlive us all, I'd bet. I think the good Father is already older than me, but why Pekka Pyykönen isn't dead already, I don't know. Maybe there are exceptions. I'm one, I suppose. I ought to live another forty years, but I don't want to face them.

This whole celebration serves me morose-pie, plenty sweet but leaves an aftertaste that gags me. It spells the end of everything. See? There I go. Morbid. Perhaps I expected more of a lift from my little poems. Maybe something more with Biz. There's the grand presentation (my well-deserved honor), but who really cares about that? Brass plaques, kind-words-you-cannot-mean, long speeches, too much applause.

Well, they're not going to clap for Denise. She won't be mentioned. And huzzas for me will be more eulogy than praise. Just go shoot yourself, Snub.

> Oh, Sir! the good die first,
> And they whose hearts are dry as summer dust
> Burn to the socket.

Wordsworth, you old stodgy brooder. You were much better as a young man. Well, who wasn't? Go wear your trousers rolled!

Hell. For all it's worth, I can't take much more.

32

Finn and Jamie

He heard them talking low. They moved the grate, stirred the fire into life, and tramped about, packing their things and loading their car. One of them worked over the fire, the other taking down the tent. "The pot must be inside," he heard Inga say. He tracked her approach and sang out before she knocked.

"Come on in, Inga."

She poked her head in, and as if she hadn't noticed Elizabeth's convertible was gone, looked around the cabin. "You alone?"

"Yes, Inga, I am alone." He sat up in the bunk, climbed down, and kissed his daughter's cheek. "Good morning. I'm afraid the coffee pot needs cleaning."

Inga brushed aside his practical comments. "What happened to Biz?"

Finn worked at the sink in his pajamas. "Nothing. She's probably still asleep at her hotel." He handed her the pot and percolator basket, smiling thinly, mostly to himself.

"What happened?" Inga asked. "After such a close call, you didn't make her drive the road in the dead of night."

"My dear child, you are terribly out of line." Finn feigned anger. "Actually, Liz insisted on taking herself home."

"Oh, it's Liz now?" She brandished the pot and turned to go. "So shall I set out three plates or four?" She left before he could answer.

Not four. Not yet.

Inga wouldn't convince him, of course, but she would force him to think about Elizabeth. She didn't have to do even that. Since the previous day, since Elizabeth's first visit, he had thought of little else. Years had not altered people much, that was true, but over time the circumstance, maybe the perspective, had certainly changed.

He had thought about Doug, certainly, and less in his way as protector and mentor than in the role of liberator. Doug would be released. He'd done his time, but Finn wanted more than a dubious freedom for his ward. More than ever he'd grown convinced of Doug's innocence, of the injustice of his conviction and incarceration. Now, he was not alone in that belief. Even at this late date, just months before the young man's scheduled release, Finn knew the importance of clearing Doug Brandling's name and relieving his family of attendant burdens.

Finn removed the breakfast box from the refrigerator—bacon and eggs, pancake batter, some local cherries and walnuts he'd chopped fine, and bread to toast at the fire—armed himself with two frying pans and a spatula, and lumbered barefoot with his load out to the fire Jamie tended, now working from high flame down to coals.

Finn greeted him. "Nice work, son." He laid the box on the stool and the pans on the grate. "I suppose I should call you 'son' now."

Jamie beamed. "*Hijo* works, too," he said. "I plan to call you Finn."

"All right, *hijo*, you start the bacon, and I'll get the flapjacks cooking."

They worked together at the fire, sending Inga to the cabin for the forgotten butter. They talked of families and the coming gala event.

"If you're on the program at the beginning," Jamie said,

"Inga and I should arrive *muy temprano.*"

"I'll be photographing arrivals first," Finn said, "then I narrate a slide program I've arranged. That's what I've been working on since I saw you in Berkeley. I've added some images from the Delta and Solano, just to broaden the reach."

"You've been working on more than that," Jamie said. He gave Finn a sly grin.

"Not you, too. Inga is bother enough."

Jamie looked around for Inga. "Take it for what it's worth, Finn, one man to another, Dr. Moore is a very fine catch, and the way you two look at each other, I believe you're headed somewhere." He turned the bacon and shot Finn a smile. "You can't deny it."

Finn worked three cakes out of his pan and laid them to warm at the side of the fire screen. "There is a lot of history between us. Some of it brings us closer, some keeps us apart."

"The murder."

"Suddenly, after all this time, she's not sure of herself. Something is afoot. Both of us received anonymous notes and news clippings." To Finn, Jamie seemed a secure confidante. He was comfortable telling him this, maybe because he'd be sure to repeat it to Inga.

"Whoa, notes and clippings. What do they say?"

"For Liz, it calls Doug's confession into question. My note reminds us if Doug is innocent, that there's a murderer on the loose. Maybe at the reunion."

"Freaky!" Jamie said but was more interested in the resurgent romance. "With Elizabeth on your side now, that defuses that old animosity."

"It has always been more sorrow than ill will," Finn said. "She seems sincere. It's never been easy for Liz to admit error. And she's done investigating of her own, uncovering doubts and sentiments, if not provable fact."

"And who's sending out the 'love notes?' Could it be Biz, herself?"

"I really think it's beneath her. She wouldn't, but whoever is doing it is likely, I imagine, part of the 'Class of '67.'"

Jamie set the bacon aside. "Ready for the eggs?"

"Just about. Let me finish another batch of pancakes. You like the works? Nuts and fruit?" Finn sprinkled the last batch with chopped cherries and walnuts, watching for bubbling to flip them over.

Jamie's scholarly instincts led him on. "What has she found? Something that changed her mind?"

Finn nodded. "Mostly the thoughts and suspicions of others, and somehow she accomplished something I never could: convincing Warren Brandling to pay his brother a visit at the prison. I'm hoping that will bring a resolution."

"That's big."

"If Warren doesn't believe Doug murdered Denise, he still has to convince little brother that he didn't do it." Finn flipped the cakes. "*Huevos fritos, mi hijo.*"

"*Inmediamente.*"

Inga brought coffee cups from the cabin and poured. "You two bonding?" She passed the brew.

Jamie sipped his coffee, studying Inga. "Man-talk, honey."

Inga put on her pouty face.

"Don't hang your lip, sweetie. We've been discussing the investigation," Finn said.

Inga immediately perked up. "Fill me in."

"While we eat," Jamie said.

They sat around the fire pit, balancing warmed plates on their laps.

"I forgot to warm the syrup!" Finn said. Before he could rise to get it out of the fridge, Inga lifted a cover from a pot on the grate.

"*Excuses-moi, mon père,*" she said, "*c'est ici.*" She crossed her eyes and laughed.

The men looked at each other and grinned.

33

Doug

He makes a sound that wakes him. Black. Night. He listens. Coyotes moan far off in the hills. No one makes a sound in the corridor. Deep night, he thinks, far past midnight. *La madrugada*, the Latins call it. The dead of the night. The time for worry. For torture. The letter bothers him:

Re-address
what you confess.

In prison you do not react. Trudge forward a day at a time. Whoever sent it could be watching. It could not be Finn. The odd message and the news photo of Warren, Finn, and himself, the coach and the Wildcats' battery worry him. The coyotes and his outcry frighten him more. The dream he had plagues him.

He'd dreamt it again. They'd discovered him in the chapel attic. Charlie Manson, the murderous cult leader doing time at CMF with Doug, had seen to it. It was pitch up there, too. Below him, someone had tried the chaplain's office door. It shouldn't have been barred. The guards' fists ripped at the door, reverberating through the floorboards he sat on. Their fierce beating cowed him.

He heard the shouting, "Open this door. Immediately." Below him, the master scrambled, saying, "It's stuck. Give me a minute." Furniture scraped across the floor. Charlie had moved the ladder, too.

They knew who was there in the room below him. "Charlie, what are you doing in there?" It was Ransdorf in the dream.

The sly one lied, but surrounded by an amber aura against the midnight attic, Doug saw, in an absolute darkness, his master afloat in a pool of light, pointing the guards to the trapdoor above, to the attic where Doug cried.

"Bring that ladder here," Ransdorf said. The specter trapdoor swings back. Ransdorf eyes him, Doug, atop the piled contraband—ropes, hooks, crude saws and drills: escape gear. The guard flashes his evil grin. "Now you're in for term." Two dozen full.

On his cot now, in the heavy darkness of night, Doug feels, rather than sees, the leering face of Charlie, his one-time master, which softens like wet clay to become the face of Malamud's character, Doug's movie hero, Roy Hobbs. The contorted features smirk in ridicule of Doug's hopes, as if to sneer, "You'll never make it, kid."

Lying awake, Doug pats his chest, rubs there. It's nerves. Game jitters. He defies Hobbs's despairing phantom: "I won't end up like you," he whispers. And including Manson, too, he adds, "Like either of you." He tells himself: You need to rest. The dream, though, has said, "There's no rest for you." It had been the jailer curling his cruel lip in the dream to say, "Your only 'rest' is the rest of your life."

"Ragers get that." The vision of Ransdorf taunts him. "Angry, my boy? Go ahead, take a swing. What you got to lose?" Doug massages his chest a long time. He rubs away the dream, the note and clip, the jitters, Ransdorf, the master, Roy Hobbs, but Doug cannot rest.

The couplet from the note he received bounced around in his mind like a baseball hit into the empty bleachers. He couldn't even guess which way to move to be able to catch it.

The Advent of Elizabeth

Re-address
what you confess.

So much depends on Finn. On a coach and a friend. Doug heaves himself onto his side.

Much of the dream had been real: hiding in the attic; Charlie's part, turning him in; the contraband; the angry guards. But the dream made it fearsome even though it had been over twelve years ago.

The coyotes are busy far beyond the fences, up in the hills. They'd have seen through the master, his one-time friend, Charlie Manson. They'd tell him now, but he does not understand coyote chatter. The only one who would have warned him was busy with his dying wife. Finn was his friend, truly. But the note? Doug folds his blanket down. His sweat chills him. Finn can only help with what he knows, Doug thinks. You did not tell him the truth. Everything Doug knows prohibits telling.

All his life-long, telling on others was forbidden him, though not to Warren, not for Charlie.

Lying in the dark, Doug recounts his first parole hearing; half his sentence served, he asks for Charlie, his master, to attend. He begs. He appoints Charlie counsel. Yes, he'd thought he had asked. That was before. Now he knows better. When they connected him with the ropes, the saws, and drills, when he was brought out, dragged out of his cell, fighting, raging, then he began to know better. He pieced it together in solitary, though they did not call it that. His master had asked, had wondered, had suggested, had planted the seed of it-might-be-better, better to have a friend, a support at your hearing. Doug had agreed. When that friend turned state's witness, Doug understood why it had been allowed.

231

Doug rolls onto his back. In his lightless cell, still he holds his eyes shut. What shame had all his life forced his confessions? Bed wetting? Martin had said so. "You try to dry your sheets with contrition." Mother-love? That, too. Others had told him that. "You're ashamed of your love for Mom, by your hatred of Dad." It was true.

He had helped with the stash—anything for the master, for his only friend—though not the bags of drugs. He'd got the ropes, made the saws. So when they read the report, the 115, he admitted right away to his part. Not just his part. To it all. Confess, he heard his mind order. Confess. Confess. Confess.

"Mr. Brandling," the board commissioner said, "was it your intention to leave us? To break out of here?"

Though he had not really thought to try a break, he didn't even look at Charlie when he answered, "Yes, sir."

"And the drugs, Mr. Brandling? Were they yours?"

He acceded to each question, "Yes, sir."

"Are you, were you, aware that this kind of activity increases the time you will serve?"

He knew. He'd known. From the time of their initial questions that other day, when he was a junior in high school, questions about Denise, recounting the gory crime he'd confessed, to these accusations they now wanted him to confirm, he had known. "I'm guilty. I confess. I did it." Charlie sat, nodding, staring through hypnotic eyes.

"Mr. Manson," the commissioner said, "do you confirm this?"

The master only rocked his assent.

"Make note that Mr. Manson has affirmed Mr. Brandling's confession."

Now Doug is cold. He feels for the blanket edge and draws it up. He rolls under the covers onto his left side, against the wall. It is darker there, stygian coals unlit.

It's Warren's visit, he thinks. Doug does not have to see his brother, but he's already consented. Finn had worked it, he knows. I'll see him for Finn, Doug thinks. No matter, though, what Warren says, I can't undo it. Denise is dead. I killed her. I remember her screams. It's only that Finn won't hear them. He won't believe, but I do.

"Watch my back, Dougie," Warren always said. From a time before he could remember, Doug knew it was his job, his lot, his salvation: to save his hero, his big brother. "Those are your dues, buddy."

"Those are my dues," Doug says to the wall. Now he drowses. He sleeps. The coyotes are feeding. They fall silent.

This is not a dream. He sees again the infield grass is green not grizzled. There is no stadium, but bleachers each side of the wide, verdant field run toward an outfield fence, wooden slats fitted through woven wire. This is his memory: a high school game. He crouches, signals to his pitcher: low and outside. Warren shakes him off. Doug passes the same sign from the coach and pounds the mitt for emphasis. His brother grimaces, says no, again.

He sails one inside.

The batter falls back. "Hey, Blue, that nearly hit me," he says to the ump.

"Strike," the umpire says.

His brother looks in again. Doug waves off Warren's grin, calls: outside. The coach calls outside. Warren throws in again.

The batter drops the bat and starts his trot.

"Strike two."

The kid whirls. "Hey, ump, that one hit me. Ticked my button." The umpire crooks his arm and holds his uplifted fist, then points.

"Play." Blue stands behind Doug. "Two and two."

Warren is laughing out on the mound, not aloud, but his shoulders are hunched and shaking with mirth. He says something to the shortstop, who coughs into his glove, spits, and smiles. Warren scratches his crotch, comes set.

The next one sends the batter down. A ball high and in.

"One more like that, I'm comin' at you," the kid yells.

Coach calls time. Doug goes out.

"Hey, Warren, quit dickin' with this kid. He can't reach outside. Nail him there," Doug says.

Warren smiles. "Don't wet your pants, little brother. I know what I'm doing. You just watch my back."

The next one ruffles the uniform right at the waist. Doug hears it.

"Strike three," the ump says.

The kid doesn't drop the bat. He's six steps toward Warren holding his club high, yelling like mad. Doug springs up and out of the box. Mask still on, he runs after the batter.

"Watch him, Warren," he yells. The kid never makes it. Doug's on him at the grassy cusp below the mound. He tackles the batter hard and low. The kid goes down head to his bat, face in the dirt, out cold.

The pitcher hikes up his uniform trousers. "Three down," Warren says. "We're up." He saunters to the dugout.

This time Doug wakes breathless as if he's come down hard.

Night has passed.

The game has come.

34

Centennial

"This place looks like a wake, like a Halloween funeral," Farley Pike complained to Mrs. Baxter. He rolled his eyes over the roof trusses festooned with orange and black streamers, mobiles, and dangling "basketballs" that would have been fanned-tissue pumpkins had this been October the last.

"Someone was thinking ahead," Mrs. Baxter said. "Do you know, Mr. Pike, outside Giants' regalia, how hard orange and black are to find in summer?"

"I suppose I've just never liked the school colors," Farley said. "They look awful on any occasion." He crooked his supple neck to grimace at the orange and black paper carnations pinned to his lapel. They designated the ushers, one of which Farley Pike had volunteered to be—the least I can do for the school. "Allow me to show you your seat," he said, and taking Mrs. Baxter's arm, he led her to the first row of plush seats in the balcony.

Mrs. Baxter beamed with pleasure. She had pined for male escort and kind treatment ever since "Mister B," as she called him, had died. She'd been her failing husband's nurse eight years.

Farley was a gentleman, she decided as she plunked none too gracefully onto the cushion and plumped herself up against the upholstered chair back. For his part, Farley Pike glowed with the magnanimity of a newly betrothed earl, someone brimming over with love and affection for all. "If you need anything, just wave to me. I'll be stage left—on your right down below."

Farley left his neighbor reading her program. He skipped down the stairway and entered the gym proper where just days before his Elizabeth had turned her back on him and walked out. Oh, that's no matter now, he thought. Not after tea, after that sweet kiss. He touched his cheek. It's a new era, the advent of Elizabeth. He liked the phrase. "The advent of Elizabeth," he said.

"The event to bring it with? Whatever are you saying?" A large woman, the usher captain, handed Farley a stack of programs.

Farley wouldn't let this bossy petunia trumpet down his spirit. "I said, 'the advent of Elizabeth,' but you won't understand."

"Just make sure each person receives a souvenir program, Mr. Pike. Thank you." She flounced off to the other side of the stage.

Yes, the advent of Elizabeth. I don't care who knows it.

People arrived in pairs and in couples, with family groups, some in classmate ensembles, and some came in singly; Farley, bubbling with his new gusto, guided all to their seats. He handed each a brochure and swept his arm down the row. "Please fill the far end first," he instructed. Occasionally, he had to reposition one of the standoffish who left an empty chair beside his seat. "I understand," he said with sympathetic sincerity, "but please slide over. Every seat will be filled anyway." Once or twice he glanced in Mrs. Baxter's direction. She was chatting vivaciously with her neighbors in the posh seats. He needn't worry about her until the end. Perhaps he and Elizabeth would walk her home.

Really, he was looking for Elizabeth. She had not made the scene, or she was off behind the stage. I bet she's studying that speech she was having trouble with. He seated Warren Brandling in the front row.

"Good evening, Doctor."

"Mister Pike, isn't it? I'd recognize you anywhere."

Farley swept a program out of his sheaf. "The program, Doctor Brandling."

"No red letters hidden inside, are there?"

"What? I'm sorry, I don't understand." He gaped at Warren.

"Never mind. Thank you for the program."

Leaving Warren to fidget by himself, Farley approached Finn and tried to push one of the glossy catalogs into the crook of Pyykönen's arm. The coach was holding an ungainly camera at the time, a mysterious contraption Farley Pike had no interest in learning about.

"Thank you, Mr. Pike, but I'm photographing the celebration. Let's put it there on my chair by the door, under the camera case." Farley took the booklet over toward the exit to the chair Finn had indicated.

From there Farley surveyed the crowd. In the oceans of voices and seas of faces, here and there like flotsam bobbing up and down in the Pacific, familiar ones bumped each other making sounds, or one caught the light turning in his direction, and he recognized a younger lilt or the thinner features of adolescence couched in a strangely altered, sometimes ravaged voice or visage. Uncanny, he thought, looking out at the gulf of a living past.

He patted his chest with the bundle of programs, fanning a burst of air up over his face. Just now, he was feeling faint. A tingling, warm rush rose from his legs up through his groin and gut, pushing his breath forth. Farley steadied himself on the chair back to let the feeling pass. Do not cry, Pike, he told himself. He'd felt stinging at his eyes. His nose began to run.

And why not? He inquired. As he placed the brochures on the floor under Finn's chair, Farley unfurled his handkerchief—his mother had embroidered his initial on it—caught the tears and when the onslaught of emotion ebbed, blew his nose. Oh, Pike! You are waxing sentimental.

Farley swung his gaze over the crowd once more, waved to Mrs. Baxter, and sweeping up his programs, returned to work. Bowing, smiling broadly, somewhat maniacally, he worried, he funneled the milling crowd into orderly rows as the Superintendent of Schools tested the microphone.

I suppose, Farley thought, if I saw myself as they see me, I would jump out of my own wrinkles and croaking voice. Still, he was held in the strength of his sentimental rush. He cherished the feeling. It is not too late, he told himself, love can come to the old. After all, it is the advent of Elizabeth!

Warren sat stiffly at the front row just as he had during graduation. Finally, he gave in and crossed one leg over the other. He hated to risk wrinkling his trousers or flattening the crease his mother set, but nerves got the best of him. He re-crossed, switching legs again, and at last resumed his original rigid pose.

How could you let a woman do this to you? Since his visit to Elizabeth's hotel room, he had thought of nothing else. She dominated his mind. Perhaps she shared space there with his anger. Warren felt distraught, angry at his own foolishness. Why had he promised to visit Doug? Was this woman so important that he'd broken an oath he'd sworn to his dying father? No, she is just a woman, just like the rest, he consoled himself.

Warren scoffed at the letter he'd carried all the way from Beverly Hills. Despite his caustic mistrust, though, he couldn't toss it off. Who had sent it? Perhaps the same person who had seated him beside the monsignor. Or it could have been Elizabeth, certainly. He straightened in his chair. He crossed his left over right. Was something about her new? He came to her tasting the old contempt but left having breathed in an affection he had not known before, like inhaling night-blooming jasmine and feeling wholly transformed. It's the letter, Elizabeth Moore, and this damned reunion, he groused silently. They have you out of sorts.

Warren swiveled on the seat. He scanned the faces, all unknown to him, everyone a stranger. Hers was the one he looked for, but Elizabeth Moore, PhD was not to be seen. He stood and turned. Biz, that name felt better, more fitting now, where are you? He could not sit still. Warren placed his program and his room keys on the chair. Having surveyed the knots of people once more, he strode to the exit. He nodded to Finn Pyykönen, of all people, saying as if he were still in high school, "Good evening, Coach," and burst through the hall door that led to the locker room toilets. Once in the hall he passed the women's locker room, already a pre-program line there, and sidled left to the wall, toward the men's room beyond. "Don't have to go, but can't stay out there," he mumbled.

Entering the lavatory part of the men's locker room , he spied his tablemate priest. He's seen me, Warren decided, too late to back out. The heavyset Berach Phelan, chin to chest, stooped, jouncing and jiggling at the urinal.

"Cursed age," the monsignor greeted him. "Can't empty out, you know."

"Prostate enlargement," Warren said, "it's ordinary."

"You would know, of course," the priest said. "Urology?"

"Related. Gynecology, really." He pulled in two slots down.

"Not to rush to heavenly rewards, but aging is not all it's

cracked up to be."

Warren noticed that, here in the locker room, Phelan's brogue had vanished.

"I might have to piss another time before the benediction," Phelan sighed. Then he smiled, "It's a long one."

Warren ignored the joke and the innuendo. "It will match the program, then. This will take hours." Monsignor Phelan, facing Warren now, was zipping up, having stepped back better to lean over his paunch. He grunted at his work and at last floated up on his toes like a bloated ballerina, with the zipper-tongue's rise. Then everything slumped into place again. Warren tried not to watch.

"Anxious to be off to Westwood? Or are you staying a day or two?"

Warren considered. What am I doing? "I'm not sure. I've a rental car and may see some of the area. It has been a while."

Monsignor Phelan patted Warren's shoulder as he passed. "Enjoy yourself here," he said, "you owe it to yourself. I'm getting some air." And chuckling loudly, he shuffled out to the hall.

Careful to let the priest move off, Warren said, "Always, the cad, aren't you, Father." How easily Phelan's lewd suggestions fed Warren's superiority. My own feelings, he concluded, are wholesome by comparison to that scheming old man.

I suppose abstinence is agar for the lascivious. Something was wrong about the monsignor, that was sure.

His thoughts returned to Biz. Perhaps it was he who had changed. It mayn't be her at all, he mused. I intended, simply, to use her. Warren felt a pang. Yes, I would turn away afterward and not look back. He shook his head and puzzled over the idea. Why can't I do that? Simply never see her again. That thought troubled him. He touched his wrist. Your heart is racing. Take it easy.

Now he wanted to sit. He'd return to his seat and rest. In the hall, though, passing the ever lengthening line of women at their locker room, he saw her. Elizabeth Moore, PhD, was standing restive in line. She was tapping her foot, arms cradling her breasts. Warren immediately decided he liked the doctor in a mood.

"Biz, good evening." He rode over the embarrassment, offering his hand. When they shook hands, he squeezed hers gently. Elizabeth smiled.

"Can you believe this line? Is the plumbing clogged?"

Warren nodded and said, "It's the nature of things, my dear. Why not use the men's? I'll chaperone you. The place is empty."

Elizabeth gazed down the hall. She bit her lip. "All right. I don't have the patience or stamina for this wait."

They strolled together down the hall. She took his arm. Two other women who had overheard broke from the line and followed them. At the entry Warren signaled Biz and the others to wait. He performed his reconnaissance, then waved them in as he posted sentry in the doorway. While he stood there, three other desperate women approached; he let them in. A minute later, a man with a teenager came up and behind them an octogenarian, shambling along on his cane. "Gentlemen," Warren said, "there are six fugitive women inside." He indicated the line down the hall. "It will be just a few minutes."

The old man pounded the terrazzo with the butt of his crutch. "Well, I ain't going to wait!"

Warren soothed him in his best bedside manner, "They are younger women, sir."

"All the better." He tried to push by.

Warren smiled at the man, "I hope they don't scream."

The old man relented. Still, he didn't like it. "I'll give them something to scream about if I wet my trousers!" He giggled in a high whinnying timbre and wobbled back the way he came.

A man coming in held the door for the old man. It was Snub Randall. He approached without extending his arm in greeting. "Warren Brandling," he said, "great minds think alike." When Warren stood his ground, Snub went on, "You're on janitorial duty? Are we closed for cleaning?"

"I'm chaperoning the feminine overflow." He pointed down the hall.

Snub stood facing Warren. He jiggled some keys or change in his pocket. He drew close, confidential. "I don't know how you feel about this event, but the whole thing is making me tired." Snub laughed, fell to coughing, and after a minute managed to clear his raspy voice.

Warren stood erect, watching Snub's act, running a diagnostic eye over the tired old drone. He had never liked Mr. Randall, and despite the change that had come over him after meeting Biz in her room, his feelings about Snub remained, were perhaps even stronger than ever. The day of Denise Hagerty's wake rose to mind. Biz had arrived with this sordid Don Juan. Snub was always one to take advantage, even of a murder. If I've been self-centered with Biz, this bastard has been absolutely pernicious.

When he heard the tap of heels nearing, Warren moved to one-up old Randall. "My date couldn't wait," he said. The woman who emerged was not Elizabeth.

Snub said, "Good evening, Mrs. Marshall." He winked at Warren and whispered, "Like the seasoned ones, Warren?"

Just then Biz arrived. She took Warren's arm immediately and said, "Snub, be sweet and take over for Dr. Brandling, would you?" Then to Warren, "All right, on with the show."

The two washed past the line-up, toward the gym doors, leaving Snub jiggling his change.

"Hussy," he murmured.

"Mr. Randall?" A woman who had emerged from the biff said. Another with her glared. "The last two are washing their hands." She hesitated then added, "Thanks for standing guard."

Finn Pyykönen burned through his digital shutter. He snapped photos of families, duos, and the curious, coming in droves, and those wandering in alone. These last, perhaps, looked to renew a friendship or a courtship. Each scanned the scene awkwardly, innocent of Finn's lens. Is that why I'm here, Finn wondered? Ostensibly, I'm a journalist covering a story, but what truly drew me here?

He caught a new arrival in his view-finder. He snapped a few shots as the man looked over the crowd, obviously searching for friendly faces; Finn caught him sighting, approaching, then embracing one who must have been an old flame. The two hugged a long while, then melded eyes, and finally kissed. Finn recorded the entire sequence.

Though he continued working, he sensed in himself a mantle of want descending as if warm fingers slid across his forehead and down his cheeks, then spread like soft hands, caressing his collar and chest. Were those Elizabeth's hands? He was clicking wildly, without composing, really, or aiming. The warm palms, now over his heart, waxed hot. They leached from his eyes an empty moisture; he broke a sweat, then a chill whipped his spine. He snapped photos but felt only that which was overtaking him.

Inga spoke.

"You caught us coming in, Dad," she said. "Let me see what you have there." Not recognizing them, he'd photographed Jamie and Inga arriving. "Oh, my, it's you." Finn stared dumbly. He caught himself, forced a smile.

"Yes, Dad, it's us." She took his hand, turning the camera screen toward her and Jamie.

Finn recovered. "It's complicated. Let me show you." He fumbled with the gadgets and knobs on the camera, moving, then reversing their positions.

"Dad, are you all right?" Inga said. "You're perspiring." She touched his cheek. "You're burning up."

"Take the camera, Jamie," he said. He mopped his brow. Inga watched him. Jamie studied the photos on-screen. "I'm fine, Inga. A rush of nostalgia is all."

"No surprise there," she said. Jamie handed her the camera. "Oh, we like this one. Look, Dad."

The accidental, unconsciously-directed shot struck them all. "It's beautiful," Finn said and laughed. "True genius."

"All right, then, turn your talent on that couple," Inga nodded toward the two entering from the stage-side doors.

Finn raised the camera. He needed to hide behind it. A new rush, this one rising from ankles turned rubbery and legs suddenly weakened, flowed through, electric and sharp: Liz and Warren Brandling had arrived arm in arm, smiling into each other's eyes. What is going on? Full tears sprang out suddenly. The shutter cycled incessantly, open, closed, flashing over again.

"Enough!" Inga said. Finn stopped. He used his handkerchief again.

"Here, you take a few. Just shoot anyone who moves." Finn, head down, left the way Liz and Warren had entered. They passed at a distance, and Finn, not pausing, raised a hand and hurried out to the lockers.

He entered and splashed his face at a tap. He was not alone.

"The ladies have evacuated, thank God. Getting into the swing of things, Pyykönen?"

Finn sighed to the mirror and dabbed at his face with paper towels. "Pardon?" He felt perturbed to see Snub Randall standing beside him.

"I don't know about you, but this reunion is making me jumpy," Snub said. "Faces are practically crawling out of the grave and all but saying, 'boo'!" He laughed as if it was understood he spoke of himself. "One minute I'm in 1949, the next in '67, and suddenly in 1984." He punctuated with a wicked snicker.

Finn inflated his cheeks and blew a long whistling breath. "I don't go that far back, but, agreed, it's time compressed. Hard to follow, and impossible to stay, except on film."

"Without a doubt." Snub said. "And then there were women in the men's john. Now that's never happened here before."

Finn felt freshness in his own laugh. "Well, get used to it, Snub."

"I won't have to," he said, "and that's a blessing."

The cool water had revived Finn, but suddenly he felt as if he were slipping down a corridor, detaching from himself. Snub Randall, though he was standing right beside him, receded, moving backwards to the far end of that stretching, extending hall. Suddenly, Finn and Snub weren't chatting in the men's locker room but were bumping heads a mile apart over an Elizabeth Moore of thirty years before. Dizziness enveloped Finn. He grasped the sink ledge. He filled his cheeks again and blew.

His sharp breath cut him loose of the spell, and his image in the mirror snapped back. Stay in the present, Finn. Let the past alone.

"You all right, Pyykönen?"

"Yes, thanks. I've got to get back."

Snub Randall watched Finn go. "That boy hasn't changed," he said. Broad shoulders, erect, righteous as they come, and probably happier for it.

In his mind, he turned over the evening Finn had paid his little visit. I thought I was a goner. I always figured I'd die at the end of a shotgun. But that little, not so little either, punk did worse than that. There's nothing more formidable or dangerous than a man with a conscience. Or virtue.

Snub could trace back to Finn's visit the slow leak of confidence that had over the years deflated his lascivious balloon. I could never again undress a co-ed without looking over my shoulder for Pyykönen. I had to check and recheck the darkroom lock, even though the signal light was on. Thanks to you, Pekka-baby, I lost the thrill, the unmitigated excitement of the hunt, the chase, and the kill. Pooh. Virtue. Like a cat circling my pants cuff, it sullies everything it rubs against. Well, tonight will be my night. Probably not in bed— one must be realistic in these latter days—but I will shine at the podium to the consternation of some, the amazement of many, and the adulation of all. Ha! It might be my swan song, but I will stand before them righteous in my own way and intact, glowing, in fact.

He inspected his image in the mirror. The dash of gray Betty left at your temples—well worth the hour's drive to San Francisco—becomes you, Mr. Randall. He put on his reading glasses to search for nostril hair. Betty had routed out his ears, so no worry there. The manicurist at the shop had smoothed and rounded his nails. Snub removed the spectacles and held his hands out to admire them. He didn't notice the thought slip in until it couldn't be stopped: A mortician couldn't do as good a job. "Goddamn!" Snub said. Leave that morbid crap behind. He straightened his tie, buttoned his jacket, and stood as erect as his stiff frame allowed. Again the thoughts came: Rigid in the casket and looking fine. He snorted at the thought.

Snub Randall patted the jacket lapel, just to make sure the acceptance speech he'd tucked in the pocket there hadn't disappeared. Lifetime achievement, teacher of the year. I've earned it, he thought, perhaps not from hard work but certainly through sheer talent.

The speech was magnanimous, hardly gloating at all, he'd judged, but Snub didn't mind a modest lording-it-over-them phrase or two. He'd looked forward to the event just for that reason. All the gossip and rumor about him all these years made the moment sweeter. Patience before virtue, he thought. That motto's served me well.

Snub returned to his seat—at the far end of the first row (thank the stars) from Warren Brandling—feeling tired but better than ever. Elizabeth was to introduce his award. This, he thought, will be a great night.

"'T'ey gathered t'em up, and filled twelve baskets with t'a fragments of t'a five barley loaves,'" Monsignor Phelan said. "Like the loaves and fishes, you will gather t'a fragments of t'is feast and t'ey will multiply in all of you."

The Monsignor droned on in an overly deep brogue. The ushers, including Farley Pike, had to put a search on for the priest, found him wandering off toward the music room, and had to argue convincingly that he was needed in the gym for the benediction. Once back, under civil guard, Phelan seemed disoriented by the crowd. When he began, though, his sermon seemed cogent enough, though long.

God Almighty, thought Elizabeth Moore, the man could put both Judas and Herod to sleep. She sat behind and to the priest's right on the stage, looking, she hoped, young, pert, and professional. Behind her attentive façade, she ticked her paramours off her list. Finn was the one she wanted. And I'll have him tonight, she promised herself. Biz had settled on Finn at a distance, even long before Ellie had died. How to resuscitate the romance was a problem the centennial had solved. She had sensed for years that Finn's love for his wife stood guard, warding off any approach, but once his children reached adulthood, she'd have a chance. This reunion proved perfect timing.

Then Snub, a near miss with Farley, and Warren.

Snub had been unavoidable and meant the least to her. An old man at his end. Pitiable, pathetic in his worn lust. This night would be the last time she'd have to think of him. Her brief speech would be a paean not for Snub but for her freedom from him, less praise—let him do the praising as was his wont—than farewell. Goodbye? Good riddance, more like. Fitting that I should lie for him just one more time and, as he always feared, leave him behind for Finn.

Though Snub had never told her exactly what Finn had said to him that night, nor had she ever got it out of Finn himself, she'd imagined the old faker groveling for his life. For once he'd been on his knees.

Phelan had raised his voice, his brogue deepening. " 'He wrote on t'e ground with His finger, as t'ough He did not hear,' and so should we ignore t'e accusations of t'e past," he said. "Let bygones be. 'Neither do I condemn you,' t'e Lord said, neither convict each ot'er now."

What is he preaching about? Biz wondered. She had no idea, but drifted with his words. Keep on, Padre, give me time to think.

On her end of it, Farley was hardly a passion. She'd needed to get his information and felt thankful for his care.

Warren she used for jealousy's sake. Finn needed something to push him toward his destiny. It had worked in the past; her little hints about Snub and others seemed to soften his righteous forbearance. Ha! A man is a man, and none can stand the heat. Anyway, she'd seen Finn's face, despite the big camera and his dodging her eyes. Warren had done the trick. Now she could dispense with him, too. Send him to meet his brother. That is my gift to Finn and maybe to Warren, too. And no gift passes without gratitude. Finn will be grateful.

"And so believe in each ot'er. Cherish and commit one t'all. In His words 'Peace be with you.' Amen." Phelan closed his notebook, nodded to the superintendent, the next speaker, and climbed down the stage stairs. His back to her, Biz watched the priest hobble down the steps, past Warren sitting at the end of the first row, to limp toward the hall beyond. Something about his bent-over gait worried her, but it was lost with Finn's appearance, snapping pictures of Phelan, the crowd, and the dignitaries, including her, assembled on stage.

Tonight, she thought, I'll follow Finn to the cabin. Inga and Jamie will have gone. I'll have him to myself. She smiled inwardly. It won't be difficult. Everything I've known leads to this. I will have Finn, and I'll keep him, too.

35

Attack

Farley wasn't going to listen to Snub Randall. He didn't even want to hear about him. Not from Elizabeth, not from anyone. So as Dr. Elizabeth Moore took the podium to announce the California Lifetime Teacher Award—it had to be Randall—Farley Pike stood, and when Elizabeth looked his way, during her well-deserved applause, he held up a finger, pointed to the rear hall doors, and nodded. He felt sure she comprehended. Farley would wait for her near the side exit. He had something to tell her.

Once away from the crowd, Farley felt better and took up his position, leaning against the radiator in the vestibule. The sound system was such that he could hear muffled growls of amplified speech, and when a young lady came through the doors on her way to the toilet, a snippet of Elizabeth's speech rang clear: "He was everybody's favorite teacher, a champion of learning in and out of the classroom, a true friend of the student body . . ." she was saying. The door closed on the rest. His Elizabeth had had trouble with that speech, but after all, anyone speaking publicly about the man could only lie about Snub.

The unfairness of it all, Farley thought. The man was popular. What charlatan isn't, at least for a while? Of course, Snub could tell the same stories over and over, to one class and then to another, and be believed; his classes actually expected, anticipated the lies. Students who couldn't even begin to suspect him of balderdash sucked in his baloney like spring air. They refused to choke because they wanted to believe.

With a bravura that filled the auditorium and the hall where Farley stood waiting beyond the doors, Elizabeth's announcement ended. Farley felt gratified at the brevity of her speech. I'm glad, he thought, but not surprised she'd cut him off short, at the knees. Serves him right. Though he did not actually hear her ending, the PA swelled with the name, "Stephen 'Snub' Randall, Teacher of a Lifetime." There had been something about "consistent achievement," followed by booming applause that drowned her final words.

As he had for years across the hall from Mr. Randall, Farley Pike stood conspicuous in his discomfort, trying to ignore what he knew but didn't see: Snub's hand jiggling around in his pocket.

Elizabeth got off the stage as tactfully as possible, sweeping her arm toward Snub and the audience, adroitly avoiding his grasp and his sally toward a hug. Public touch she would not allow. So backpedaling, she gave the audience their favorite son, turned on her heel, and strode off the stage, down the stairs, and directly out the rear gym doors.

Too late. Pushed by swelling applause behind her, she fled one bore and remembered the other, kind though he may be, awaiting her arrival. Farley is in here. And yes, he was hovering at the end of the hall. She lifted a finger to stay his advance, turned, and marched directly through the women's lavatory entry.

By God this is one place to get a little privacy. She moved straight to one of the line of sinks to daub her face with a moist towel. Farley seemed to be sticking to her like cheap makeup. Biz lifted an eyebrow to the mirror, "Oh, you'll soon be rid of him." She heard something like a shambling growl and turned to it.

"We'll be rid of you, Dennis and I, we will."

Elizabeth Moore could not comprehend what Father Phelan was saying as he advanced from the shower room toward her, but she felt danger echo in the rumbling voice. Still, his ludicrous figure drew a laugh from her as she spoke: "What the hell are you doing in here, Phelan? Have you lost your mind?" Immediately, she regretted it. Now his hunching retreat down the stage stairs leapt up and melded both with his surge toward her and with the figure escaping from Denise Hagerty's attack years before. "It was you!"

He was on her then. A sickening mildew odor mixed with boozy breath choked Elizabeth, even before Phelan grabbed her throat. He twisted her arm behind her and pressed her backwards toward the shower room whence he'd appeared. In her face he snarled, "You, you and that girl tried, but you can't keep Dennis away. Never again." And as he loosed her throat reaching beneath his coat, Elizabeth kneed the good Father hard in the groin. Even doubled over, though, he did not let go of her arm.

Talk Biz. Talk to him. She wriggled in his grip and rasped a question at him. "Dennis who? Berach? Who do you mean?" Get him talking. Work him, Biz.

Sickened, Phelan moaned, still fumbling inside his coat. "Sweet Dennis," he said, as if soothing the woozy gut she'd inflicted on him.

"It was Dennis Hagerty," Elizabeth said. "Denise was only protecting her twin. From you, you bastard."

Elizabeth Moore struggled furiously, kicking and missing but breaking free of the priest's grasp. She was cornered, though, at the rear of the showers, but even when he drew forth the knife from his coat, she couldn't stop herself, "You beast! You are an animal!" She feinted as if to kick, and as he lunged, adroitly slid away and levered the shower handle on. Her actions and accusations were drowned out by what began as a shriek and boomed forth in a series of horrid screams echoing around the women's shower room, bouncing past the sinks, out the entry and into the hall where the sounds grew sharper.

Farley Pike, who had just swung open the door to the auditorium, retreating from Elizabeth's snubbing, paced long strides back to the entry of the locker room. There he hesitated, but when the screams continued and were punctuated by shouts of "bastard," "stop right there," and "oh my God, my God!" he dashed in. Just as Farley Pike hurled himself into the short tiled hall toward the screams, the yells, and the banging of partitions, the tumult of struggle burst into the hall and ricocheted through the door Farley had opened into the then quiet and expectant auditorium beyond. Transfixed at first by Farley's dash, then by the wailing from the toilet, Inga's Jamie caught hold of the open gym door. He'd recognized his girl's voice.

The auditorium was stilled, first in expectation of Snub's acceptance, but then by the amplified screeching from the locker room that soon threw a tide of scrambling people into a torrent of rescue. The crowd streamed through into the hall.

Snub Randall, arranging his notes, had not begun to speak.

It was Inga who had shrieked and screamed. She'd slipped into the last cubicle in the long row ahead of Elizabeth's entry. She'd heard the interchange between the priest and Elizabeth and followed it into the shower room.

She screamed when Phelan lunged and continued wailing as the priest whirled momentarily under a sudden shower. Inga stepped forward.

Biz stood confused, flushed from struggling, from the

lies in her speech, from Farley's weird presence, and finally, from the sounds screaking all about her. The screams came at her from all directions, silent from the past, too, as well as from that moment. Biz heard the voice of fourteen-year-old Denise Hagerty, pleading for her life. Inga swept Elizabeth behind her, still screeching, and this time it was Inga, facing the knife. Father Phelan crazed, sopping wet, and demented, slashed, and Inga, though she deflected the attack, went down, her forearm bleeding profusely. Inga's cries froze Biz ghostlike to a scene she'd known before: gore and urine and blood and horrid death.

Then Farley Pike was there.

Finn crouched below the stage in the auditorium, strobes of flash bursting from his camera. He'd captured Elizabeth's introduction and exit, snapped a few frames of Snub at the mic waiting for applause to end, but then turned to the eerie sounds emanating from the hallway. He knew that voice, that scream, the timbre of that shriek.

"It's Inga," a man shouted, rushing past Finn. It was Jamie, running.

Finn followed Jamie, disappearing past the doors. Somehow it seemed that they both arrived at once. A herd stampeded in behind them.

Standing before the priest, "Halt!" Farley Pike commanded. "Stop it right there."

Behind Inga, Biz wobbled, reached out to anything for support, and Finn grabbed her before she fell. He saw exactly what had swept her consciousness away. Before them all—Biz, Finn, Jamie, and the host pushing in from the gymnasium behind—the squat, hunching figure of the priest, Father Phelan, raised a butcher knife above his head shaking it, aiming now at Farley Pike's chest.

"Halt, I said," Farley Pike repeated. His voice in the tiled room boomed gigantic as the Holy Ghost's Himself. The priest glared red-eyed at him and hiked the knife an inch higher. Then faster than anyone then or later could believe, Farley Pike himself shrieked and flew, a catapulted saint, directly to Phelan's raised arm. Those two spilled to the floor kicking, writhing, and sliding through Inga's blood, scuttling away from Phelan's erstwhile victims. Jamie was at Inga's side that instant. Finn cradled Biz. Farley rose over the priest; the knife clattered across the floor.

Warren Brandling pushed through the crowd. Snub Randall followed, clutching his chest. Both stopped short, staring not at the bloody scene, but at Elizabeth Moore in the arms of Finn Pyykönen. She was alert. She pointed at Phelan.

"It was him. All these years, it was the goddamn priest." She shouted it. Hysteria clutched her throat, but Elizabeth Moore fought free of frenzy to screech to heaven, "You sinning, rotten pig." She repeated it until Finn rolled her in his arms snugly, and she hid her face in his chest.

Brandling said, "Jesus," turned and pushed back through the crowd.

Snub Randall rubbed his chest, hung his head, and followed Warren out.

Someone from the throng yelled it, "Hurrah for Farley Pike." All joined in refrain.

Farley Pike stood over the heap that was the parish priest, glancing in bewilderment from one cheering face to the next.

36

Snub Speaks

You'd suppose I would complain. There at the height of achievement, a pinnacle I'd not deserved or dreamt of, *Fortuna* swept me off the dais. I basked in adulation a final moment. I thought she was shining her face upon me, but a eunuch stole my thunder. A man of the godforsaken cloth, as rotten as they come, pissed on my parade. And to think I'd confessed to *him*.

In case you're wondering, these are descriptions, not complaints. Were I to rail against the goddess, that would be a foolish beef, a futile waste of the labored breath left me.

All those faces rapt and expectant lifted to me. Politeness rather than adoration? I suppose. After all, I was the final act of the night. I was to be the last gasp of the evening.

Did I say one word? I was in mid-inhale, about to launch into my well-rehearsed and vaingloriously modest acceptance. I planned to snub them all without them knowing. Thank you, my friend, Berach Phelan-of-the-phony-brogue. An Englishman if ever there was one.

I'd have screamed myself had the Pyykönen girl and Biz not done it for me. It is unjust.

Not the tarnishing of my glory, the lost opportunity to gloat and goad, that will be in the record, the glory that is. What is against the kindness of nature is this fearsome burning in my chest I'm talking about. What's the use of seeking an opinion or help? Medicine will not cure me in time. They'll say, "It was the excitement." Hell, they don't know what excitement is! Try a trio of seventeen year-olds on three successive nights. I'll bite my tongue, maybe my rubber gag, but I'd rather go a-sudden than in a waste of cancer.

I left the stage and fought through the crowd packing itself into the women's john, my heart on fire, pulsing electricity up my throat. And for what? To see my Elizabeth, after years of devotion to me, finally, in Finn Pyykönen's arms? To discover the good Father Phelan, appropriately undone in his own piss? He wept, like Jesus, for sins, his own, of course. There wasn't even another corpse. Phelan had missed his mark more than once.

What burns me most? Not the lightning bolts running down my arm or congestion beneath my shirt. Not losing out to Finn in the end. Not my lost opportunity to bask in shining light.

What is it? Farley Pike! That's what. I am the honored guest, but he is the hero. I cannot stomach that for anything. It's not worth it.

37

Elizabeth

Elizabeth Moore's blissful ride in Finn Pyykönen's arms did not last long. He carried her like a bride over the threshold into the nurse's office between the men's and women's locker rooms to lay her on the wide divan of the exam room.

Perhaps because she'd suffered a shock over twenty years in the coming, she circled his neck, clasping herself like an engagement necklace, drawing in his scent and exhaling tenderness against his chest. "Finn, I've been so wrong for so long. Now I won't let go again."

He pressed her body lightly to his chest. "Don't worry, Liz. You've had a scare. Everything will be all right. Inga will be all right." He lowered her to the firm couch and looked around the room.

"The blankets are in here." Mrs. Baxter had followed, puffing from her rush down the auditorium balcony steps. She'd sensed she would be needed. "I know nursing, my boy."

"Don't leave me, Finn," Elizabeth whispered to him.

He knelt to her and held both her hands in his. "I wouldn't, but I must see about Inga."

"Fine. I'll come to the cabin."

Mrs. Baxter shouldered her way between them. "Give me room. I have the blanket." She set the folded wool over the feet of Elizabeth Moore, PhD and opened it methodically, crease by crease, covering her new patient. "Mr. Pyykönen, you leave her to me. I've much more experience than most doctors." She'd found a pillow to augment the rise of the

259

headrest and carefully tucked it beneath her ward. "You'll be fine my dear. I'll get you water and a warm, damp towel for your head."

Finn spoke to Mrs. Baxter on his way out. "Take good care of her."

Biz watched him go a second time. As before, she held her breath, but at the doorway of the nurse's room, this time, Finn looked back, caught her gaze firmly in his, thinned his lips toward a faint smile, and left. She closed her eyes beneath a sigh and the second blanket Mrs. Baxter unfurled. Her nurse spread a warm cloth over the patient's forehead.

Biz listened to Mrs. Baxter hush someone at the door. "Mr. Pike," she whispered, "were you hurt?"

He murmured, "No."

"We must let her rest."

Farley wavered before Mrs. Baxter's direction. "Well, please, Mrs. Baxter, give her this," Farley said. "It's a new pen."

"Very well, Mr. Pike, now go along, and thank you for the escort, but I'll find my own way home," she said, as if she believed he'd come to see her and not Dr. Moore. The house was just down the block in any case.

Elizabeth Moore kept her eyes closed then and for a long time, warming herself at the fire of expectation and in the glow of Finn's parting glance. Even in the face of a new uncertainty rising in her, Elizabeth thought: Nothing will stop me now.

It was almost ridiculous, but she insisted on giving Mrs. Baxter a ride home. The walk through the lot to the car was nearly the same distance as a trek to the Baxter house. But the old woman was glad to see her charge up, around, and grounded enough to maneuver through the maze of police and on-lookers.

"It would have been safe to walk home with all this going on, I'm sure," Mrs. Baxter said. She gazed at the spectacle of police, television, and lookie-lou's. However distracted, she seemed glad to accompany Elizabeth.

When they were turning out of the parking lot, Mrs. Baxter said, "Oh, there's Mr. Pike. They're interviewing him."

TV crews and lights jammed around Farley. He attracted microphones like moths in the descending night. The reporters had drawn most of the crowd away from the squad cars, and a second ambulance parked nearer the gym doors waiting for the downed priest. Inga had already been whisked away to the hospital.

"I'm sorry I can't stop, Mrs. Baxter," Elizabeth said, "you'll have to see it on television." The woman drew her nose slug-like along the window as they passed the interview, smudging a line, arrow-like, watching Farley Pike.

"I've always known he was a fine man," she said.

Biz smiled. "Yes, Mrs. Baxter, a very fine man."

She pulled round the block, a block made infinitely longer by curiosity, and at Mrs. Baxter's front walk, insisted on escorting the woman to her door, as much to prove her recovery as to bring Farley's neighbor home.

"Thank you, Mrs. Baxter. I'm fine, all because of you." She found herself hugging the woman.

Elizabeth returned to the car. And perhaps because she did not think she would find him there, she headed immediately toward Finn's cabin.

Elizabeth Moore did not find Finn at the cabin. He had followed the ambulance carrying Inga, with Jamie at her side, to St. Francis Hospital, the better of two in town. He would not return until very late that night.

Biz knew that. In any case, she had come for herself

rather than for Finn. It might be better without him here. She parked and rifled through her bag in the trunk of the car, bringing it and a flashlight to the cabin.

"Shit," she said. It was locked. "I haven't come all this way just to turn back." She checked the windows, all latched. She scoured the cabin front with the Eveready. Searching atop the door, under the mat, around the corners, and up into the eaves where, finally, she spotted it, a complicated-looking key hung on a spike, high against a rafter tail. She reached up with a redwood stick she'd found and lifted the key from its nail. You're becoming a regular camper-detective, my girl.

Five minutes later she was ready to take the thought back, ready to scream and to stomp. The lock would not give way. She slipped the key through the keyway this way and that, turned it clockwise and counter, hard and softly, but it would not turn. She put her bag on the camp stool beside the door and charged the thing again. Elizabeth Moore was shaking in a frustration on the brink of rage. Once again she slipped the key in, and like a palsied crone, nearly dropped it to the ground, hardly able to control its rotation, and it turned. So much for campfire bravura, and it serves you right.

Inside, the cabin was chilly. Cooler than the air outside. "All right, Elizabeth," she said and drew in a long breath, "time to break a nail." She opened the stove and, as she had seen Finn do years before and just a night ago, crumpled newsprint, then piled the kindling from the box by the door, which she lit as he had done. What else? Something else, she thought. As smoke flowed from the stove door, it came to her. "Oh, God, something else." She found the coiled damper handle and turned it. The fire leapt, dragging the smoke with it up the stovepipe.

Biz opened the cabin door, and using it as a bellows, rid the cabin of most of the billowing smoke that had filled the single room. Once she cleared the air, she sat, plopped down, wiping her eyes of smoke and tears. A familiar voice whimpered, "You're not cut out for this." Another, soft, full, low, but feminine replied, "In time, dear, in good time."

She rose, took up Finn's huge gloves hung above the wood box, and fed the fire, first sticks as big around as her fingers, as her wrists, then larger, and finally loaded into the stove, as she'd watched Finn do, a split quarter of oak. "Not too much," she told herself. The chill was already out of the room. She shut the cabin door.

As the slab door swung to, the room widened, seemed larger to her but felt close in a tender, palliative way, like the blankets of Mrs. Baxter spreading spaciously over a troubled soul. Elizabeth felt rather than heard that womanly tenor touch her thoughts. "You are able."

Was that Mother's voice? So long since I've heard it. She decided not, but like the genial commands earlier that night, Mrs. Baxter's directives, this utterance enveloped her in a world she'd privately longed for but never allowed herself to enter. The sensation felt strange, childlike most surely to Elizabeth Moore, PhD, but the allure had promise of caring that she could not resist. The firelight played about the room and on her arms. Elizabeth realized she had never before been alone in this place, not in the cabin, not in this presence.

Though Biz did not feel alone, neither did anyone disturb her privacy. She took from the trunk-bag the folded outfit she had worn the previous night and laid the items out on the bunk, smoothing the jeans and western shirt and standing the boots on the floor below, dangling new socks over them. She bent to the stove door, checking the oak faggot inside and reached another from the box with ungloved hands. This second quarter flamed immediately above the embers. Heat surged into the cabin corners.

Biz wet, then dried her hands at the sink and languidly but without reluctance slipped off her shoes, unzipped her skirt, letting it fall, rolled down her hose, and turned each button of her vest and blouse through its stitched hole, carefully laying aside those garments, finally unhooking her bra, and dropping her panties to her feet. Elizabeth stood naked in the firelight, bathing in the warmth of Finn's cabin stove and in a new glow from within her. The unstated encouragement she had heard pitched the tenor of change. "All will be well," it told her now. Unbothered, Biz crossed her arms embracing herself, bringing her hands down, smoothing her sides and thighs in amber-coated luxury of the fire and said aloud, "Yes, all will be well."

Now Elizabeth made pert movements, folding her shed clothing into the bag, taking up the camp duds and slipping into them in unhurried, crisp turns. She finished with the long socks and boots and buttoned up the plaid shirt over her bare breasts. She put her hands on her hips as if to say, "What are you waiting for?" and began her chores.

Without gloves she washed and stacked the dishes left in the sink that morning. Setting them to dry in the rack, she took up the rag and cleaned the little counter and stove top over the hissing protests of the wet cloth. She smoothed sheets, straightened pictures, arranged shelved items primly, and took the broom to the floor, the small open area and the hidden reaches under the table, bunk, stove, and rocker. She swept a sizeable pile of detritus into the dust pan and dumped it in the bin outside. Elizabeth marveled at her work, even more at the humming melody that wrapped itself around each task she accomplished. She amazed herself; she was singing.

At the end of this joyful labor, Biz stowed her utensils and stretched out in the rocker, resting her boots on the little leather ottoman. She'd opened the door. Through the screen, drawn in by the draft of fire, the sharp air swept up her nostrils, bringing on a sneeze that cleared them to a tannic tingle. "Oh, my. This is new," she said and half-heard a refrain, "Yes, this is new and good, as well."

The fire was out. The moon sunk behind the redwoods. The rush and ruffle of a night heron or, perhaps, an owl swooping by the screen away to the hills beyond Finn's place woke Elizabeth Moore. Strange as this dark cabin was to her, the work she'd invested in the place soothed what might an earlier time have been fright at the eeriness of waking there alone. She opened her eyes suddenly but felt untroubled. Elizabeth woke to the dark cabin, following the bird's path with her ears, piercing the gloaming shadows with dim sight, and breathing in a freshening faith from the woods that she had not felt in fifty years, or, perhaps, ever. Is this contentment? She wondered. Without waiting for the reply she knew hovered nearby, she said, "Yes, I am content."

She rose, stretched, and sighed happily once. She shouldered her bag and, stripping a sheet of paper off the tablet Finn kept on the table, wrote to him by the light of her torch:

> I hope you don't mind, Finn, I tidied up a bit, but decided not to wait for you now. You'll be tired. I'll likely return home tomorrow. I trust Inga will mend quickly. She is healthy and young (and beautiful). Don't worry too much.
>
> My love,
> Your Elizabeth

She went to the door, returned to the table for the key she'd left, and kissed the note. At the doorway, she turned one last time, summed up her work, and nodded approval. I can see why Finn likes this place so much.

Biz closed the door, slid the key into the slot, jiggled it gently, and turned the bolt. It slid gracefully into place.

Late that night, Finn scoured the ground at the cabin corner. His exhaustion played tricks. Three times he lunged at a stripped redwood frond on the ground, once at a root, thinking he'd found the key, before, finally, abandoning the bare nail in the eaves above, to go to the door he thought he'd locked that morning and found his one-of-a-kind key resting in its lock. He jiggled the key and turned the latch.

The warmth of the cabin woke him fully from incipient sleep. Someone had been there. Finn lit the lantern and saw the note. He had to read it twice to understand.

"Oh, Elizabeth. I don't think I can," he said to the note. He was too full of Inga, of family, of children, of his life with Ellie. Berach Phelan's attack on Inga had wiped away all thoughts that had seeped up from his Santa Reina past, including his thoughts of and resurgent feelings for Elizabeth Moore. His daughter's hurtful brush with mortality blocked all his thoughts of reconnection.

Finn read the note a third time. Even though her name was written there, it did not sound like Liz. He looked around the cabin, at the touches she'd left. He felt glad she had not stayed, had not waited. Still, he looked again, smiled to himself as he shook his head. He folded her note and tucked it in his shirt pocket. He decided to think about it in the morning.

He undressed and climbed into the bunk made up by Elizabeth Moore, the bed where Ellie had died.

Spent as he felt, though, Finn did not sleep. He lay in the bunk, surrounded by Liz's ministrations. He searched for the feeling that Ellie had left with him in the cabin, her cheerful music, like morning in the woods. Ellie's lyrical tenor had buoyed Finn each day he stayed at the ranch, like a scent of jasmine lingering at the screens, fleeting on the breeze though always present. Now he could not sense her. Finn failed to feel anything of Ellie here; the mayhem of the evening, too, had cut into the reviving affection born here long ago, long before Ellie.

Finn gave up. The day before him, the drive to Doug's game, demanded rest. For the first time at the cabin since he was a kid staying there after his father died, Finn Pyykönen fell asleep lonely.

38

The Morning After

Mrs. Randall

I'm shouting up the stairs, "Rise and shine, Snub!" I'm not going to burn my toast or chalk my yolks for the likes of him. I'm not.

"Hey, Mister! Breakfast!" That usually does it.

I'm not going to waste good bread or eggs on a loafer. So I set aside the pans and leave his bread in the slots—who cares if it dries out and burns before it pops? I stomp upstairs to his study, as he calls it, where the old wag sleeps. I'm not the quiet type. I might not say much—why rock the boat? It usually capsizes—but you know I'm there, bustling and bunging about, making my presence known. So I bang on the door. "If you want to eat, get out of that bed."

It's quiet in there. Absolutely silent. I beat on the door again. "Have you died on me? Finally?" At this moment I don't care he doesn't want me snooping, looking at his photo albums and masturbatory pinups. I'm getting hungry. So, I open the door and push my face through. "Snub, I cannot wake the dead every morning. Breakfast in five minutes, take it or leave it."

He doesn't twitch a whisker. And then I smell it. Worse than old-man scent. I'm used to that. This is bad. And I have to see what. "Snub? What have you got into now?"

Mr. Randall won't be having breakfast today. Not

another day, either. I make sure that he isn't drunk. He's cold. I press a finger into his side, and I'm sure. No give. I should call someone, so I go downstairs.

I'm shaking. Not trembling, just shaking my head. You expect it, and finally, there it is. You'd think I'd be shocked, but I'm hungry is all. So I make breakfast.

I toss his burnt toast and scramble my eggs in the bacon grease. I like them scrambled; over easy for him, always. Well, that's going to change. I sit at the little table by the kitchen window, butter my toast and add a touch of strawberry jam.

On the lawn this morning, a robin cocks his head. He's listening to the ground, they say, for worms tunneling beneath. That might not be true, but sure enough, between the crunch of bacon and the sweet mush of eggs, up he pulls a long one. We swallow together. I guess he's like me, no more mouths to feed than one's own. The bird hops off to part of the lawn hidden from me.

I have dishes to do. I don't eat right off the ground. I suds up the frying pan and whisk the water over my plate and silverware. I'm using the Marley Brothers Department store plates Snub bought when we moved into the house. Over forty years, now, and only three broken. You can't raise kids without cracking some plates. I dry the few things on the red-striped cloth and set his unused plate in the cupboard on top of mine. The sun has broken through the morning mists. The robin hops out from a shadow.

I look at the phone as if it has rung. The phone. Like a sleepwalker I go there and pick up the receiver, like I'm curious to see what it will do. I listen to the buzzing tone. It sounds odd. I don't know who to call. Who do you call? The police? That doesn't sound right. So I call Kitty up in Portland. She's home with the children. She'll know who to call.

The Advent of Elizabeth

Upstairs again, I walk by the study. I open the linen closet and stare in. Finally, I kneel low to loosen from the stack an old queen-size sheet I've saved—both of us went to single beds after the kids left, when Snub moved in there. Now I'm glad I didn't cut it up for rags. I'm playing this by ear, from knowledge gained at the movies, I guess. Haven't had much experience with this.

Now I'm sitting with my draped corpse of a husband. Merciful and swift. Stinky but done. It's another jumble Stephen "Snub" Randall has left for me to clean up, not that I interfered with his messes unless they threatened to rub off on me—three children to feed, a house to keep, appearances at school events, and while he thought he was the dandy and I was the dupe, I stoked my own fires for the younger men that filled in for my wandering husband.

"Snub, you old fool. You never looked at home to see. Too intent on your doings, on your little chasers, to find out what you left right here. Were you afraid you couldn't satisfy just one woman? You had to move on and on. There might have been truth there, if you thought long enough about it. Well, I waited. I waited my turn. When I was sure you'd vacated my bed, I filled in where I could.

"I'm sitting with you now, just to tell you what you would not have listened to before. That night Finn Pyykönen came unannounced, I thought he'd shoot you. You had a hard-on for his girlfriend, that Dizzy-bit Moore, everybody knew that. Some folks even told me they'd seen it. That night, I was ready to sweep up the kids and to run out the back door. I didn't want to be in the way of the gun.

"Finn, though, had come to ask kindly as you please. He was known for that. Still, when he left, you looked worse than you do now. White as a sheet and sweating buckets. It served you right. That was when I decided to stay and to play. You were having so much fun, I thought I'd invite the neighbors. And I did. No need to name names or tally them. Tit for tat sums it up.

"So is this what comes of love?

"You and I had quite a whirl, that's for sure. Over at The Music Box I'd thought we'd never stop dancing. We were the couple. So what it lasted only a few years beyond the wedding? I suppose that's about all any young wife can expect. Two years. In reality. Of course, my poor baby, most couples live on fiction. The more a husband heaps lies on, the more the wife shovels the shit higher, too.

"It started with that most sincere, 'I love you,' neither of us understood the meaning of, but who cares at first? Later, though, you wonder what the phrase really means. You love your breakfast? You love the house? You love those settled accounts?

"I did love you, Snub. At one time. I didn't care what it meant, but a bit at a time, I learned not to love you. Blame it on Finn if you like. We had settled in. We'd discovered who the bad guys really were. Us. We'd adapted. We'd accepted. We moved on in place. I'm not going to say it's harder when your husband is chasing teenage skirts. You can figure that one out.

"I wonder about the couples who grow old together, not that we didn't. Sounds sweet, doesn't it? Only a few grow to resemble each other. Maybe those are the extremely fat and the very thin ones. Look alike or not, sooner or later, one dies. The other follows, quickly if it's the man survives. Widows, as I'm like to do, hang on for years and years. Why is that? Relief! God, the thing that comes to mind is 'you don't know what you've got, until you lose it.' Was that a song?

True? Well, not if you look at evidence. I, for one, knew what I had. Most of us do.

"Now you really have moved on. This is new. You would expect to feel grief. I'd expect to feel relief. And maybe that's what this is, a kind of queasy, uneasy turn of the gut, a scary little flutter at the heart. 'I'm alive,' you say. I say, 'That's grief enough.' You think: get shut of this kitchen, this house, this town, and definitely this school. Get out the dancing shoes, for Christ's sake, even at seventy-two. Move to Portland, help Kitty with her kids.

"That's relief enough. That is not for you. No more. Falling in and out of love is like living and dying. No different? You can answer part of that. To me they seem the same. You think it'll never end. Then? It does. And soon. Do you know it, Snub? Judging from your mooning around the last few days, I'd guess you saw it coming.

"I touched you once. I had to be sure, but no more. One little finger told me. We're done. I'm leaving you under our old sheet. This is it, Snub. I'll wait down in the kitchen. When they come, I'll just point to the stairs. And for what it's worth, when last night's plaque and certificate arrive, I'll hang them on the wall. For a little while."

Farley Pike

Farley Pike lay in bed. The sun had been streaming in for a good, long time, but he did not want to rise. He'd heard the Sunday *Republic* thump on the landing nearly an hour ago, and was that Mrs. Baxter he heard clipping the hedges that separated their properties down there, below his window? He lay on his back in the exact middle of the bed, his head propped on two pillows, a bolster beneath the sheet under his knees, the way he always slept. He knew, though, and very well, that something had changed. Imagine, I've been interviewed on television. Yes, that had something to do with it. And they'd called him a hero. That's new. Perhaps they'll stop calling me Farty Pants. That'd be nice.

Farley Pike, though, did not feel like a hero. He barely remembered what he'd done, what he'd thought right before and right after. I just wanted that screaming to stop. What an outrage. I wonder what I said to the TV. I don't think I want to see it. He'd easily overcome that priest. I never liked him anyway. "Creepy-to-the-max," he said, quoting his tenth-grade students' favorite phrase—they say that in reference to me, I believe. Fame? Heroism? Attention?

These were not the thoughts that kept Farley Pike in bed. Obviously, the advent of Elizabeth was over, if it had ever begun. He thought of Dr. Moore in his apartment, in his mother's bedroom. Just two days ago? Was it his self-delusion he avoided, here in bed, languishing two hours beyond his usual time? Or did a new vision of his life, something unlike anything that he'd given himself to, worry him so that he refused to meet it squarely? The clacking of garden shears grew louder, and with it, Farley rose, removed the knee-pillow, turned the sheets back, and, standing over his bed, tugged them tight. He fluffed each pillow and went to the window.

Yes, it was Mrs. Baxter down there, happy as could be, squaring up the hedge. He almost called down, but her appearance, something new about her seen from up here, stopped him. Less stout? Energetic? More musical?   He heard, again, her last-night's voice speaking to Elizabeth, firm, kindly, and in command. Then, she'd turned to him: "Mr. Pike," she'd whispered, "were you hurt?" Her tone was so, so . . . so soft. Motherly? No. Softer than that.

He went to the bathroom, washed and shaved. He folded his pajamas into the second drawer and dressed, approaching the window twice to look into her garden. He buttoned up his shirt as he moved to the door, then unfastened the top two, took a look in the hall mirror, removed his keys from the hook, and strode lightly down the stairway, wondering: Is this what they mean by "jaunty?"

Outside, on the apartment doorstep, Farley Pike took in the morning air, the dappled sunshine, the gentle breeze. Why didn't I rise earlier? His sojourn in bed now seemed a waste. He took a step, then marched around the corner to the side of his building where his neighbor played over her hedges.

"Mrs. Baxter. I thought that was you clipping your hedges. Good morning."

She turned, left the shears sitting on the flat top of the hedge, and came to the little gate that led to his sidewalk. She stood there sweeping her eyes over him from top to toe. "Oh, Mr. Pike, I am so proud of you."

"Thank you, Charlene, may I call you that?"

"Yes, Mr. . . . . Farley. We've been neighbors long enough." She giggled, then smiled.

She has nice teeth. And her cheeks are plump. He looked at the hedge, not wanting to stare. "I heard you clipping and wanted to see you. So I came down."

"See me?" she asked. "What about, Farley?"

"Do you have any more of those wonderful scones left?" You are not handling this well, you old fool, asking about scones right off.

Mrs. Baxter left one hand atop the gate and with the other reached over and touched Farley's arm. "I'm sorry, I have no peaches now. But I made some lovely lemon bars this morning, lemons fresh from the tree. Are you hosting a

Sunday tea?"

Farley Pike placed his hand over hers on the gate. "Yes, tea for two, at three o'clock. He stood tall—heroic, so he thought. "I was hoping, Charlene, that you would come."

Finn Pyykönen

The phone rang a long time. He wondered if she might be at church, but, finally, her uncertain voice sounded through the receiver. "Good morning, the Brandling residence."

Finn had wanted to make this call but had also postponed it until he had confirmed what the scene in the locker room had meant. He had risen far past dawn, packed his gear, and closed the cabin—who knows, he'd thought, when Jamie and Inga will really come up again—and returned the key to Gary at Glen Ellen Gas. He'd eaten breakfast across the street from Gary's shop and had driven all the way to the freeway on Highway 12. He couldn't afford the time to take the scenic route, especially with the phone calls he'd have to make.

From a gas station in Fairfield, Finn called the Santa Reina police chief. Yes, Berach Phelan had confirmed it. He had murdered Denise Hagerty. He'd confessed to the Sheriff and Chief of police together and wanted, he said, to publicly confess. He wanted to be punished. This was the news Finn wanted to carry to Mrs. Brandling and, once at the game, to Doug. He wouldn't depend on Warren to be curious enough to check or kind enough to say anything.

"Mrs. Brandling, it's Finn Pyykönen. I'm sorry to call on a Sunday morning, but I wanted to tell you personally."

She was silent.

"Mrs. Brandling?"

"Oh, yes, Mr. Pyykönen from Santa Reina High School.

Is everything all right? Is Warren all right?"

To Finn, she seemed confused. "Yes, everything is fine. I saw Warren last night at the centennial festivities. He seemed well."

"Good." Her voice trailed off as if she had forgotten who she was talking to, but recovered her manners, "How can I help you?"

"When I visited you at your home—Warren arrived late, we sat in the kitchen—you told me you had nothing for me to tell Douglas. Well, several things have happened since then."

Mrs. Brandling's voice grew more distinct. "Yes? And you think I should know about them?"

"If you are willing to hear them, yes." Finn did not want to intrude. "Both, I think, are good news."

"Mr. Pyykönen, this time I will hear you out. Tell me your news."

Finn wondered what to say first. "A mutual friend, Elizabeth Moore, persuaded Warren to visit Douglas at the Medical Facility. I believe Dr. Brandling is there now."

He waited for her reply. Finn wondered if she had heard, but he stayed quiet. Finally, she said, "What is the other news?"

"There was an attack at the school. Actually, my own daughter, Inga, and a former teacher, in addition, were accosted by a man with a knife. Both women survived and are all right, Inga defended herself well. The man was arrested and admitted not only to this attack but to the stabbing murder of Denise Hagerty. I confirmed this with the police chief this morning. Douglas had nothing to do with it."

"Why, then, why, Mr. Pyykönen, would Douglas have confessed to such a horrible crime?"

Finn was ready for her inevitable query. "I believe, as I did years ago, that Douglas was covering for his brother. He thought, for some reason, that Warren was the murderer." Finn again waited. Mrs. Brandling said nothing. "I should find out more this afternoon when I see Douglas."

"Thank you for calling," she said returning to the dreamy, absent manner in which she'd answered his call. She hung up the receiver.

Her silences and abrupt termination of the conversation troubled Finn. *Maybe I should not have interfered. I should have let Warren break the news. Even this good news could not have been easy for her to accept. After twenty-four years, the son she'd abandoned could come home. That would change everything in Mrs. Brandling's as well as in Warren's.*

Finn had to wonder that she hadn't asked who'd attacked Inga and then confessed. *Perhaps it didn't matter to her.*

Elizabeth Moore

She woke very late, near noon. It was already after checkout time. *I don't care.* She called the desk. "I'm late leaving," she said, "obviously." The desk captain assured her it was all right. "Good. Please send up a pot of coffee. And a bit of toast, if you would."

The long sleep had done her good. She seemed to have sorted out the whirl of the last three days and all the feelings that had cascaded along the step of each day.

Elizabeth watched out the window. The people of Santa Reina, below on the sidewalk and street, were going about their Sunday business, walking home from church no doubt, picking up picnic supplies, driving out of town for the afternoon. She wondered who'd said mass at Sacred Heart this morning. *The day of rest, of reflection would soothe her,* Elizabeth thought.

The Advent of Elizabeth

Biz watched a girl of about six prancing in a flowered summer dress, a ribbon dangling from her ponytail, holding hands with her mother, dressed in similar fashion, thin dress swaying with her gait and lifting slightly in the breeze. Those two walked to the corner, crossed the street, and, chatting merrily, the girl raising her face to her mother's gaze, disappeared round the corner of the mercantile building. Elizabeth Moore tapped the windowsill with her nails, staring at the empty place mother and daughter had left.

Leave. Now is the time. The reunion is over. She spun around, putting her back to the window. She took her luggage from the closet and opened it on the bed.

Biz laid a few garments in her suitcase. She put on a robe. She washed and dried her face and returned to the suitcase. She looked at the thing awhile, then closed it. She glanced toward the television, moved toward it, and stopped. She returned to the window.

Let me see the town this way, through my own window. Let everybody else blurt out their say. Hold counsel with yourself, Biz. She felt lighter, happier than she had in years. And it has, she smiled to herself, nothing to do with a man!

The coffee arrived. "Please set it on the desk there, and thank you," she said. She tipped the bellman.

He'd brought her a paper, *The Chronicle*, which had a front page story covering the mayhem at Santa Reina's Centennial, coupled with a compilation of excerpts from 'the event,' including 1967 quotations of the then yet-to-be Monsignor, Berach Phelan, holding forth about the family's loss. "Hypocrite. Bastard," she told the paper. Centered on the bottom of the page, a startled Farley Pike faced the camera, wide-eyed, gawky-looking as ever, his eyes bulging. He smiled crookedly, uncomfortably. "Unlikely hero" the caption began. Elizabeth laughed out loud. Photo credit was Finn Pyykönen.

"Now when did you snap that one?" Elizabeth asked an absent Finn. She did not read either article but tossed the paper into the wastebasket.

She rose from the desk and again opened the suitcase. Between sips of coffee and nips at the toast, she continued to pack. "You do not have to stay," she murmured, thinking another time that Sarah Petroski had taught her that. "What does she know?" Biz said and stopped in the middle of folding a skirt and closed the case again.

Elizabeth fished up the paper, sat, and finished another coffee and piece of toast while leafing through the news section at her desk. She held her head in her hands, elbows on *The Chronicle*, massaging her scalp. No, Biz told herself, Sarah was right. I don't have to stay. Snub had taught her what she knew of love; that could not be undone. She did have choices, though. Elizabeth Moore, PhD threw her hair back and scrambled in the desk drawer for stationery and a pen. In determined, quick strokes she wrote a short note and sealed it in a Stanford Hotel envelope. Let this be the last.

She rose to watch the afternoon sun scrub and warm the buildings along the street. She looked at her luggage, the newspaper, the envelope, then tossed off the robe and strode to the shower.

Let me start over at a good beginning. She shut the bathroom door on the half-packed suitcase and leavings of her breakfast.

39

Warren and Doug

Ransdorf spoke in a gruff voice. "Visitor, Brandling. Belly chain and cuff required." In no way was this a visit from Finn.

Not since Finn's very first visits had guards required this protocol. Doug knew better than to speak. He simply offered his wrists to Ransdorf and stood quietly as the guard harnessed him in chains. His escort grabbed his elbow more to inflict pain than to guide him.

"Mind switching off my throwing arm? Could affect a play at second," Doug said.

His escort said nothing, loosened the grip only slightly, but at the first set of doors let go, and when the gate opened, took up his other arm.

The visitor's room stood without ornament as if to remind outsiders of the barrenness of their visit. They could bring nothing, could take nothing away.

Warren, waiting since before Doug was summoned from his cell, sat tall. His brother, Doug thought, had aged considerably, though more slowly on the free side of the thick glass cage than anyone within. Still, he looked fit and appeared on the younger side of forty, though he was nearly forty-five. Ransdorf guided Doug to his chair and scooted it in behind him as he sat. The guard activated the microphone. "You have ten minutes, Brandling." He took up his position near the entry door.

Doug slouched in the chair, working to avoid the rasp

of the chain. He waited as only one who has learned to pass time in prison can wait, patient, quiet, without fidgeting or ticks. He watched Warren through the glass, without saying a word. Doug felt the younger, servile brother within him stir and squirm. He wanted to comfort himself, to touch his chest, to rub, but he would not show Warren any weakness. Instead, he loosened his breathing.

Ransdorf, as if to prod them into conversation approached and repeated, "You've only got ten minutes." Doug remained as before.

Warren leaned in toward the microphone. "You can thank Coach for my presence here."

Doug nodded. "I will. I'll tell him I appreciate it." Doug did not explain what he meant by "it."

Without preamble, Warren went right to work. "Did you think you were covering for me?" Warren said. His gaze burned through the glass. "Is that why you confessed?"

Doug looked softly at his brother. You get to say it once and once only, he reminded himself. He straightened in the chair, let the chains ripple over his spine, and spoke quietly, "I knew you were there. I had your back."

"I was not there."

"I heard you get up, Warren. You pretended to jog off toward school."

"I pretended?"

"You wore your loafers."

"Spying?"

"Observing. Remember." Doug paused long enough for Warren to finish his thought.

"You had my back. Yeah I know, but I wasn't there."

"Then where? Just jogging around town in street shoes?"

"Not exactly."

Each minute that ticked by in silence stilled the already

stagnant air in the booths, but neither brother moved quickly.

Doug looked at Warren carefully, without accusation or anger. "Can you tell me, then? It would be nice to know." The wheels were turning on the free side of the glass. Warren kept his head steady, but his eyes darted from his brother to his hands and back again. Doug had paid with twenty-four years of his life to hear Warren say this, something, anything. He waited.

"You knew I was seeing the music teacher, didn't you?"

Doug considered. "Not from you, but, yeah, I'd heard." It seemed as if his brother would never finish. Doug, though, was patient.

Warren moved in on the mic. "Well, a dozen times, I'd met her in one of the practice rooms, the one with the baby grand in it." He could not suppress a whimsical smile. "We'd have a quickie, and I'd come back home to shower before going to classes."

Doug considered the information.

"You were with her? That morning?"

Warren said nothing. Finally, he nodded slowly. "That's where I went. It must have been after I left that Elizabeth, Miss Moore, witnessed the stabbing."

Doug was shaking his head, looking down at his cuffed hands. Then he rifled his gaze at his brother.

Warren did not smile now. "Look, Doug, I had nothing to do with Miss Moore accusing you." He fingered the glass between them with a surgeon's touch. "I didn't know she'd identified you until after you confessed. Then I thought it was too late to do anything about it."

Doug Brandling retreated into his prison, behind a glass thicker, enforcing more silence than that separating him from Warren at that moment. He'd have time to think, that he knew. There was just one more thing to say. He glanced over his shoulder at Ransdorf. He nodded to the guard, rose, rasping the chain against the shelf below the mic, and looked at his brother once more. "You haven't told Mom this."

If Warren was capable of showing regret, his eyes would have betrayed him. "No. I never told her."

Doug nodded. He pushed the chair away with the back of straightening knees. He turned away, Ransdorf switched the off mic, and guided his charge toward the door, touching him softly, lightly on the shoulder—was it a caring response? "You have a few minutes left," the guard said. Doug walked on. He stood before the door, waiting to be let out.

On the free side, Warren followed his escort. Once in the fresh air, he thought of Berach Phelan and all else he'd withheld from Doug.

40

The Game

It was not far from his telephone stop to the California Medical Facility, but Finn lingered and drove slowly to make the trip last. Even the good news he'd had about Inga from Jamie did not quell his unease over Mrs. Brandling's part of that call. Finn mulled it over. There'd been no response. At least on the outside, he thought. What had happened after he'd left them? Had Warren raised hell about Finn's visit?

Doug's mother might well finish her days in controlled silence, tending her clippings from *The Chronicle* and *Santa Reina Republic*, adding the latest news and the reprints of old stories that would soon again find their way into print, perhaps all across the nation but surely all up and down the Pacific coast. She'd keep the scrapbooks separately, of course, like two sets of accounts, secret and illicit, hiding them from Warren, definitely, but perhaps also from Doug. The weight of Brandlings threatened Finn, weighted him down.

He left the main road. I need more time, he told himself; I need to step back, get perspective on all this. Finn fixed his mind on his wife. Those were safe, stable thoughts.

His years with Ellie in Pasadena, in love, raising kids together, then without her, seemed right—had always felt that way—an island of light and love surrounded by a darker, turbulent sea scudded by murderous Santa Reina winds of treachery and lust.

In the years before Ellie, his plans for a future under a baseball sun and green-field freshness were bent by his romance with Elizabeth, then by distance from her (the Giants' organization followed by Viet Nam), then again in the rekindling of their romance that, finally, ended the day of the murder, the moment of "the event." That day, Elizabeth seemed evil, hard.

Now, driving away from a furious attack on Inga by the same man toward a fulfillment of his devotion to Doug, the blending of the far past, his life with family, and a new longing dizzied Finn. Was this trip some sort of penance he'd imposed on himself because of the catastrophe at Santa Reina High? Had he failed or simply tangled with the messiness of people struggling through dire and wretched lives ?

He'd suffered: the truncated baseball season (much like his own minor league ending); a romance ripping itself apart from within on a wind of duplicity and Elizabeth's wayward habits taught her by a seditious, old man; a sudden leaving, carrying away the taste of blood in one's mouth; his desire to go far from his hometown, to become lost out there, away, far away. Finally, what had felt true was his marriage of love that was often at odds with life as he'd found it, anathema to what horrified him.

Maybe you were just lucky to find Ellie, to live in a charmed place, enveloped by her lustrous nature. Finn knew that was untrue. The success and competence they'd both won in the world told him their lives had been more than good fortune. Her death had proven that; palpable good spilled over far beyond her own life. Still, in contrast to his years at Santa Reina—restive, jostled by people and their events, including these few days of the centennial—his marriage, even though marred by early death, was far from a ruin. Everything, though, about Santa Reina, about Elizabeth, about Snub, and about the Brandlings, each and every one, perhaps, even Doug, moldered in a fearful darkness, stank of despair. Was that all that would eventually remain? He longed for Ellie's joy.

Finn turned his thoughts to Inga. Her wound, though not superficial and very bloody, would heal. She had already begun to throw off the trauma of the attack. She and Jamie held fast their investments in the sunshine of the heart, in doing good for others and themselves, in the light of the future. Finn could not, right now, bask in their optimism. Have I tainted Ellie's legacy? What have I brought Inga to? I involved her with Liz, with the centennial, with murderers and misery. What else waits in darkness that I cannot see, can't protect against?

"All right, Finn Pyykönen, stop it right there," he said aloud. "You're low on sleep, slumped in misery, and lost in life." It wasn't the first time—he recalled the drive two and a half decades past from Santa Reina to Los Angeles, fleeing the grisliness of murder. He would survive; he had found Ellie that time. He would figure it out. As if in cold defiance of his hope, though, the daunting twin prison compounds of Solano State Penitentiary and the California Medical Facility stepped forth from behind the trees.

Surrendering to a gloaming authority, Finn turned into the prison yards. The parking lots were jammed for the games. A guard on duty, moving traffic along, directed him to the very edge of the lot. There were few spaces left.

Finn shouldered the Nikon and stood, shaded by the huge oaks defining the lot. The prison spread before him wrapped in giant-height chain-link fence and razor wire, its wide-open spaces barren, towers looming over them— like stationary hawks hunting the inmate mice housed in a monumental rise of the warren of cell block buildings that screamed a silent doom: Move into the open and die.

As if he'd never seen the place before, in all the years

visiting Doug, Finn suffered waves of despair, perhaps fear at what lay before him. Despite the unusual and even festive occasion arranged by a new-style warden intent on positive public relations and whom some styled "touchy-feely," the California Medical Facility had never looked as dismal as it now appeared to Finn. He had to prod himself to get going. Get this over with, echoed in his mind.

The entry ritual, much of which had been softened for his many visits, especially after he'd written positively about the place, seemed tense. The guards were not party to the new warden's openness. To the jailers, the staging of an inter-prison competition was wrong and dangerous. The guards acted according to their belief. Finn had no end of trouble explaining the workings of his special camera capable of transmitting pictures over phone lines and had to endure searches and questions he'd never encountered before. Incarceration. He felt like an inmate, helpless, caught, kept. He waited for escort in a holding area, which emptied only after it grew overcrowded with later-comers. The second game of the double-header had already begun.

Despite flags, team banners, and bright uniforms, the field looked all a prison. The families on each side were themselves imprisoned, assigned to bleachers between high fences. The crowd on each side faced guards at the ready. A second fence, accessible only through one of two locked gates before each team bench, held the nine fielders and no more than four offensive players, their numbers doubled by twenty-six guards around the perimeter, four more acting as umpires, and two pair manning the entry gates. A guard tower loomed beyond and over center field. This was like no game Finn had ever covered.

After some wrangling on the phone between the warden and the captain of the guard, Finn was allowed onto the field to catch some action photos. The warden wanted less of fence more of baseball in the news. That Finn could manage.

The first seven-inning game, 9-3, had gone well for Doug's team. The second game of the twin bill, now in the third inning, looked to be more difficult. The Solano Prison team scored twice in the first and were up now 3-0 with men on first and second. Though Finn snapped a few photos of Doug behind the plate, he had no way of talking with him. Warren was not in the stands. Had he visited? What had Doug heard from him? Finn would have to wait until later. For now, he stood on the sidelines near left field, between two guards and Ransdorf, who manned the gate. Finn balanced his camera on a collapsible pole.

The right-hander coming to the plate was gigantic. He played catcher for Solano and hung a huge gut, rounded-out, rolling over the plate. The big batsman crowded in. Doug's pitcher, Kettner, caught the big guy swinging at a curve outside. Then he slid one low across the plate just above the knees. Strike two, but the steal from second was on. The giant in the box stood firm, and Doug had no play at third. He held the runner at first. Finn caught the steal on camera.

Kettner yelled in to the plate, "Interference."

Blue signaled safe.

Doug flashed a 2-4-1 series and tapped his right thigh. Kettner shook off the outside curve. Doug insisted, running a 4-4-4 series and slapping the outside knee.

His pitcher came set and fired hard a brush back pitch. This time the batter did move. Fast. "Go talk to your pitcher," the umpire said.

"Okay, Blue." Doug went out.

"Hey. Pitch to the signs. No head shots, Kettner," Doug said. "They're looking for a reason to yank you."

The pitcher laughed. "Did you see that hog move? He's

fast when he wants to be."

"Just pitch to the signs, will ya?"

"I'll make him move another way," Kettner said, but he fell in line. Doug's call, the curve outside, dribbled off the big man's bat. Kettner ran in, scooped it up, and turned a 1-6-3 double play. Fast as he ducked, the man couldn't run. Side retired.

In the top of the third, Doug sliced a double past the center fielder. His right fielder loped in ahead of the shortstop who scored from first, 3-2. Kettner came to the plate. He switch-hit on the right side and dug in deep and tight. When the pitch came low inside, Kettner didn't move, but Doug was off before the pitch. He took third easily. Kettner waltzed across the plate and set up as a lefty. He took a swinging strike. The next pitch bounced on the plate and got away from the catcher. Doug went for the score, but fatso smothered the ball when it came off Blue's shoe, and blocked the plate as Doug slid. Finn caught the collision on the Nikon. He moved on instinct toward the plate, but the guards held him back. The plate ump called Doug out. The impact had shaken Doug. He didn't get up right away, though when he did, he signaled that he was all right. Kettner went down swinging and the left fielder popped up to short.

Behind the plate, now the bottom of the fifth, Doug is sweating. The water he's drunk sits heavy on his gut, and he labors to breathe. The score stands.

Doug knocks his glove on the mask. The infield grass has drained its color, grizzled, now, not green. The fences have bled away into a grayed lawn past empty bleachers aside a wide open field. The outfield fence has dissolved. Doug taps the mask again.

Blue stands. "You all right kid?"

"Yeah, fine." He crouches, signals to Kettner: low and outside. The pitcher shakes him off. Doug passes the same sign and pounds the mitt for emphasis. He squints at the endless field all gray and now undulating like his own labored breath. It is his brother, Warren—not Kettner, now—who grimaces and says no, again.

He sails one inside.

The batter falls back. "Hey, Blue, that nearly hit me," he says to the ump.

"Strike," the umpire says.

Kettner has flown. To Doug, it's Warren on the mound. He looks in again. Doug waves off the grin, calls: outside. Warren throws in again.

The batter drops the bat and starts his trot.

"Strike two."

The opposing catcher whirls. "Hey, ump, that one hit me. Ticked my button." The umpire holds his uplifted fist, then points.

"Play." Blue stands behind Doug. "Oh and two."

Warren, again, is laughing out on the mound, not loud, but his shoulders are hunched and shaking with mirth. He hollers something to the shortstop, who spits and grins. Warren scratches his crotch, comes set.

The next one sends the batter down. A ball high and in.

"One more like that, I'm comin' at you," the big batter yells.

"Talk to that pitcher of yours," Blue says.

Doug goes out, looking around, hoping for prison, but seeing only gray open fields and his smirking brother on the mound. He cannot shake the vision. His head pounds. He staunches vomit.

"Hey, Warren, quit dickin' with this guy. He can't reach outside. Nail him there," Doug says.

"It's Kettner?" His prison-mate smiles like Warren. "Just watch my back."

"Yeah, I remember." Doug shuffles back to the plate. He mumbles, "Just watch my back."

Blue looks at him. It's Doug's father. "One more like that, and you're done."

The next one ruffles the uniform right at the waist. Doug hears it.

"Strike three," the ump says.

Now the batter moves. The big man isn't fast, but Doug can't get out of the crouch before he's gone. Then Doug's up, grabs the bat left behind and runs, holding the stick high, yelling like mad.

Finn is yelling, too. "No, Doug, don't!" He drops the camera and breaks from the guards.

"Watch him, Warren," Doug yells, but Kettner is already off the mound, headed for the dugout.

Finn runs for all he's worth. "You didn't do it Doug! It was the priest!"

Doug looks over at Finn but gains on the fat man, stumbles along, but is narrowing the gap.

Finn, cutting across the infield closes in on his catcher. "It wasn't you," he shouts.

Doug has nearly caught the big guy who is now running for all he's worth.

Finn throws himself at his friend and wraps his arms around Doug's ankles. They go down together.

The opposing catcher—just now, called out on strikes— moves to his own dugout gate. Doug calls out, "Warren, I've got your back."

On the ground, Finn hugs Doug then looks him in the eye. "Doug, Warren didn't tell you. You've been cleared. You're innocent and free."

The Advent of Elizabeth

The game is over.

All through the clearing of the field and stands, Doug's hysterical mantra played in Finn's ears. Suddenly, it seemed to him, he was outside, in the parking lot again. A lockdown had at once been announced by the head jailor, with the tacit agreement of the shocked warden. Ransdorf had confiscated Finn's camera which likely had been broken in its fall. Finn, who couldn't visit Doug, had no reason to stay, but he waited for something. The lot was organized chaos, dwindling from full, with the shouts and gestures of guards, toward empty. Sheriff's deputies, racing up the roadway outdistancing wailing sirens and practically beating their flashing lights, took over the show. Still Finn stayed.

What did he want? He hoped that someone from inside would come with news, but news of what? Of Doug? The other catcher? Finn wondered. What of Warren? Had he been there? Finn had only guessed the brothers had met. Had Warren's visit something to do with Doug's behavior? Finn's head swam with questions. His stomach churned. For twenty-four years, Finn had worked for this day, but now it had come, the prison would release no answers. A sheriff's deputy tapped on the windshield.

"You can't stay here. Game's over. Time to go."

Finn could say nothing.

He drove in a stupor. It seemed like hours. Had he stopped to fill the tank? Had he eaten? Nothing seemed real.

I need to see Liz. He pointed himself back to Santa Reina and drove. The horror and discord that had dislodged him from his hometown a quarter century since, now hurled him onward in return. The answers to his life's dilemma at graduation, again in '67, and right now, remained out of reach. "You only thought Ellie's love was your salvation," he mumbled. Now he felt nothing had been resolved, only postponed like Father Phelan's penance, like Snub Randall's comeuppance, perhaps, like Warren Brandling's incipient confession to his mother, like his own facing of facts with Liz. What he would do for Doug would have to wait, but he must, right now, square with Elizabeth.

So lost in thought that Finn did not know how he came to be there, he parked in the Stanford Hotel lot and went directly to the front desk to ask for Elizabeth Moore.

"Dr. Moore checked out hours ago," the clerk answered his query. "Are you Mr. Pyyk . . . onen?"

"Pyykönen," Finn said, "yes."

"She left this for you."

The note said simply, "I'm sorry, Finn. I couldn't wait for you."

That was all. No encouragement, no reason, nothing. Finn left the lobby without a word. Now he felt alert. In San Rafael he did not take the exit for the East Bay where Inga and Jamie would be but held course toward San Francisco, toward Elizabeth's apartment.

What drove him to go there felt to Finn the only thing worth knowing right now. He had been coy. He'd thought freeing Doug was his mission, and all the time, as Inga had said, it was the business of Elizabeth Moore that needed settling. Everything else to do with the reunion was over. His uncertainty had to end. This was his chance.

He drove, over the Golden Gate, on the same road he'd traveled twenty-four years before, escaping tragedy. Back then, he'd decided to leave for good. And now? Finn wasn't sure. He felt an emptiness in Santa Reina, in Pasadena, in all his life. He drove toward Elizabeth. There seemed no other place to go.

The Advent of Elizabeth

At the top of Elizabeth's street, looking westward down the hill, the mid-June sky outshone the nascent glow of street lamps. Below and away toward Santa Reina, the Marin Headlands and the water between shimmered in summer's late sunset. In a few minutes a fog would shroud the hill and wreathe the streetlights in their own dim radiance.

Finn sat in the car, waiting, perhaps for the cover of fog, perhaps for a rapacity that he'd never enjoyed. He watched Elizabeth's apartment windows redden from gold, then fade with the sky to pink, then cloud over in an opaque, gray sheen. When the sky darkened to a purple hue, the globes of streetlights blushed against the sunset and dimmed, tempered in cloud. He waited for her windows above to glow like the street lamps. There seemed no light inside.

In a hazy twilight now, Finn left his car to cross to Elizabeth's building. He lingered there under the portico before the door and watched the night descend. The sky had closed in and was dark gray. He rang her top-floor bell and leaned against the pilaster beside the door. He waited. No signal returned. He pushed the button again, then, having counted heartbeats like minutes, he rang once more.

Finn Pyykönen sighed. Regret, a deep weariness, and sorrow flooded his chest. He pushed off from the pillar.

Above, on the still dark third story, Elizabeth Moore parted the sheer curtains, pausing to view the street. She marked Finn Pyykönen down below, his broad shoulders hunched, hands in his pockets, walking straight ahead through the descending fog.

CPSIA information can be obtained at www.ICGtesting.com
Printed in the USA
BVOW08s1301070916

461102BV00002B/4/P